Danger,
Sweetheart

Danger, Sweetheart

MaryJanice Davidson

St. Martin's Griffin

New York

DANGER, SWEETHEART. Copyright © 2016 by MaryJanice Davidson. All rights reserved. Printed in the United States of America. For information, address St. Martin's Press, 175 Fifth Avenue, New York, N.Y. 10010.

www.stmartins.com

Library of Congress Cataloging-in-Publication Data

Names: Davidson, MaryJanice, author.
Title: Danger, sweetheart / MaryJanice Davidson.
Description: First edition. | New York : St. Martin's Griffin, 2016.
Identifiers: LCCN 2015048999| ISBN 978-1-250-05315-2 (trade paperback) |
    ISBN 978-1-4668-5543-4 (e-book)
Subjects: LCSH: Man-woman relationships—Fiction. | BISAC: FICTION /
    Romance / Contemporary. | GSAFD: Love stories.
Classification: LCC PS3604.A949 D36 2016 | DDC 813/.6—dc23
LC record available at http://lccn.loc.gov/2015048999

Our books may be purchased in bulk for promotional, educational, or business use. Please contact your local bookseller or the Macmillan Corporate and Premium Sales Department at 1-800-221-7945, extension 5442, or by e-mail at MacmillanSpecialMarkets@macmillan.com.

First Edition: May 2016

10 9 8 7 6 5 4 3 2 1

This one's for me, and for you: lovers of romantic tropes everywhere. Whether it's an amnesiac sheriff or an uptight city boy trapped in the country or a feverish hero being tended to by the heroine (three of my faves), this is for readers who not only defined the genre but also demanded more and never tire of it.

Author's Note

I love *Shaun of the Dead*. It is, possibly, one of the finest movies in the history of cinema, second only to *Starship Troopers*. It's got everything: a clueless hero, a puffy sidekick who can imitate an orangutan, Bill Nighy (my old-man crush), a supernice mom, a nerdy bespectacled frenemy in love with the hero's ex, Queen on the sound track (Is there a more beautiful sight than a bunch of British twentysomethings whacking a zombie with pool cues while "Don't Stop Me Now" blares in the background?), debunked dog myths ("Dogs can look up!"), and innocents getting hit by darts.

Oh, and zombies. Lots of zombies. I love everything about *Shaun of the Dead,* but I love how they handled zombies the most. Their love for the genre shone through virtually every minute of the film as they poked fun at themselves and the genre, and I never once felt like they were mocking me or the movies I like: we were in it together. It was the first movie I ever thought of as a conscious gift to the audience: here's something we liked; we think you'll like it, too.

So: this book. My editor and I love the romance genre (not atypical for writers and editors who work in the romance genre, and thank goodness). We love historicals and paranormals and contemporaries and Regencies. We love the silly stuff and the BAMF stuff and the sexy stuff. We love kick-ass heroines and damsels who need to be rescued every twenty minutes. We love alpha heroes and beta heroines, and we love it the other way around, too. (We're dirty girls, and so flexible, too!) We love heroes who are SEALs and farmers and sheriffs and doctors. We love heroines who are biochemists and Vikings and captives and wardens. We love third person and first person and audio and electronic and paperbacks and classic hardcovers.

And the romance tropes, oh God, the tropes. We love those most of all; for us, tropes make the romance.

For the uninitiated, Wikipedia defines "tropes" as "the use of figurative language—via word, phrase, or even an image—for artistic effect such as using a figure of speech." Did that help? Because it didn't help me even a little. I had to keep reading: "The word 'trope' has also come to be used for describing commonly recurring literary and rhetorical devices, motifs or clichés in creative works." Oh. Okay. That's a little better, Wikipedia. Stop trying to impress me and just define stuff, okay? Maybe with pictures next time? I like pictures.

A "trope" is when you're watching a new show about a cop who's set to retire next week/month/year and you know that cop will never retire. It's when the slutty pretty teenager in a horror movie says, "I'll be right back!" and you know she's toast. It's knowing the hero and heroine who at first loathe each other will fall in love. It's a way for the writer to let the reader/viewer know what to expect without having to, you know, write. (Shut up! We're doing the best we can.)

A trope is the thing that brings you back to the same genre again and again, because the stuff you loved in the first book will pop up in other books and you're always chasing that feeling, the giddy excitement of reading about a hero and heroine, or hero and hero, or heroine and—you get the picture; whoever they are, you know they are destined for love, and you want to watch. (Not in a creepy way.) Even more: you want to fall in love, too.

And while we were listing our fave tropes (and everyone in the office was getting in on it, and when I mentioned it to my book club they couldn't wait to list theirs, too) my editor said, "Wouldn't it be great if there was a book that paid homage to the romance tropes? Not in a mean way, like the *Scary Movie* movies."

"In a fun way," I replied, "like *Shaun of the Dead*." And wouldn't it be great, we thought, if the audience was in on it?

And that's how *Danger, Sweetheart* came about. A romance novel that pays respect to romance novels, where the readers are in on the joke. Unless you skipped this Author's Note, in which case I cannot help you.

For those of you in a hurry, I've listed all the romance tropes used in the writing of this book at the end, so you can peek and see if any of your favorites are there. Dunno about you, but I can never resist a hero with a high fever, all delirious and adorable, being tended to by a (reluctantly) adoring heroine. I also like the fish out of water trope and the first sex is perfect sex trope. I even got to have some fun with tropes I find annoying (I'm looking at you, Hero Keeping a Big Secret).

If you're new to the genre, this is a fun place to start because: tropes! I'm basically throwing you into the deep end, but unlike when I was tossed into the deep end at the helpless age of twenty-seven, I think you'll enjoy it.

Other things you might want to know (or things I want you to know and your feelings on the matter are nothing to me, nothing!): No tropes were harmed in the creative process. Also, I'm not as gross as readers might assume: it really did rain urine in the bathroom at the Plaza Hotel and Casino, courtesy of a leak one floor above. I did not make that up. God, I wish I had made that up. "Urine" and "rain" and "hotel" are three words that never belong in the same sentence.

The T-shirt Natalie wears ("One by one the penguins slowly steal my sanity") is a thing! You can get it at Amazon. As I did. And the pink-and-black skull leash sported by the White Rose of York also exists in real life.

Finally, as of this writing, you can't hop an Amtrak from Las Vegas to Minot, North Dakota. This is a crime against humanity. Long train rides rock. Minot does, too (my bias: I was born on the Minot Air Force Base).

Quotes

Armed with only a cork-topped plastic tray, I encounter the best and worst people on Earth. Every night.
—SARAH VENTRE, "Why Your Cocktail Waitress Hates You"

If we are to feel the positive feelings of love, happiness, trust, and gratitude, we periodically also have to feel anger, sadness, fear, and sorrow.

   —JOHN GRAY, *Men Are from Mars, Women Are from Venus*

The fish are watched working their way up the shallows . . . when they come to the shelter of a ledge or a rock it is their nature to slide under it and rest. The poacher sees the edge of a fin or the moving tail . . . instinct, however, tells him a fish ought to be there, so he takes the water very slowly and carefully and stands up near the spot. He then kneels on one knee and passes his hand, turned with fingers up, deftly under the rock until it comes in contact with the fish's tail. Then he begins tickling with his forefinger, gradually running his hand along the fish's belly further and further toward the head until it is under the gills. Then comes a quick grasp, a struggle, and the prize is wrenched out of his natural element, stunned with a blow on the head, and landed in the pocket of the poacher.

—THOMAS MARTINDALE, *Sport Indeed*

[My daughter] starts walking out toward the ponies, she's like "Can I go?" I'm an idiot . . . "Go on out there, honey, you're only outnumbered fifty to one. What could possibly happen?" And there's this one beautiful speckled pony . . . she walks up to the pony . . . the pony bites her on the fucking leg. And she screams: "Why, Daddy?" She calms down . . . she wants to look [ponies] up and learn about them. And we go look up ponies. And it turns out they're assholes. They bite all the time.

—LOUIS C.K.

Pretendian: A wannabe American Indian. Usually exhibited by white people but blacks do it too. Claims to be ¼th Native American or a lesser percentage, but usually have no definitive proof of it or of what tribe they're from . . . if such ancestry exists, they tend to exaggerate the very small amount that they have after generations of their family neglecting this heritage.

The most annoying thing about these people is the smugness that they claim this lost heritage with. Upon being told by some senile relative or actually finding proof, they suddenly claim to know EVERYTHING about Native Americans and press for tribal membership while buying ambiguous, commodified Indian-themed jewelry and merchandise like dream-catchers. It's usually the first thing they put on their MySpace biographies, and they get miffed when people don't refer to them as Native American or take them seriously as such (but say that they don't want people to "judge them for embracing their ancestral roots"). They also spend their time discrediting other white people who display Indian Princess Syndrome or people who actually have accountable Native ancestry.

These people often have no grasp on Native culture and issues, both historical and contemporary. In the end, most people with accountable ancestry don't whore their heritage in order to look "exotic" and interesting.

—*The Urban Dictionary*

There's nothing trashy about romance.

—Parry in *The Fisher King*

Danger, Sweetheart

Prologue

"Wow."

"I know."

"That was the best awkward sex I've ever had."

"Yeah, baby, it was good for me, t— What?"

"A new winner." Shannah Banaan sat up in bed and began rooting around for her clothes. One good thing about a lackluster performance: her stockings were intact. "Pride of place went to the awkward sex in Madame Tussauds Wax Museum, right next to Hugh Hefner and his life partner, Michael Jackson." At his puzzled stare, she elaborated. "My date and I rearranged some of the couples, mostly because I thought Madonna and Elvis deserved a chance to be together. And I honestly thought I'd go to my death with unsettling wax museum sex in the number-one slot. But you fixed it."

"I don't get it."

"Mmm." She climbed into her clothes while keeping a wary eye on her surroundings. She'd been hot—and he'd been gorgeous (if somewhat selfish and unimaginative in bed)—but not so lust crazed that she would let herself forget that she worked, and now had sex, in a hotel where it had once literally rained urine.

"You liked it," her now-disgruntled bang pro tem was grumbling. "My ears are still ringing; that's how loud you were."

"I had little choice; you weren't responding to my hand signals. No need to get miffed. You got off. I almost got off." She shrugged. "Now we're off on our separate ways and ne'er the twain shall meet."

"You don't talk like a waitress."

"Incorrect, since I am in point of fact a waitress." Ah, the beloved *all cocktail waitresses are slutty and stupid* cliché. And that observation from a man who was unable to calculate 15 percent of $150.15.

"Huh?"

So gorgeous, she thought with mild regret, *and so dim.* He really was almost stereotypically handsome: penetrating blue eyes, deep blond hair with gold glints, long, long legs. She'd always had a weakness for the tall ones with good shoulders.

"Don't call me," she said as she threw him a smile and gathered up her de rigueur overtly sexy uniform, "and I won't call you."

He had by now managed to sit up in bed and looked adorably rumpled and confused. He rubbed his (blue, *bleu, azul*) eyes with the heels of his hands and squinted up at her. "Look, we can't see each other again. I'm sorry, but it was one of those boats passing in the night things."

"Ships." She managed not to add *you gorgeous moron.*

"Huh?"

"I will never understand how men are struck deaf post-orgasm." She pulled on her underpants, then wriggled into the rest of her uniform. The rest = a long black satin suit jacket that buttoned low and fell high. Someday she would have a job that required her to wear pants. *Hold fast to your dream*, she thought, then straightened, turned, and spared a look at the gorgeous moron she had taken in a moment of insanity/horniness/loneliness.

He was blinking up at her like a confused, handsome possum caught in headlights. "So, going?"

"Yes, going. Thank you for six minutes of your time." She was grumpy and anxious to get home where she could let her Hitachi, Sir Shakes-A-Lot, finish her off. But no need to be an *utter* bitch. She'd keep it at 30 percent. "It was nice to meet you." And it was. He was all superficial charm and classic good looks: trim and tall, with eyes of direct Monet blue (post the artist's cataract surgery of 1923) and a brilliant smile she had first felt in her knees and then . . . higher. But not too high.

"Sorry it didn't work out. Listen, I come here quite a lot—"

"Yes. Your coin-bucket collection was a giveaway. As were the many times I've brought you Sea Breeze after Sea Breeze over the last few months. A bold choice for a straight man, by the way."

"—and if our paths cross again, even though I'd love to see you again, I'm hoping we can be adult about this."

"Right. Because nothing says adult like an exchange of bodily fluids followed by pretending the other person never existed to avoid conflict." She managed (barely) to soften the observation with a smile. "Don't worry. I guarantee you will never, as long as you live, *ever* see me again."

"I have to see you again."

"How come?"

"Idjit! Not you," she added when she heard his affronted huff, "me." She couldn't believe her accent had slipped. Never had the word "idjit"—argh, "idiot," she meant "idiot"—been hurled so accurately.

"Are you going to invite me in?" She looked around at the gold wallpaper, gold gilt mirror, and slightly less gold carpet as if seeing them in their tacky glory for the first time. "Or are we going to have this discussion in the hall?"

Benjamin Tarbell's bemused expression never faltered. "Look, I understand what you're going through," he began, shifting immediately into practiced soothe mode.

She blinked. "In fact, you don't."

"But what we had was too magical to cheapen with regular sex."

She made a fist, then bit it to swallow the hysterical guffaw the word "magical" brought forth. "Ggghh. Mmmm?"

"So I'll have to ask you to leave," he finished, swinging the door closed, "with only your precious memories of a lost love. It's killing me, too, baby! But it's the only way."

Pretty rich boys should never take on country girls; she shoved past him, into the suite, and after a long nonplussed moment he shut the door and followed. She took in the dirty clothes draped on the desk, his wallet and rental car key, the room service cart, and the devastation that had once been his meal. The man had the table manners of a farrowing sow.

"There are French fries," she observed, "on every surface of this room." Then she stuffed her fist back into her mouth. She needed to wrap this up before she hit bone. Or vomited. Maybe both. "The reason I— What are you doing?"

He looked up from shrugging out of his robe. "Don't worry; I changed my mind."

(don't ask, What mind? *don't ask,* What mind? *don't)*

He sat, crossed long, muscled legs, then patted the bed, which boasted rucked-up sheets and French fries. "I'm glad you came. Pretty soon I'll be glad *I* came." He punctuated his idea of a bon mot with a lopsided leer as he stroked his burgeoning erection, which, she hated to admit, was impressive. *Ah-ha! Now I remember what I saw in you.*

She tittered around her fist. Was this really happening? "Listen to me, you beautiful dolt. I am not here for another five-minute sweaty interlude."

"No?" He wiggled dark, perfectly groomed brows *(my first tip-off; what had I been thinking? he has the eyebrows of a cologne model!),* then took a firmer grip on his penis and angled it toward her, as if it were a microphone and she his interview subject, or as if he was afraid she would have trouble finding it. Unfortunately, that would never have been difficult. The lovely dumb ass was hung like a steer. "You sure, um . . ." His inability to recall her name put an end to her giggles, for which she was grateful. And at least he had the grace to be embarrassed.

"I'll give you a hint: it means lily."

"Is it Lily?"

"No," she sighed/groaned (grighed? soaned?). "It's not Lily." Their chat had the welcome side effect of softening his erection.

Shannah (English/Hebrew origin; diminutive of Shoshannah, meaning: "lily") had confidence that her next statement would wilt it entirely. "It's not Lily, you're not getting laid tonight—by me, at any rate—and I'm pregnant. By you."

Going, going, gone. *Farewell, Benjamin's erection. I barely knew ye.*

"No."

"I understand," she said kindly, "because that was my exact response when the stick turned blue. No, and then there may have been screaming. Followed by sobbing. But it's true. I've since had a doctor confirm."

"It's not mine."

"No need to take my word for it." Never, she would never, *never* let him see how that hurt her. His reaction was expected, knee-jerk from a quintessential jerk.

And it hurt.

"No need," she said again through clenched teeth, "to take my word for it. A blood test will show the baby has two dolts for parents and they're both in this room. Which stinks of French fries and your hair product. In fact—" She held up a finger, then bolted for the bathroom. She could have made it to the toilet but spitefully chose the sink. Then felt bad: *It's not like he'll be the one cleaning this up. Well, he'll have to call the front desk. It'll cost him seven seconds of his life.*

From behind her, a hollow, "Aw, man," followed by the whump of him falling back on the bed. She heard rustling and assumed he was putting his robe back on.

She rinsed her mouth and left the bathroom, pressing the heels of her hands to her eyes, hard, to shove back tears. She would cry; it was as inevitable as Tarbell's instinctive ducking of responsibility. But not here and not now and never in front of Benjamin Tarbell.

"So, rather like two people in a car accident, we should exchange insurance and contact information the better to wade through the legal and moral ramifications. Here's mine." She pulled the paper with her contact info, along with a picture of the ultrasound, out of her pocket and offered them to him. When he didn't reach for them, she put them on the dresser beside his wallet. "Too soon?"

"Um . . ."

"Yes, I understand. I've had the better part of two weeks to adjust. In fact, I'm still adjusting. You need time. *I* need time. Once you are satisfied the babies are yours—"

"Babies?" He said it the way she would have said, *There's a rattlesnake in my soup!*

"Yes. Twins." The doctor was certain she had the date of conception wrong. When she explained, at length, that she well remembered her only sexual experience in fourteen months and thus was quite, quite sure about the date, he'd given her an ultrasound on the spot. And there they were: twin harbingers of the coming destruction of her youth.

"Oh, fuck."

"Exactly." She nodded. "That is the perfect response." She absently patted her stomach. *Sorry, babies, I'll probably come to love you in time.*

He sighed and his eyes narrowed. "So you want money."

"I want," she replied with care, "support. From the other *half* of this equation. To which I am lawfully entitled." She summoned a smile that felt as sour as her post-barfing breath. "If you're going to be nasty about it."

"I'm not giving you a fucking dime."

"Please don't make me get your address, credit card information, and phone number from the nice people at the front desk." A bluff. The nice people at the front desk thought she was a stuck-up bitch, and she thought they were boring and small-minded (in every sense of the word).

"You think you're the first bimbo to try this?"

"To 'try' getting impregnated with twins by you when we were both in our right mind and fully consented? Yes. I think I'm the first bimbo to try this, unless you have other illegitimate children out in the world—then God help the world. And it's Ms. Bimbo, jackass."

"I'm not giving you a fucking dime," he said again, doubtless assuming pregnancy hormones caused selective deafness.

"That," she replied, stepping to the room service cart and sticking her index finger through the hole in the metal plate warmer, "remains to be seen."

"You fuckin' women, you're all the same."

"Double X chromosomes?" she suggested. "Vaginas? Physiologically weaker but longer lived? Lack of prostate cancer?"

"You dress hot and flirt and then go out and get yourselves pregnant—"

"Behold, a virgin shall conceive!"

"—and then comes the money grab, fuck!" Benjamin Tarbell hit her with every ounce of contempt a man who had never worked for anything was capable of. His expression was that of someone ankle deep in cow shit who blamed the cows and not himself for walking through the field in the first place. "Don't any of you sluts have any fucking pride oh God *ow*."

"Oh yes." She had hit him with the plate cover, which made

a lovely *bwoonngg* as it connected with the side of his (possibly hollow) head. "Too much pride, in fact. How do you think I ended up in this mess?"

He staggered, straightened, then seized her arm in a pincher grip and hauled her toward the door, ignoring her pained yelp. He was holding the side of his hand over the rapidly swelling bump and mumbling, "Oh God ow that hurt so bad fuck fuck God that hurt fuck ow," as he shoved her into the hallway, then slammed the door.

"What?" she asked the door, hands on her hips. "No tip?"

A shattering clatter—his dinner plate imploding against the door?—was her answer.

"Not even a lousy eight percent? Fine," she said to the empty hallway. "Fine. All right. Plan C." Plan A: abortion, tell no one, resume her life. Plan B: confront Benjamin; make child-care and/or custody arrangements, or arrange for a monthly check if he wished to support, but not love, his sons. Plan C: crawl.

But where? And to whom? Back to Sweetheart and disapproval and small-town gossips who thought they knew her but never would? To the casual insanity of her hometown? No. To her father, who thought her motive for leaving was to trap a rich man? Other women could rely on their birthplaces for support, but as she had known long before the pee stick foretold her fate, home wouldn't have her, and she wouldn't have them.

She thought Robert Frost, the city boy who came to love the country, put it in a way most people could grasp: *Home is the place where, when you have to go there, they have to take you in.*

Mr. Frost probably meant well, but his father had died when the poet was eleven and his mother when he was in his twenties. His sister and daughter had been institutionalized and the family was plagued with mental illness, mostly depression. Of course a man with that background thought home was a mythical place both magical and beautiful, stuffed with forgiving loved ones who were always happy to see you and never dropped hints about when you should leave again. The man's entire career was a love letter to the power of wishful thinking and a denial of his sorrowful life.

Shannah preferred Stephen King's take on the poem about a dying handyman and his grudge-holding employer: *Home was the place where, when you have to go there, you have to finally face the thing in the dark.*

Even if *you're* the thing in the dark.

So she would crawl, but not back to Sweetheart. She would start pulling every shift she could; she would become a most helpful, charming cocktail waitress. She would cultivate her acquaintances into friends—she could do that, could force charm and warmth when she had to. She would make friends and find a decent obstetrician and call in favors and keep Benjamin Tarbell's contact information handy. She would do these things and be a mother—good or bad remained to be seen—and if nothing else she would do a better job than her parents.

"Maybe set the bar a bit higher," she murmured, and started for the elevator. She glanced through the wallet she had palmed and big surprise: no library card and not one but *two* Hooters gift cards.

"Oh, boys. Or girls. Or one of each." She sighed with another pat to her stomach, and stepped into the empty elevator.

One

Blake Tarbell rolled onto his side and eyed the long, lovely naked back beside him. He could tell by her breathing that she was awake, and ran a finger from the top of her spine to the last bit of it just above her *fossae lumbales laterals*, the Dimples of Venus.

"God," she groaned into her pillow. "You know that gives me the shivers."

"More effective, perhaps, than an alarm."

"Forget it." She flopped over and jackknifed into a sitting position so abruptly, he put out a hand, thinking she was going to tumble off the edge of the bed. "I've gotta get back, so just holster the morning wood already."

He chuckled and let his hand drop. "Holster it where?"

"Dunno. It's a guy thing; you figure it out." She bounded from the bed like a gymnast on crack and he fought down a shudder. *Morning people, dear God in Heaven.* He liked Ava's company, and last night she was as she always is: energetic and hungry in bed. It had been fast and urgent and delicious; they didn't get together for long tender interludes.

They'd met in the lobby for drinks, never dinner.

("Don't ask me out. Don't buy flowers. That's not what this is."

"What is it, then?" he'd asked, amused. They'd met at Mc-Carran four months ago; she was a pilot for Southwestern; his flight had been delayed. Drinks at the club had turned into a delicious sweaty tumble back at the hotel.

"This is me enjoying my divorce. This is you being the sexual equivalent of a Fun Run. Less talking, Blake, and a lot more stripping.")

The evening had ended as it always did, with both of them agreeably sweaty and out of breath. Ava called him whenever she was in Vegas longer than three hours. If he was free, they met for drinks. If he wasn't, Blake imagined she called someone else. He was bothered by how that didn't bother him.

"—the run to Boston," she was saying. She'd done her usual efficient cleanup in the bathroom and was now wriggling back into her clothes. "God, sometimes I think it'd be easier to keep a spare set of clothes and some toiletries here. Ah-ha!"

"What?"

She pointed at him with one hand while zipping her slacks with the other. "You should see the look on your face. I've only seen people go pale that fast when the oxygen masks drop."

He opened his mouth to

(lie)

protest, but she ran right over his words. " 'S fine. Really. I was teasing. I know you're cemented in your bachelor ways."

He opened his mouth again.

"Nope. Don't even try that. And don't go on about how you're just waiting for the right girl, and maybe that girl could be me—"

"I wouldn't have used the word 'girl.'"

"It's *fine*. This—" She gestured, indicating the suite. "What we do? It's great, really."

Two reallys in twenty seconds: it's not fine (really) and it's not great (really). He knew the signs.

"It's just . . ."

You need something more.

". . . I need something more. And . . ."

There's this guy.

". . . there's this woman—oh. You didn't know? I'm pretty flexible between the sheets."

"Figuratively and literally," he managed. Discovering his soon-to-be-former lover was bisexual was not helping his nocturnal penile tumescence. "Why would you wait until now to bring that up?"

She laughed, bent, gave him a quick kiss. "For a chance to see that look on your face. Hey. You're great, Blake. This was, too, y'know? But I never go back for seconds."

"Fourteenths," he couldn't help pointing out.

"Right. But I want to keep liking you, if not fucking you. So: You don't pretend you're going to miss me, and I won't pretend you can't fill my spot in your sex suite with one text." He couldn't help smiling, at both her astute observations and cheerful bluntness.

"Fair enough." She was fully dressed now and looked clean

and pressed and like she'd had a full eight hours, when he knew she hadn't. "Might not see each other again. But if we do, it'd be great to keep it friendly, okay?"

"You're wrong," Blake replied. At her surprised expression, he added, "I *will* miss you when you're gone."

"Awww." She bent and gave him another kiss, the last kiss. "But not for long, I bet."

On that point, he conceded as she bounded out his door, she was correct. Though it was flattering that she assumed he could pull a companion *de la nuit* with a single text. He would never text for something like that; he wasn't a (total) barbarian. A phone call, now—

His phone rattled on the bedside table and he leaned over to grab it. Glanced at it, then looked again. Keyed in the password, saw the entire text, and thought: *shit.*

Two

Too soon, far too soon, he was in a terrible restaurant (French/Japanese/Cuban fusion) sitting across from his terrible twin, Rake.

"Not that I don't love being treated to your scowling face in the wee hours—"

"It's ten thirty in the morning."

"—but why am I here?" Rake had the ability to use any piece of furniture as a bed, and now he was lounging with no regard for his posture. All Blake could see was a shock of dark blond hair and bloodshot blue eyes. "Is Mom okay? Please say Mom's okay. A hangover plus Blake plus Mom is just exhausting to think about." He straightened and rubbed his temples. "My head *is* still attached to my body, right? It didn't blow up or anything? My brain feels really explodey."

"Stop making up words, you hungover troglodyte."

"I will if you will."

"'Troglodyte' is a real word! God, why do I ever reach out to you?"

"Dunno. But it makes you nuts, so I don't know why you don't quit it." Rake had drained his water glass upon sliding into the booth and now snatched and slurped Blake's.

"Unlike some, I cannot simply jettison my responsibilities when they become tiresome." *But oh, in a perfect world . . . one where Rake isn't terrible . . .* "Not that I haven't been tempted; surely I've done nothing to be saddled with you."

"Did so. It's your own fault for insisting on being born first. You probably elbow-checked me on your way out of the womb. Now c'mon, why are we here? Why'd you call? What couldn't wait until our birthday?"

"Our mother is in Sweetheart and she needs us. She hates it, but she needs us."

The wiseass grin dropped off like it had been slapped away (which, Blake had to admit, he had been tempted to do on several occasions) and Rake's teasing mien was replaced with utter seriousness. "Tell me," he ordered.

So Blake did.

Three

One year earlier

"I don't understand you, boy," Shannah said, shaking her head. She was as slim as she had been in her twenties, twice as willful, fifteen times as wealthy.

"'Boy,' really? Don't you normally save that for Rake?"

"He's not here yet," she replied, as if that made *any sense at all.*

Blake sighed and stared into his scotch and soda. "We're not actually interchangeable, you know."

"Hush," she told the frowning man a head taller and forty pounds heavier, and he hushed. "Look at you."

"No need; I could just look at Rake when he arrives. It's the same thing."

She ignored that. "Handsome, smart, rich, well-read."

"Well-read is last on your list?"

"Fertile, ready to settle down and spread your seed."

"I am not. Discussing my seed." Blake hid his head in his hands, the better to shut out the restaurant, the bright lights, his mother's relentless interrogation about his seed, and his sudden desire for self-inflicted felony assault. "Please kill me instead."

"My point—"

"Oh, good, you have one."

"—is you don't have to do your silly lone-wolf thing."

"That," he said, taking a careful sip of the scalding tea, "is a relief. I'll stop immediately."

She smacked her knuckles, hard, on the table, an attention-getter he'd been familiar with since toddlerhood. When the knuckles hit the table/counter/top of his skull, it was past time to pay attention. "What was wrong with Carrie? Or Sandy?"

"Terry and Mandy wanted things I didn't."

His mother just looked at him, and after a long moment he elaborated: "Every girlfriend I've had—"

"Some of them were older than you, boy, and not *girls*."

"Every womanfriend I've had—"

"No, never mind; that sounds idiotic."

"Every female chum I've had liked my money far more than they liked me." *A little more* would be tolerable, probably; *somewhat more* he could live with. How unfortunate it was never a contest. It was always far more. *Far more.* Faaaaar more. And yes, he could hear the chorus of *poor baby!* in his head, thank you very much. They all sounded like the fiercely loving woman sitting in front of him. His self-pity, he often thought, was matched only by his self-loathing.

(He would never say such a thing to his mother. Also on the list of things he would never say to his mother: The ones who didn't care about his money liked him for his cock, and only his cock. And unlike the women interested in his checkbook, the ones who liked his cock were up front about it. On the whole, he preferred the latter.)

"All right," his mother was saying, "you haven't found the right female chum yet; it happens. It doesn't mean you won't fall in love tomorrow." And never in a hundred years would Blake point out his mother's hopeful-yet-defeated tone to her. She had given up on herself, yes. But never on him. Never on his brother.

"Love is an illusion fostered by the greeting card industry."

His mother opened her mouth. Closed her mouth. Shrugged. "I can't think that's true," she said at last. "It's too sad. And someone your age definitely shouldn't think it's true."

He would never point out she hadn't found The One, either. In the beginning, she was living on tips and finding out about the world. Then she'd gotten pregnant, and the following years had been spent finding out what the world thought of single mothers.

Then, of course, their father's wealth. From Burger King to Trattoria Reggiano in one day, thanks to their absent father's determination to re-create the erotic food scene from the *9½ Weeks* remake (he had choked to death on a kiwi).

And in all that time, Blake's mother had dated here and there, and apparently having twins wasn't nearly the baggage for a rich cocktail waitress as it was for a poor one (she still waited tables one night a month to "keep my toe in the cesspool of humanity"). But the men all left eventually, or she left them, and Blake knew why, because it was the same reason he hadn't settled down: two Tarbells would never *settle*. The third

Tarbell had structured his entire love life around settling. And see how that turned out.

"In your own way, you're just as much a hound as your brother."

"You take that back!" he nearly roared.

"You both go through women like a pig through slop."

"Enough of the farming homilies."

"That's fair," she admitted. "That's how I can tell I need a nap. I start to sound like Sweetheart."

"Change of subject?" he asked. "How was the Louvre?"

"Terrible." She pouted. "Security was far too tight."

"Mother." He shook his head and gulped at his drink. "You're going to get arrested."

"Why are you using the future tense?" she teased. "I've *been* arrested. And stop calling me Mother."

He shook his head. His mother had the strangest hobby: She enjoyed changing museum exhibits. She would put Egyptian jewelry on a mannequin in the Western exhibit. She would put a kimono on a mummy. Blake had been thirteen before he realized all mothers did not do this.

"I don't want to talk about those unyielding, uptight Louvre employees. I want to talk about why you're alone."

"Leave it."

"Oh, goody! Here just in time for the 'I'm rich and cute and life is sooooo hard' followed by the 'shut up about your problems that aren't problems, boy' section of our program. Thank God I didn't miss it."

Blake didn't look up. "Apologize for calling me cute. Right now."

Then he did look up and saw, as expected, Rake grinning

down at them. Further proof Rake was clinically insane: He was happy to see his brother, and tolerated their mother's loving criticism much better than Blake could. Because Rake was terrible. "And come on. Sushi? Are we really having bait for supper again?"

"Breakfast, I think." His mother glanced at her watch. Four fifteen A.M. "Sit down, boy. Give your mother a kiss. Stop pretending you don't like Japanese cuisine."

"I love Japanese cuisine." He slid into the booth beside their mother and kissed her cheek with a loud *smek!* that she pretended to dislike but blushed over even as she wiped it away. Blake admired his brother's ease in social situations almost as much as he found the man as irritating as a recurring hemorrhoid. "The Japanese are a subtle people when it comes to their meticulous cuisine. This?" Brandishing the menu like a whip. "This isn't Japanese cuisine. It's blasphemy wrapped in rice and seaweed. And you'll *still* make us tip forty percent."

Blake grinned. "He's right, Mom. The Japanese deny responsibility, rightly, for the Philadelphia roll, the California roll, and frushi."

Rake snorted. "Thanks, Encyclopedia Blake. But see?" he asked, turning to their mother. "That's how horrible this is: Blake and I are on the same side! We *agree*. That hasn't happened in . . . uh . . . When did *Lady in the Water* come out again?"

"Ah . . . 2005? No . . . 2006."

"Enough." Another rap on the table; Shannah was ruthlessly wielding the Knuckles of Doom today. "I have news and we need to get down to it. I'm an heiress."

"Again?" They spoke in unison, then glared at each other. They loathed all twin clichés and wouldn't dress alike if someone stuck a gun in their ear. They never tried to speak in unison. Rake lived in T-shirts and leather jackets; Blake felt more comfortable in anything from Savile Row (he occasionally slept in his suit). Rake was a Democrat ("Ironically," he'd explained, "I vote Democrat ironically.") solely because Blake was a registered Independent. And on. And on.

Rake had continued solo: "Seriously? You've inherited a bundle again? And we couldn't meet on our birthday to talk about this while pretending we don't drive each other nuts?"

She shook her head. "It can't wait four months. And my inheritance . . . it's not as much fun this time."

"Well, it hardly could be." Ah, the memories. From living on tips and the kindness of friends, to millionaires, and literally overnight. It was juvenile, Blake knew, but his most treasured childhood memory was the week after their mom had explained about their father's death. A six-figure wire had hit her account to "tide them over" while the estate plodded through probate. She had stared at the balance, staggering like a sailor back on land—he and Rake had to hold her up—and then burst into fierce tears.

Blake had been frightened

(she never *cries!)*

and Rake had been angry

(who made her cry and what part of their face can I fit my fist into?).

As her sons stammered in confusion and tried to comfort her, she had bent (not much—even at thirteen they were almost as tall as she was) and swept them both into a hug so swiftly all three skulls banged together: "Mom, don't—ow!—cry."

Then: shopping spree. Since it was Vegas, baby, land of a

thousand daily bachelorette parties and gambling addictions, all sorts of places were open. They started at a gas station to top the tank of their always almost-empty Volkswagen ("Fill it up! Fill it allll the way!"), and from there to a dealership to buy a new one. From there, Home Depot for a grill ("Why d'you want to make fire in the desert, Mom? Can't we get a walk-in freezer instead?"), the grocery store for things to cook on the grill ("I want, like, a dozen kebabs of marshmallows."), and finally ended up at the SassiPants nightclub guzzling Shirley Temples at 5:00 A.M. All the while their mother giggled and cried and giggled some more, and that was the day Blake found out his face could actually hurt from smiling so much.

"This time," she said, yanking him back into the present, "it's a little more complicated."

"Who died?" Even as Blake asked, he realized he had no idea how many relatives he had from his mother's side of the family. He and Rake had never met any of them. And she never spoke of them, but that, at least, Blake understood.

It wasn't until much later that he realized she'd avoided the question.

"I'm inheriting land."

"Amusement park land?" Rake asked, ever hopeful, as well as eternally thirteen.

"Abandoned farmland."

"That you can build amusement parks on?"

"No, dolt." A smile softened the rebuke. "Farms formerly owned by several family members—"

Blake straightened so fast it was almost a spasm. "That's impossible. We do not have family."

She sighed. "Blake."

"Yeah, they made that clear enough when you needed help."

"Rake."

"This is your inheritance? Our father at least left something useful, even if he himself wasn't ever useful."

Rake picked up the rant. "They left you— What did you call it? Abandoned farmland? The same assholes who disowned you when you went home for help? The ones who ignored you for years, then had the balls to get angry when you wouldn't fix their lives with money they never dreamed you'd have but didn't hesitate to ask for once they found out you had it?" Rake had to stop and gasp for breath, and their mother seized the opportunity.

"I don't know," came his mother's steady reply. "You'll recall we haven't kept in touch."

"And I'll recall why: They shut you out. They shut all of us out, so my advice? Keep it that way."

"I'm not seeking advice, boys!" she snapped. "I'm telling you what I'm going to do. The reason I left Sweetheart in the first place was to earn enough money to buy my own farm."

"It was?" Rake asked, catching Blake's glance for a moment. Blake shrugged; he'd had no idea, either.

"Yes. And now I've inherited several." She paused while the waitress delivered refills, and resumed when she left. "And why would I do to them what they did to me? Turn my back in strength as they did in their weakness? How does that solve anything? How does that *help* anything?"

"All right," Blake replied mildly. "I apologize." He glanced at his brother, whose mouth was set in a stubborn line all at the table knew well. No apology forthcoming, that was fine.

Sometimes Rake needed coaxing. Blake kicked him under the table.

"Agh! You fu— You bas—" Rake jerked his leg away and bent down to rub the no-doubt-throbbing shin, which gave Blake a clear shot at the other one. "Agh, that *hurts*, fuckwad!"

"You both stop that. *Now.*"

Cowed, they complied. Blake cleared his throat. "What will you do?"

"Go home. Again. This time for longer, I think." Shannah nibbled her lower lip, a rare external indicator of stress. "And I have no idea how long that'll be; I don't know when I'll make it back."

"*If* you make it back," Blake pointed out.

"Of course I'll make it back; stop making it sound like we're in a horror movie."

"My bleeding legs are in a horror movie," Rake muttered, sitting as far from Blake as he could while still remaining in the booth.

"You're not speaking with strangers, you know. 'Of course I'll make it back'? Mom, you've been a nomad for over a decade. You rent, or you buy and then rent, or you buy and sell, or you stay in a hotel suite for months at a time."

"As do you," she pointed out.

"Not me!" Rake added with cheerful spite. "Same shithole apartment for the last four years. Location, location, location." He didn't mention, and Blake didn't volunteer, that Rake loved his apartment because it was walking distance to several strip clubs/prime rib buffets, because Rake was terrible.

"You've never put down roots," his mother added. "I have long put it down to you and Rake being restless spirits."

"And lovers of low rent and cheap sirloin. And pretty ladies."

Don't engage; stay focused on Mom. "But really, all this time you have been waiting to go back? You've wanted to buy a farm? You've had the funds for years. You don't want *a* farm. You want a Sweetheart farm. And now it seems you have several."

A long silence, broken by, "Maybe. If I'm right, I'm fulfilling a family duty. If you're right, I'll have found my true home again. Either way: I'm leaving."

"Well, we've done our best to talk you out of it." Rake was indulging his loathsome habit of helping himself to everyone's water glasses, and finished draining his mother's. "But you're set in your ways, old woman."

Blake failed to hold back the all-body shudder. "I love you, little brother, and if you ever call her that again I will throttle you."

"Nice way to talk to your bro, Bro!"

"Until my fingers ache. Until they're in spasm from the strangling."

"Enough." Their mother was wisely signaling for the check and the waitress came over at once, laden with a brimming water pitcher.

"Is it a Tarbell thing?" Rake asked. "Wanting a Sweetheart farm? Needing to go back?"

"I think it's more like a Lifetime Movies for Women thing," Rake suggested.

Their mother shook her head. "I don't know. It's something I have to do. Perhaps it's just a Shannah thing. And so I leave you to your Edward the Fourth biographies, Blake, and your occasional arrests for assault, Rake."

"Don't forget his impending case of alcohol poisoning."

Shannah quirked a curl of a smile at him. "Yes. That, too. You can always find me, boys. Or call me, and I'll come. As I always have."

She ignored her sons' protests and paid the bill for the three of them. They left their customary 40 percent tip and went their separate ways. That was a Tarbell thing, too.

Four

Back in the present . . . (remember, the last chapter was a year ago!)
(I need to remember how to tell a linear story one of these days.)

"It's too much for her, too much for anyone; she keeps getting in deeper and deeper. You wouldn't recognize her voice if you took her calls."

"Hey!" Rake yelped. "World traveler, remember? Show me the cell tower on Lopez Island or the Travaasa Hana or the Aran Islands. I always call her back—"

"At three A.M. Sweetheart time, when she's semiconscious and barely coherent."

"She's completely coherent! It's our mom! She'd be coherent if she was dead!"

Blake sighed. "You disappoint me." Unspoken: *again.* "If anyone could recognize barely coherent, little brother, I'd think it would be you. And the racket when you pulled in! Like this town isn't barely tolerable as it is. A motorcycle *and* a leather jacket? How original. Lovely periorbital hematoma, Marlon Brando."

"Blow it right out your ass, Benjamin Tarbell Two-Oh."

Blake hadn't realized he had slammed his fist on the table until his knuckles began to throb. "I'm nothing like our father."

"What's the new one's name? Carrie? Terry? Gerri? Foferry? Fee-fi-fo-ferry? *Ferr-ee!*"

"*Ava.* And she's fine. I have reasonable certainty she's fine. As couples often do, we came to a mutual decision to give each other—"

"—some breathing room," they finished in unison, and now Blake's temples were throbbing in time with his knuckles. "And you're one to talk, little brother," he added.

"At least I'm open about what I want from them and what they want from me. You, *you* think you're a gentleman because you insist they spend the night instead of calling them a cab. You're just fooling yourself, pal. And they know it and I know it and Mom knows it and everybody but you gets it."

"Wanting the lady in question to spend the night rather than showing her the door once we've stopped sweating isn't a character flaw, Rake, though it's telling that you think it is."

The twins glared at each other, nothing new, but remained seated, which was. Only a matter of enormous concern would get—and keep—the men in the same room at the same time outside of their birthday, or house arrest. *My brother is a cavalier man-slut,* Blake thought with dismay, *and he thinks I'm a closed-off tight-ass with the heart of an Anglophile. And we're both right. Because Rake is terrible and I'm no better.*

He pulled in a long, steadying breath. "This isn't helping our mother."

"No." Rake was suddenly very interested in stacking all the Splenda packets on top of one another. He was trying to take care, but the Tower O'Splenda was wobbling. "It's not. So. What, then?"

Relieved at their temporary détente, Blake leaned forward. "I propose we join forces. Hear me out!" he added at Rake's shiver of terror/revulsion. "You know she has a harder time dealing with us when we're united."

"Truth. It's like the Roadrunner teaming up with Wile E. Coyote. You never see it coming, and when it *does* come it's creepy and weird and everyone's taken off guard."

"Yes. 'Creepy and weird' is an outstanding way to describe the situation. Let's initiate a conference call and let her know we're going to work together to help her through this mess, no matter how complex."

Rake was nodding slowly. "Yep, yep. That would definitely disarm her into allowing us to interfere. Help! I meant help."

Blake nodded. "So: we will reach out at a time early enough that she will likely be in her room getting ready, but not so late she has left to deal with the judgmental farmers brigade. Eight A.M. ought to do it. Can you be at my place in time?"

"Sure."

While pleased by his brother's unexpected attack of sense and cooperation, Blake paused and, because he was a masochist, asked, "So when would that be, exactly?"

A shrug of leather-clad shoulders. "Fifteen minutes early to work out the script. Say quarter to ten?"

"She is trapped in the Central Time Zone, Rake."

"Right. Center means more toward the middle. Noon is the middle. So she's two hours closer to the middle: ten A.M."

"I don't understand." As Rake opened his mouth to explain more of his demented logic, Blake continued. "You have a high school diploma. You have a college degree. You're a polymath."

"Not anymore. The doctor gave me some antibiotics and it cleared right up."

"Very funny." Argh, his jaw hurt. Forcing words past clenched teeth was harder than it looked. "You are not a complete imbecile."

"Awwww. So sweet!"

"How do you not understand how time zones work?"

"Christ, Blake, will you back off my dumbassery for once?"

"But it's so fascinating. Like studying a new mold spore no one knew existed."

"Aw, jeez." Rake had forgotten his bruise and rubbed his eyes with a wince. "Just tell me what time to be at your place."

"Five forty-five." To be certain, he added, "In the morning. Tomorrow morning. Morning is the opposite of evening. Not today. Tomorrow."

"What?" Rake straightened and the motorcycle jacket was just a hair too big, so he looked like a horrified turtle popping out of its shell. "But I'll have just gone to bed!"

"So assist me with our mother, and *then* go to bed!" Blake snapped. "It's not rocket science!"

"You're just saying that because you studied rocket science! You're forever running around telling people this isn't rocket science, that's not rocket science. Nobody elected you the namer of things rocket science!" A pause. "What's wrong? Why is your face doing that?"

"I have no idea. I can't see my face." He swallowed another

sigh. "Either I'm getting a headache or my brain is trying to eject from my skull in pure self-defense."

"Bummer! Need some Advil?"

"Advil," he said, rubbing his temples, "is not what I need." He glanced at his brother's face, then away. "You all right?"

Rake shrugged, then indicated the puffy flesh beneath his eye, which had swelled slightly smaller than a Ping-Pong ball and displayed an impressive range of green bruising. "It's just sore."

"I assume whatever damsel you rescued was appropriately grateful?"

Another shrug. "I dunno. Never got the chance to ask. I saw a couple of assholes harassing the kiddo, and when I rolled up one had her purse and the other was about to have her. So . . . you know."

He did know. Rake had their mother's quick temper, as well as an inability to tolerate an unfair fight. When they were eleven, he'd grabbed a Wiffle ball bat and rushed to defend a classmate trying to hold her own against two high school students from the next trailer park. If it had been a real bat, he might have killed them. As it was, both boys had odd Wiffle-shaped welts all over their backs and legs and fled, yelping, never to be seen again. Because Rake was terrible, but most people were even worse.

"She took off before I could make sure she was okay. The way she was moving, she was probably okay."

"If you're going to let people smack you, you might at least tend properly to the injury." He waved the waitress over. "Could I get a clean washcloth and—"

"Blake—"

"—a bowl of water? And some ice?"

"First off, they're not bringing you bowls of water and cloths. This is not business class on a flight to Tokyo. Second, this happened two days ago. Anything you do now will be window dressing."

"And some duct tape for my brother's mouth," he finished, then turned to Rake. "If you sit still and take care of this, I'll schedule the call to Mom for an hour later, so you can get a nap first."

"Awwww. You *do* care!"

"Shut up."

"I feel safer already."

"Stop talking."

"Such big, strong arms! To go with your big, strong feet!"

"I hope you get blood poisoning and die."

"No, you don't." Rake was positively radiating smugness. It was as sickening as it was (slightly, very slightly) amusing.

"No," Blake sighed, waiting for the bowl and the ice and the cloth, "I don't."

Five

Amtrak wasn't horrible.

Blake had expected to dislike a twenty-hour train ride through the vanilla-bland Midwest. Instead he had been pleasantly surprised; the countryside was beautiful, the food wasn't dreadful, and the sleeper cars were equal parts efficient and interesting.

After a pleasant night, he felt refreshed and ready to solve problems as the train slid into the station. He pulled down a bag for the thirtysomething redhead in the seat opposite his and automatically flirted back when she made appreciative noises. He counted the freckles sprayed across her nose while they chatted, and instantly thought of many more uses for a sleeper car. The slow glide, the gentle rocking back and forth while the cars wound their way through the countryside as he figured out where to touch and when, and how gently or . . . not gently. He walked with her off the train and bid her farewell, not a little reluctantly.

Business first, he reminded himself as he found himself in Sweetheart, North Dakota.

Well, not exactly. Amtrak didn't go to Sweetheart, but the good people at Enterprise understood and were happy to rent him a sober, sensible vehicle with excellent gas mileage.

Well, not exactly.

"I don't understand." It was an hour later, and he was in a near-empty parking lot with an unstable stranger. He eyed the thing he was expected to drive with no small amount of trepidation. "This is not a car."

"Technically," the unstable stranger agreed, "that's correct. It's a truck. A Supertruck!"

The thing that wasn't a car was the largest vehicle he had seen outside of a Greyhound bus. Tall (*very* tall; he would have to stretch to reach the handle)) and long (*very* long; he had never seen a truck with a four-door cab before), it was deep blue with a pattern of waves streaking the paint all along the side. On purpose, apparently, and doubtless to give observers the impression that, even parked, the Supertruck was a vehicle to be reckoned with.

"You promised to rent me a car and I promised not to destroy it." He dragged his horrified gaze from the Supertruck to look at the woman foisting said Supertruck on him. "Those were the terms of the contract we just signed. This"—he pointed, since she didn't seem to be getting it—"is not a car."

"I thought you might like to take advantage of our free upgrade," the out-of-college-maybe-a-month agent explained cheerfully, her "Hi, I'm Dara!" name tag twinkling in the early-morning sun. Despite her extreme youth, Blake was seriously considering seducing her solely to get a car upgrade (downgrade?). He ought to be ashamed. He tried not to be so coldhearted about his bedroom trysts. It was something Rake would have done (he'd once seduced the manager of the local fried chicken eatery for free wings, and when Blake pointed out he was whoring himself for chicken Rake just laughed at him). "And look! There's a little bitty ladder, right here, to help you climb in."

Blake eyed the little bitty ladder with trepidation. "The wheels come up almost to my thighs."

"I know, right? Isn't it the best?"

"No." He took a slow step back from the vehicle. It would never due to appear as if he was fleeing. He must not show fear! "I'd like a car now, please."

"Look, I can't." The overly cheerful attitude vanished, and in its place was an overly harassed attitude. "The Great Outdoors Band is in town and this is all I've got."

"Who? Never mind. Would you like to get a drink somewhere?"

"It's nine A.M."

"I'm aware of the time," he replied grimly. "Listen, Dara, it doesn't have to be drinks; I happen to be—" *Stop. Stop, you heinous douche! Were you really about to blurt,* I'm a big-city millionaire and not exactly hard on the eyes, please let me make love to you so I can drive a sedan? *Wow, stay classy, Blake.* He hated when his internal voice sounded like Rake. He forced a cough and tried again. "The thing is, this, ah, vehicle isn't—"

"And I didn't charge you extra for the upgrade."

"I would hope not." Then: "It's *not* an upgrade."

"You should definitely gas up at least twice before you get there."

He gaped at her, impressed yet annoyed that a young woman barely of drinking age (if that) was dominating him so completely. *Once more unto the breach.* "Listen, forget about drinks. It may be possible you don't understand what a contract is, so I'm going to take you through ours, step-by-step, until—"

"Enjoy!" Exit Dara. Cue the agony of defeat.

He sighed and tugged on the door handle, which was almost nipple high, then put a foot on the ladder and heaved himself inside. The Supertruck swallowed him and he managed to yank the door shut with a grunt. At once he felt like he was on top of the planet, staring down at everything else on earth. Was this how God felt? Did God, in fact, drive a Supertruck? Per the contract, which had been crumpled in his fist during his Dara wrangling, "Supertruck" wasn't a description; it was what the thing was called. One word. He shuddered; he couldn't help it.

Never mind. He and the Supertruck had work to do. He started it, then began to familiarize himself with the instruments. Thanks to trysts with Ava, he'd seen the cockpit of an airplane, and the Supertruck's was bewilderingly close to that. He leaned across the wide seat and managed—barely—to open the glove compartment and extract the manual. A quick skim, some prudent test-driving, and he would be in Sweetheart in no time. By lunch, at the latest.

Fear not, Mom! The Supertruck and I are here to help. Now then, I can skip the index, I think, since time may be of the essence. . . . Chapter One: "Understanding Your Supertruck" . . .

The countryside was impressive. What little he had heard or read about the Midwest had left him with the impression that it was like a desert with grass and trees and very few people. Except in North Dakota, where there was only grass.

Patently untrue. Grass, yes, trees, yes, even hills. Farms and small towns and big cities, trains and trucks and commuters and kids. The third time he had to stop for gas, he asked the attendant what the huge building shaped exactly like a carton of milk was. He got an eloquent look (*How dumb are you, exactly?*) and a reply ("Grain elevator.") that wasn't as helpful as the attendant no doubt believed. Still, the thought of a three-story carton of milk stuffed with grain was almost enough to make him chuckle.

In short, he was pleasantly surprised by not only the abundance of greenery and farms but also the wildlife. He had never seen so much roadkill in his life. Deer, raccoons, skunks, possums, and once even a beaver: all were easy prey to cars and Supertrucks. He had slowed to observe a bald eagle with a six-foot wing span perched atop a dead fawn, enjoying breakfast. *I have no idea how to feel about this. It's my first live bald eagle. Majestic bird! But it's devouring a dead baby deer. Revolting bird!*

And in this way

(someone hit a beaver? beaver, why were you even trying to cross the road? the lake is right behind you!)

the time whipped by. He was almost sorry to pass the *Welcome to Danger, Sweetheart!* sign.

He knew his mother was staying at the UR A Sweetheart! bed-and-breakfast (*ugh*), and the fact that she had family in town yet wasn't welcome to stay with any of *them* would be addressed later, when he was sure he wouldn't smack anyone.

Thoughts of vengeance, however juvenile ("You were mean to my mommy"!), were for another time. Meanwhile, thanks to the good people at Google Maps, he found his mother's temporary home in no time, a three-story rambling white Victorian perched on the east end of town.

The outside of the B and B was standard, the de rigueur white with black roof and shutters to be expected. He was surprised it was so long—the few Victorians he had seen were tall, not wide. The UR A Sweetheart! (yes, complete with exclamation point) B and B was exceedingly wide, almost fat.

He also hadn't expected the sight of people in various somber-colored suits bustling back and forth. Some sort of fancy business-dress family reunion? Was the B and B under audit?

One young woman in particular caught his gaze—though from this height ants could conceivably catch his gaze— because she wasn't scurrying like the others. She was lurching like Frankenstein's monster. It took him a few seconds to understand what he was seeing: she was staggering under a load of manila folders, each bulging with breeze-caught papers fluttering. She had caught her sensible heel on something and was trying not to pitch forward and be doomed to spending the rest of the week catching and refiling at least two reams' worth of minutiae.

Anxious to prove chivalry wasn't just a collective hallucination from centuries back, he lunged for the door and leaped out. Well, not really. He fell out, forgetting he was driving a vehicle that required the use of a ladder to embark and disembark. The fall was so high that if he had planned he would have had time to do a full somersault on the way down. As it was, it was only high enough for him to do an unplanned half somersault.

He felt the air leave his lungs in an explosive gasp, and

everything from his shoulders to his knees went numb. "My coccyx," he groaned, staring up at the gorgeous midwestern sky. He had the vague suspicion the clouds were laughing at him. They sounded like Rake. A chorus of cumulous Rakes.

The gorgeous midwestern sky was blotted out by the woman, who had—quite without his help—righted herself and held on to every file. He gazed up at her like a stunned beetle. "My coccyx is numb," he told the lovely stranger, and would have been appalled, except: *ow*.

She snorted, a sound that should have been inelegant but was instead charming. "D'you want me to call a doc?"

"Please don't." He shivered at explaining any of this to a physician. "I'm begging you."

"Well, at least let me help you up. You were diving out of your truck to help little old me, right? My hero!" She fluttered her eyelashes, which Blake hadn't realized until that moment could be done sarcastically. "It's the thought that counts, or something." He grunted his agreement and proffered his wrist; she seized it. What followed was tugging and a series of grunts and groans until, after an impressively long time, she surrendered to the inevitable. "Get up, maybe?" she suggested.

"Can't. Numb coccyx: still in effect. What did you trip on?"

"What *don't* I trip on?" she said cheerfully. "If it's on the planet somehow, I'll trip. And, y'know, these didn't help."

"These?"

She swept her skirt suit beneath her and squatted beside him, somehow making it look graceful. Her small, close-set pale blue eyes seemed to almost sparkle at him. He knew they weren't sparkling, not really. It was a phenomenon brought about by how the light caught her vitreous humour* and bounced off the retinas. "It's my own fault. They seduced me," she explained, as if what she was saying made sense to him, a stranger. "Wedge shoes are the ultimate in style and comfort, they said." She pointed down at the offending brown wedges and puffed glossy bangs out of her eyes. "As comfortable as walking shoes, they said."

"Who are 'they'?"

"*Them*," she replied darkly. "The devil's messengers. Soulless creatures, all of 'em. The editorial staff of every single fashion magazine for women. *Heads will roll!*"

Lovely *and* insane, an unfortunate combination.

From a distance she had been pretty, which, now that they were face-to-face, did not do her justice. Shorter than he by several inches—he was fairly certain; they hadn't been standing at the same time thus far—with deeply tanned skin and a sturdy, slender body. Her deep brown hair was cut short, curving about her high cheekbones, and her bangs ended just above dark eyebrows. She had a broad, clear forehead and a wide, pretty mouth. *Native American, certainly. What else? The eyes, those light eyes . . .*

She grinned. "Trying to figure the mix?" He glanced away, embarrassed to be caught gaping like a teenager, and she laughed outright. "Irish and German on my dad's side, and—"

He tried not to interrupt her, tried to stop himself, but the thought had hit him and come right out of his mouth like he was Rake, or five. "You—" *Are lovely. Are intriguing. Are carrying too many folders.* "—have high cheekbones." At some point

---

*Eyeball jelly.

in the festivities, she had carefully put the folders on the sidewalk. A prudent move.

"It's good that you told me that," she replied, sounding perfectly serious, then shattering the illusion with a snicker. "Hadn't ever noticed."

"I think my brain is also numb."

"You *really* shouldn't leave the door open like that. You're basically demanding to be made fun of. It's entrapment!"

"Please," he replied. *Please stay here and keep talking to me. Please don't take two trips when you can barely manage one, because otherwise we'd never have met. Please tell me how a stranger's smile makes me want to smile, too. Please.* "Mock away if you like. My brother is one of the world's greatest mockers and he's been torturing me for years. You have no power over me." *Lie.*

What is wrong with me? We've only just met. It's not even sexual—or not entirely. I just like hearing her voice and watching her eyes. Did I hit my head on the way down, too?

She squatted again to help him, and this time as he grasped her small, cool hand he was able to rise to his feet. "Naw. Too easy. Don't say, 'That's what she said.'"

He snorted and managed—just—not to rub his coccyx. "What year do you think this is?"

"Touché." She bent to scoop the folders back into her arms, blocking him with her coccyx when he moved to help. "Nope. Confidential, sorry."

"Oh." *Do not leer at her lovely behind. Do not.*

"I've . . . you know." She jerked her head toward the rambling white house. "Gotta get back to it."

"'It'? Do you work here?"

"No, it's a temporary setup. The Great Outdoors Band is in town, so . . ."

He should not, he thought as she trotted off after a parting smile, but he did. He liked how she said things that made no sense, then assumed he understood everything. It should have been annoying. It absolutely was not.

He watched her until she went around the side of the house

(a temporary setup, but she eschews the front door?)

and then went to find his mother. If he'd known what was coming, he never would have left the driveway. If he'd known he'd just had the best part of his month, he never would have left the Supertruck.

Six

"Couldn't help yourself and I blame myself. Took your offer to help and didn't think about what it meant, what you'd do, and instead of actual help you went Martian and doomed this town!"

Blake, fluent in four languages (including English), had no idea what his mother had just shouted. He tried to parse the sentences; surely the answer was in there somewhere. *Couldn't help yourself . . . blame myself. Active voice, suggesting current events in which I played a significant part. Think about what it meant: she had anticipated another outcome. Actual help . . . Martian? Several theories: 1) my mother is an alien, 2) my mother thinks I am an alien, 3) my mother is drunk at eleven A.M., 4) my mother has gone clinically insane, 5) this woman isn't my mother; she is a hologram programmed by alien scientists to mimic my mother exactly, 6) if not alien scientists, then perhaps programmed by—*

A sharp *crack!* an inch from his left ear; his mother had

crossed the room while he ruminated. The sound sent him rocketing back into his body and (unfortunately) back in his mother's room.

"Come back here right now," she ordered. "No sneaking into your brain when I'm talking to you."

Talking? Then, the even more perplexed thought: *sneaking?*

"I apologize. You were ranting?"

"We were discussing your giant cock-up."

Blake blinked. *My mother said "cock." Yes, it was part of a hyphenated word, but she could have said "screwup." Balls-up. Even fuckup. Any of those would have been fine. Perhaps not "balls." What is happening?* "I don't understand."

"Exactly!"

"You seemed—we only—you were besieged. On the phone, all those talks we had, you sounded . . ." *Broken. Bereft. Lonely.* ". . . overwhelmed."

"It was good of you to call," she replied, calming. "You always called right back, no matter when you got my messages. You're a good boy, when you're not killing me with blood pressure spikes brought on by stress."

"I—" *No.* He had no follow-up to that. Best to stay quiet.

His mother let out a short bark of a laugh. "And yes, over-whelmed, that's putting it—are you saying I inferred I needed you to rush to my rescue?"

No.

Don't, Blake.

Do not do this.

"Actually—"

Blake!

He shut out the increasingly hysterical inner voice. "—I

inferred, as I was the listening party; you implied. 'Infer' and 'imply' are opposites."

You care nothing for living. Definitive proof at long last.

Pretending not to notice his mother's reddening forehead, he doggedly followed the line of thought to its logical conclusion. "The speaker implies. The listener infers. I inferred."

"Not. Now. Blake."

"I'll put the badge away," he agreed at once. Even when Rake wasn't there

(Hey, grammar police! Shove that badge right up your ass!)

he was there. And it bought him a smile, thank goodness, however brief. Time to get back on track. "During our conversations I *inferred* you felt overwhelmed. You *implied* you were plagued with problems."

"Stop using the past tense!" she snapped back, but the fingers that had jerked him back to the present now affectionately ruffled his neatly combed hair (fun fact: she affectionately *smoothed* Rake's eternally mussed hair) before pulling away so she could resume her pace/rant. Her pant. Her race? "And the only thing I'm plagued with is sons."

Hands shoved wrist deep in his pockets, Blake scraped his toe along the green floral carpet, scowling down at it as he mumbled, " 'M not a plague."

An inelegant snort was his mother's rebuttal. He looked up to watch her pace and was disoriented—again—by the décor.

Flowers, had been his initial thought upon entering the room. *Flowers everywhere. But not in a charming meadow way. A funeral home way.* Flowered carpeting (green, with sizeable pink cabbage roses). Flowered wallpaper (white tea roses over pale pink stripes). Flowered curtains (sunshine yellow background and tiebacks littered with roughly eight million daisies). His mother had been pacing back and forth so quickly, her small form darting from floral-curtained window to floral-curtained window over floral carpet, that she reminded him of an irritated hornet trapped in a vase with flowers not at all happy to be in there with her.

"Do you know what I'm trying to accomplish here?" she asked after another minute. But she shook her head even as he opened his mouth. "No, that's not fair. I never told you boys in so many words. I spent decades never talking about this place; I can't put that on you two."

Thank God! Blake, you idiotic bastard, you just might live through this! "Then why—?"

"I thought that when you said you were coming to help . . . I thought you meant *help*."

"I *did* help!" he protested. "You don't have to worry about the farms anymore. They aren't your responsibility anymore." *Why are we still discussing this? Why are you so upset when the problem was easily solved? Why am I overnighting in the world's oddest bed-and-breakfast?*

"Yes. They. *Are!*" She whirled on him so quickly, Blake experienced a sympathy dizzy spell. "That's the whole *point*. That's what you don't *get*."

Dear God. More italics talk. Not good, most emphatically not good. It forced him to say three words he loathed, words he tried never to say aloud if he could help it, a bad habit that had led to much unpleasantness: "I don't understand."

"No. You don't; that's clear to me like it never was before. That's on me, too. But you will, boy. I promise."

"All right." Blake pitted every shred of self-control into not sounding terrified. "Enlighten me, if you please. I'm all yours. Here, I'll . . ." He looked around, spotted nothing to sit on that wasn't embroidered, topped, or near flowers, and sank into the overstuffed chair near the fireplace.

"Now you listen like your life depends on it, Blake." Unspoken: *because it does.* "What you've done in your Martian arrogance is . . . is . . ." His mother was trailing off in confusion (he could count the number of times that happened on both hands) and staring into space.

"Mother?" She was too young for Alzheimer's, he thought in a panic. Wait; was she?

"Oh!" she gasped, slapping herself on the forehead like a gothic heroine. "I promised Roger I'd help him deworm the White Rose of York!"

Blake stared up at her from the chair that was making a valiant effort to suck him in. If there was such a thing as flower quicksand, this chair was the physical manifestation of such an entity. "You promised who? To do what?"

"Deworm the White Rose of York. She's a pig," his mother added impatiently, clearly irritated with Blake's continual stupidity.

Blake began to give serious thought to the theory that the train had crashed, that he was even now in a canyon somewhere with train cars piled everywhere, slowly bleeding out. All of this . . . whatever it was . . . it was just a hallucination conjured by his dying brain to divert him from the fact of his own death.

"Mom, I don't—"

"To be continued!" she snapped, jabbing a bony finger in the general vicinity of his face before sweeping out the door.

"We are *not done!*" she italicized, her voice getting farther away with every stomp. She didn't slam the door—Shannah Tarbell would never indulge in such childish behavior, no matter how tempting—but the weight of her displeasure was much worse.

Blake, never a fan of casual profanity *(everyone does it; there are so many more interesting ways to express shock/anger/surprise/ sadness; how dull)*, managed a, "What the *fuck?*" before allowing the chair to suck him the rest of the way in. If he was lucky, it would suffocate him.

Seven

The terms, the hideous impossible terms of his withdrawal from disgrace and reinstatement into his mother's affections, were made horrifyingly clear over dinner that evening.

Blake, suspecting nothing, arrived five minutes early. Used to the teeming masses of the greater Las Vegas area, he had overestimated the time to traverse from UR A Sweetheart! (God, that exclamation point unnerved him) to the (why? why?) Dipsy Diner.

He had parked the Supertruck at one end of the neatly kept downtown area and, as he walked the streets, he began to get an inkling of what had so disturbed his mother.

Everything was dead, or dying.

Not the few people he saw; they were lively enough, if quiet, keeping their distance and watching him pass with wide-eyed curiosity. *Small towns,* he told himself, surprised he wasn't made uneasy by the scrutiny, *and strangers stand out. Is my mother a stranger to them? I think yes. I think she was even before she left the first time.*

There were many *For Sale* signs on lawns. There were many Going Out of Business sales advertised in windows. The few cars and trucks parked on the streets were old, though neatly kept. He didn't see a single vehicle from the twenty-first century. That could have been a matter of personal preference but, as he took in obvious signs of a town sliding into the void, plus the lack of car dealerships, Blake doubted it.

His phone buzzed, alerting him to a text. He plucked it off his hip and read: *R U in town tonite? 3rd month-aversery of divorce let's fuck!*

Jeanine! In Vegas and feeling sentimental; how charming. He wished she would have called instead; he found texting for sex (or to turn down sex) to be a little cold for his taste. He wasn't Rake, dammit. He wasn't a goddamned barbarian.

So sorry, out of town for a few days. Congratulations again. Your ex was a fool.

He hadn't had a chance to put his phone away when it buzzed again. *U R a sweetie!!!! Sorry to miss U LV not the same when U R not here!!!*

He sighed; he loathed text-speak (another reason why he preferred the more personal touch behind a phone call). Was it so difficult to spell out words and use appropriate punctuation?

Sorry again. Hope to see your lovely face next time you are in town. Ciao, bella.

And that was that, and just in time, because here was the Dipsy Diner

(God!)
on the corner of Main Street
(there are main streets literally named Main Street? outside of nineteenth- and twentieth-century American fiction?)
and Elm, across from a Realtor's office and beside a drugstore with a *For Sale* sign in the windows on either side of the door. He stepped inside, rolling his eyes at the cheery *ka-jang jang!* of the bell hanging directly over his head
(like a scythe, one that sounds cheerful as it separates your head from your spinal cord)
and spotted his mother, seated in her favorite location: a booth equidistant from the kitchen and the restrooms. She nodded and waved him over and, as he couldn't see a weapon, he crossed the room to her.

"Mother."

"Blake." She shook her head at him but found a smile. "We've had this talk every year since you were three."

"Right, too formal. Mom? Mommy. Mama. Madre. *Mère?*" He could remember explaining to his mother on his third birthday that only babies used "Mommy" or "Mama," while Rake laughed and laughed in the background. Now Blake only used "Mother" ironically, except when he honestly forgot.

Distracting her with multiple languages would work, but not for long. But here came the waitress with menus and their water. Excellent; his mother would never eviscerate him in front of a witness. Blake thanked the waitress and gave himself over to the luxury of enjoying a water glass his brother wouldn't steal and drain in three noisy gulps. Meanwhile, the waitress, who was likely sixteen due to employment laws but looked a harried twelve, was bending an attentive ear to Shannah Tarbell.

"Multitask, dear," she was suggesting, accepting the menus. "You have to go back to the kitchen anyway, so grab dirty plates on your way. You've got to refill drinks for another customer; ask the new customers if they want drinks right away, since you'll be over there anyway."

"Oh! That's . . . yeah. D'you want drinks? I mean besides water?"

"Mom, you're not in charge of her training. Leave her be." He didn't even have to look to know he was getting The Glare. *I have literally faced death and walked away unmoved. And yet I'm terrified of my mother, a petite woman in her fifties I'm almost certain I could take in a fight. If I had any sort of a life, this would probably bother me.*

"Milk, please," his dictator-for-life mother was saying, "and more ice water."

"Okay. Yeah. Those are good. . . ." The small brunette flapped a hand at the tables behind and around them, over half of which were empty. "Thanks for being nice about it. I'm just . . ."

"New, yes. You'll get it."

"Hope not," she muttered, already heading back for drinks. "Want *out* of this town."

Shannah sighed. "You and several others." Her gaze settled back on Blake. "Which brings me to the subject of this meeting."

"I'm impressed you waited this long, Mom," Blake said. "Such restraint!"

"My first and last favor to you this evening."

He smiled at her fondly disgruntled tone. "Shall I take that to mean you'll decline to pick up the check?"

A stifled *hmph* was his reply; then she leaned forward to catch his gaze. *Like a cobra hypnotizing a sparrow,* he thought. "You get a chance to look around Sweetheart?"

"Yes."

"Not a lot going on?"

"That was my impression, yes." *Minefield. This entire conversation is a goddamned minefield.*

"This restaurant is a prime example of what's gone wrong here."

"They don't recycle?" His hip buzzed; he ignored it.

Here came the scowl: "I'm serious, Son. What have you seen?"

"Mom, please. I've been in town less than a day, and in this establishment less than three minutes, and—" His phone buzzed again; he ignored it.

"And talked about tea for most of it, yes, but you don't fool me, boy, and you never have. You— Why don't you take that?"

"It's fine, Mom. Here, I'll shut it off."

She shook her head. "Not necessary. And it might be your brother."

He shuddered. "Then I'll definitely shut it off."

"Forget it. Listen, I know you see it and if you don't—for God's sake."

He pulled his phone, glanced at the text. *Conference over; don't have to head back till tomorrow, dinner?* Kelly. Her skills as a veterinarian had creative applications in the bedroom, something he thought he would never know, much less appreciate. *Alas.*

"Er—" He indicated the phone. "May I?"

"Politely turn down one of your random lovers for sex? Yes."

"It could have been work related," he replied, stung.

"It never is with you, sweetie. And I thought you put a stop to the texting."

"Unfortunately, if they have my phone number they also have the ability to text. I told them my preference, but it's not for me to dictate the terms of their communication." *Lovely to hear from you, but so sorry, I'm out of town for a few days. A pure crime; no one with legs like yours should have to wait for anything or anyone.* Send. Shut off. Put away. "You were saying?"

"I was saying you should pull your head out of Edward the Third's bio and really look around this town."

"I left Edward the *Fourth's* biography in my Supertruck," he mumbled.

"Your what? Never mind; we've got to stay on track. Surely you've noticed that it's six o'clock on a Friday night and there aren't more than a dozen people in the only restaurant still open on Main."

"I *had* noticed that," he admitted.

"Which is why what you did was such an unholy disaster."

"Let's be clear. I paid off mortgages so you had less on your plate. I did not kill a chicken, make a pentagram with its blood, then try to call up the Beast. Not that I would, even if I could. The Beast is also my brother, because Rake is terrible." His took a gulp from his water glass, already annoyed and rattled beyond belief. "But please continue explaining the unholy disaster I brought about through love of my mother. Specifics, please."

She rolled her eyes. "God, the guilt. All right. Specifically,

these people don't need money; they need their property. Specifically, duh. Right? Is that what the kids say?"

"I have no idea."

"Why would I have called you if money was the solution?
You boys have always been generous; you could have challenged
the trust anytime after you turned eighteen, then twenty-one,
then twenty-five, but you never did."

"And never would. You deserved every penny, then and now."
A rare moment of agreement between the twins. Of course
their mother should keep enjoying their inheritance, even after
the twins were of age. It hadn't been a matter for debate.

"You're nearly thirty and could have fought to exclude
me—I'm only a Tarbell by shotgun marriage—but you never
did." Her tone softened and she reached across the table to
touch his hand. "For which I was, am, will be grateful, always.
But for God's sake, boy, did it never occur to either of you that
if I'd wanted that solution I would have paid them off myself?"

"It did," he acknowledged, giving her fingers a slight
squeeze before she withdrew her hand. "But Rake reminded
me, because he is awful, that your stubborn streak, which
mercifully passed me by, was likely to prevent you from throwing in the towel, as they say. Isn't that what the kids say? Always remember, Mom: Rake is terrible and should have been
destroyed long ago. In a way, this is entirely his fault." Blake
was vague on the details but remained convinced.

"Spare the shit." Blake blinked; his mother rarely indulged
in epithets. "Listen: Money won't fix this. The bank doesn't
need it and the townspeople won't take anything perceived as
charity. Some of the families have been here longer than North
Dakota has been a state."

"It's been a state less than one hundred thirty years. That's, what? Three generations?" In Las Vegas terms, an eternity. In Roman terms, a sneeze.

His mother chose to ignore math. "Some of them would literally rather die than give up their land, d'you understand? You've got no idea the things they've done to hold off foreclosure. The sacrifices they made because to them it was worth it; they knew it was to secure their children's future."

Blake was beginning to see the problem and didn't like any of it: the actual problem and his part in the actual problem, which made another problem, which was a hideous offshoot of the original problem.

"You giving money to the bank holding their lien literally made their worst nightmare come true."

Mother never confuses "literally" and "figuratively"; ergo, I really have made nightmares come true. What will be required? Amends? Likely. But what sort? An offer of a cashier's check will not be welcome. What can I give her—and Sweetheart—that would signify remorse, and also help? And why am I pondering? She'll have a solution; she always does. She wouldn't have summoned me if she didn't have this figured out. So now I am terrified.

"Three generations would be considered 'new guy in town' by anyone on the other side of the planet."

She groaned and rubbed her temples. "No 'Europe is ancient and wondrous and America is as a truck-stop restroom in comparison' crap, please."

"But when one puts the Sweetheart dilemma against radiometric dating, it's not long, and there are lots of places to live. I drove through several in my Supertruck."

"Your what?"

He ignored the dumbfounded query. "If this particular patch of planet Earth is no longer habitable, for whatever reason, they can find another one." Blake, native of a city of transients, had never understood the emotional response some people had to specific pieces of land. "It's not a matter of sentiment; it's a matter of logistics. Land is the one thing the planet will never make more of, so all parts are equally precious. So what does it matter? You always told us that home is where you hang your hat."

His mother was staring at him and Blake braced himself for angry hair ruffling, finger-pointing, shouting, or perhaps a gentle punch to his solar plexus. But she didn't speak, didn't move, and long seconds passed before she managed, "This is all my fault."

Ah, sweet relief! If she wouldn't blame Rake, who was awful, she would blame herself. Either way, he might make it out of this diner alive. Alas, relief fled as she finished her thought: "But you're still going to help me fix it."

"How?"

His mother showed her teeth in what most people would assume was a smile. "Thought you'd never ask."

Eight

"No."

"Blake."

"Absolutely not."

"Blake!"

"I refuse." He was iron; he would not be moved. "I will love and honor you as my mother for my lifetime, but I draw the line here. No."

"Blake." His mother was steel, an alloy of iron and carbon. "You have to do this."

"Untrue." Iron, dammit!

"You *will* do this." *Argh, steel. Superior tensile strength.*

Still, he hung in. "Inaccurate."

"Blake, I will activate the nuclear option."

His brain actually went off-line for a second as it contemplated the horror. ". . . you can't mean that."

"Without hesitation. I'll turn that key and you'll have to live with the fallout."

Blake stared at the alloy of iron and carbon and knew defeat, which he indicated by muttering, "Shit," into his perfectly brewed cup of tea.

Minutes later, a thoroughly defeated Blake turned his phone back on

(bring on the sex texts! bring on the awkward! I don't care anymore and have nothing left to lose!)

and began mentally composing the blistering text he would send to Rake, because Rake was terrible. The text would be a thing of hateful beauty, Blake's triumph and vengeance at once.

Face up to it: you're screwed.

Yes. He was screwed. But Rake was still terrible, and that was the straw he would grasp. Meanwhile, the bulldozer of his life was imparting more waitressing wisdom: "You can save yourself more trips if you learn to anticipate," she was saying in her frightening *(obey me or face the consequences!)* yet soothing *(I'm just looking out for you, honey)* voice. "Most of the time a customer who wants a hamburger will want ketchup. And small children—"

A sharp *ka-clang!*, followed by a tentative voice from the booth behind them: "Um, waitress? Can we get another fork over here?"

"—frequently drop their silverware."

How did she accomplish that? The timing was perfect! I didn't even know a child was sitting behind us. Once again I am in awe, and also terrified, of she who gave me life.

Their waitress began to wander off in search of flatware just before his mother put down three twenties to cover a $32.46 bill. The manager loomed out of nowhere, startling them both, like a corn-fed chubby demon emerging from the shadows of the hostess station. "You folks have a nice evening," he said, starting to scoop the twenties across the table and into his pocket. "Unlikely, but no fault of yours."

"That's not for you," his mother spoke up. "It's for our waitress."

"Yeah, no. See, I keep them all and we divide at the end of the week." The manager (black lettering on white background name tag read *Bill!* And what was with this town and unnecessary exclamation points?) was short and round, a little taller than Blake's mother and wider, and balding, which he for some reason called attention to by combing strands from one side of his head up over the top of his (bald) head and securing them on the other side with . . . what? Gel? Superglue? Saliva? A bad business, regardless.

(He recalled Rake explaining his position while they were in their teens. "If I start shedding like a husky in spring, I'm just getting rid of all of it. Fuck all that clinging to scraps garbage. It's *all* going down. I will totally rock the Patrick Stewart look. And the Dwayne Johnson. And the LL Cool J. And the Taye Diggs."

"And the Pablo Picasso," he suggested.

"Dammit, Blake, do you have to suck the cool out of everything?")

"You can't do that, Bill," Blake's mother was saying, sliding out of the booth and getting to her feet.

"Sure can, Shannah." The manager was coolly polite, obviously known to Blake's mother but not a friend. "We keep some in the pot for the holiday party at the end of the year and I divide up the rest so we all get a share. It's called teamwork, like when people in this town stick together to stick it out? Maybe you've heard of it?"

Warm delight curled through Blake's midsection. *Oh. Oh,*

this is going to be wonderful. His phone started buzzing (*Caroline? Sharon? Barb? Vanessa?*); he ignored it.

"It's called tip pooling!" she snapped. "And it's illegal. Tips by definition belong to the employ*ees,* not the employ*er.* Do you know why, Bill? It's because *you* aren't paid subminimum wage. So *you* don't get a share of their tips. Nor can you share them out with nontipped employees like dishwashers."

"I know the law!" Bill! snapped back.

"It seems," Blake said in a low, soothing tone, "you don't."

Like all bullies, Bill! ignored the larger threat and went back to trying to dominate the shorter, lighter threat. "This is none of your damned business, Shannah, *again.*"

"You're wrong, Bill, *again.* You can sue him, you know," she said, turning to the waitress, who had frozen in place with a replacement fork clutched in one fist. "He's not legally entitled to any of your tips."

"Sue?" she echoed, and then laughed. Looked around the almost-deserted restaurant, the dusty corners, the quiet kitchen, and laughed harder. "Sue! Right! Because I want a percentage of whatever all this is."

Sensible creature.

"You, get back to work." Bill! pointed in one direction, then the other. "You, get the fuck out of my restaurant."

Blake stepped up, forcing Bill! to stand his ground or take a step back. He stepped back with such speed he nearly fell into the booth with the forkless child. "Sir, I have terrible news for you. More terrible than the fact that a visit from the North Dakota Department of Labor seems to be in your future."

"You don't—"

"My terrible news is this: I don't mind that you're crowding my mother and using foul language, because I have endured a very odd day where almost everything has been out of my control. That's bad for me, because I dislike change, and being out of control, but it's worse for you. Because I am in a foul enough mood that I'm hoping you'll be suicidal enough to raise a hand to my mother. Federal assault is against the law, of course, but sometimes unacceptable actions are met with unacceptable nosebleeds."

"Jesus. You people. All *right*." With a snarl, Bill! threw the sixty dollars at the waitress, who watched with an amazed expression as the twenties fluttered to the floor, then stooped to pick them up. "Now get the fuck out. I'm serious, now."

"Did you know that over forty percent of facial injuries result in broken noses? Your nose is always in danger, as it protrudes from the middle of your face. Yours more than others. And it's not just cartilage; it's bone, too, which is why it often requires surgical correction."

"Blake."

"Sometimes if you're hit hard enough, a broken nose can even damage the bones in your neck. Isn't that fascinating?" Blake asked Bill's! nose, as the man refused eye contact.

"Blake," his mother said in fond exasperation. "Please don't. It'll be inconvenient to bail you out."

"Worth it," he told Bill's! nose. "My brother and I are the only ones allowed to contemplate Shannah Tarbell's grisly murder. Finding our mother intensely annoying is a privilege, not a right."

"If you get pinched, Rake would have a field day."

In an instant Blake abandoned Plan Deviated Septum, because she was right and he would never live it down, because Rake was terrible. "Very well, Mom. Shall we?" He stepped back to let his mother walk past and to let Bill! sidle around him to scuttle to the kitchen. Their waitress seized Shannah's forearm and mouthed, *Thank you,* with a big smile, holding up the twenties for emphasis. Blake turned to follow, and felt a big smile of his own slide onto his face.

She was there, the woman he had met outside the bed-and-breakfast, the one he had plunged from his Supertruck to assist. She was wearing the same suit she'd had on earlier, and the same brown wedges, and two older men were right behind her, also in suits (one with tan oxfords, one with brown loafers), waiting to be seated. All three were big eyed, but she was the only one grinning. It threw her gorgeous cheekbones into sharp relief, and he was absurdly happy she had caught him doing something clichéd and heroically masculine.

"The North Dakota Department of Labor, eh?" she teased as his mother walked past, intent on the street. "God help us all. The last thing this town needs."

"Evil must be stomped from existence by any means possible," he replied, wishing he could linger and talk. Alas, he had a mother to soothe and a venomous text to prepare, because Rake was terrible. And if things went the way Blake's mother planned—and as she had the nuclear option, that seemed to be the case—he would have plenty of time to strike up new conversations. Perhaps his exile to Sweetheart wouldn't be entirely wretched. He wondered if the lovely blue-eyed creature tasted as good as she looked. "A pleasure to see you again."

"Back atcha," she replied, which pleased him so much you'd think she had said, *Jeepers, you're dreamy!* or the twenty-first-century equivalent.

At the time he had no inkling, but it would be their last pleasant interaction.

Nine

Thus did Blake find himself back in his room at the UR A B and B, trying not to gulp his whiskey. Normally he took it with a splash of soda; tonight he needed it neat. And he needed a lot of it.

There was only one bright spot. He would not be tortured solo. His mother had sworn it to be so, and she never lied.

He took another sip, collapsed on the overstuffed bed, which instantly deposited him in the middle of a growing quilt crater

(like a sinkhole! with quilts!),

and fumbled in the bedside drawer for his laptop. He withdrew the dull silver rectangle, opened it, and was pleased to find the battery at 89 percent. He hit the Messages icon and gave silent thanks for iChat; it was the only way he could rage-text with accuracy and speed.

Loathsome brother,
I am being held hostage in our mother's hometown and

*cannot escape the observation that this is ALL YOUR FAULT.
She controls the keys to the kingdom, the money, and the nuclear
option. Take a moment and think about what that means.*

Send. Off it went, winging its way to wherever Rake was hol-
ing up having ungodly amounts of casual intimacy with women
he would never see again. Blake knew he was just as bad with his
flings, but at least he took the trouble to learn their names.

Now. The rest. He thought of the look on their mother's face
("This isn't the movies, Son. You don't get points for trying.")
and continued.

You'll recall we felt the best way

("No. The fastest way, and there's a difference. You wanted a
quick fix so you slapped a Band-Aid over a crack in the dike.")

*to assist Mom would be to pay off the bank holding all the
paper. This solved the immediate problem, but as a long-term
tactic it was brought to my attention that it will prove to be
a disaster. And so, though we are equally culpable in our
mother's perceived crimes against Sweetheart, I am the only
one exiled. Because you are terrible.*

His glass didn't have enough whiskey in it. Minutes later,
fortified, he returned to his texting.

*The terms of my atonement are as follow: 1) No more selling
people's homes/farms to the bank. 2) The remaining farm,
scheduled for closing next week, is off the market. 3) Said farm*

must be made profitable within six months. 4) By me. 5) With-
out my fortune, which she has pulled off the table. (You'll recall
that though she allowed access to our inheritance on our
eighteenth birthday, we are not legally entitled to it until we
are thirty, which is twenty-three months and seventeen days
from today.) 6) I cannot terminate anyone or sell anything. 7)
Resistance is futile. 8) If condition #7 is ignored, she'll activate
the nuclear option.
 Sound nigh impossible? I quite agree, but our mother

("You don't get to be the hero with an attempt. So if you're in
it, for God's sake be in it. If you're in it, here's what that means.")

does not.
 For this, in addition to many other crimes you have perpet-
uated upon me since our birth, you will be made to pay and pay.
I warn you only as a courtesy as dictated by the bonds of family.
Good night.

Later, when Rake hadn't responded to his text missive (to be
expected, because Rake was terrible, but it was annoying all the
same), Blake admitted the truth about why he agreed to remain
in Sweetheart for a minimum of 181 days: his mother was a guilt
ninja. Annoying how, even though you knew how and why you
were being manipulated, it was still difficult to resist. And though
he would never feign understanding of some people's unreason-
able attachment to particular plots of land over others, he wasn't
so clueless he could dismiss their feelings about such things.
 Meanwhile, he had to spend only one night in the bed-
and-breakfast, after which he would move to (muffled groan)

Heartbreak Farm. Only one night surrounded by chintz wall-paper, chintz overstuffed chairs, and chintz drapery.

At once it was too much, and he needed to be away from the chintz. Or surrounded by different chintz. So with one thing and another, he found himself in some sort of porch/tearoom, which had only one inhabitant.

To his astonishment, the lone inhabitant was an infant pig.

She was standing in a small box stuffed with clean straw, looking up at him with bright eyes (he would discover later pigs had poor eyesight) and making small squeaks in greeting.

"Hello," he said as he set his empty glass down on a nearby table. "No more whiskey for me tonight." Was this common in Sweetheart bed-and-breakfasts? Were guests expecting to bed down with infant pigs, or required to? Heartbreak Farm would likely not demand he bed down with livestock, right?

These are the questions I should have asked before agreeing to this.

"Er, hello. Have you eaten? Or nursed? Whatever it is you do at your age?" *Why am I talking to her? Do I expect her to answer back?* He recalled his mother blurting something about the White Rose of York hours ago . . . could she have been referring to the pig?

She *uunnffed* at him in response; he had no interpretation but chose to see it as the porcine equivalent of "come forth, fascinating stranger." After a quick peek over his shoulder to ensure they were alone, he scooped her up in the palm of one hand, then settled her against his shoulder, one hand under her tiny fuzzy rump, the other securely against her back. "You are quite personable," he told the White Rose of York, if that was her real name. "It's close to irresistible. Then again, I may be drunk."

If the *uunnffs* she squeaked at him from her box were cute, the *uunnffs* in his ear were enchanting. He would have to put her down soon. If she kept snuffling in his ear he might giggle.

"You two having fun?"

Blake whirled, clutching the piglet, who let out a small squeal, and beheld a short, stocky man wearing immaculate navy overalls and a short-sleeved shirt of lighter blue. He was older—about Blake's mother's age—with deeply tanned skin, a white monk's fringe circling his head like a fuzzy equator, a heroic Roman nose, and small smiling eyes so dark it was hard to tell the irises from the pupils.

"Is this your piglet? She escaped! But I recaptured her. That's what this is." *Do not nuzzle. This is no time for nuzzling.* "A . . . a recapture. That is the thing you are seeing now, sir."

"Mmm-hmm. Yeah, she's a friendly critter, i'n't she?" He spoke in a clear, calm voice and didn't seem at all bothered to behold a stranger holding his piglet. "Poor thing just drinks up affection like lemonade. Gotta keep Rose in here for a couple more days."

Rose? "That seems sensible." He, of course, had no idea. Porcine husbandry was not in his skill set.

"I'm Roger." He held out a brown weathered hand the size of a bowling ball and Blake managed to shake hands without dislodging the piglet. "You must be Blake Tarbell. You see your mom?"

"Yes."

"Lived to tell the tale, so that's good." Roger stepped close and tickled the White Rose of York under her fuzzy chin. "She's the one named the pig."

On short acquaintance, I like this man. Why? Some people have enough unconscious charisma to make people like them; is Roger a man with such a gift? Is liking him an error? Need more data.

"And you went along with it? With calling her the White Rose of York?"

"I just call her Rose. Your mom settle your hash for ya, then?"

Blake frowned. "How is that your concern, Roger?"

The older man's friendly smile dropped away. "Your mom's a great lady. Real classy and she's not afraid to work, neither."

"Either."

"What?"

"Nothing. You were explaining to me what a great lady unafraid of work the woman who raised me is." Unspoken: *a lady I know better than you do, sir.*

"I've known Shannah since we were kids, so you can just put that thought right out of your head."

Ye gods. A telepath! "How did you—"

"Aw, it was all over your face; anyone could've seen."

"Untrue. I'm told I am . . . I am . . .

a rock
a machine
a robot
you don't care
you only love your books
it's not you; it's me
it's not me; it's you
you don't care
can't you even try to care
do you care about anything

". . . difficult to read."

Roger shrugged. "Don't think so."

"Continue your point, please, and don't think I haven't

ruled out the dark arts," he warned, cuddling the White Rose of York closer to his chest. If Roger turned out to be a powerful warlock/farmer hybrid, he would protect the White Rose of York as best he could.

I should probably sleep soon. I am having irrational thoughts and am feeling protective of an infant pig.

Roger, meanwhile, stood his ground and continued. "I just don't like to see your mama under a bunch of grief, is all. Because of her name, the town never really gave her a chance, but that was never her fault."

Because of her name? Because she birthed the spawn of Tarbell? Before he could ponder further, Roger finished his thought: "She should be able to enjoy herself these days."

"You and I are of one mind in this, Roger."

"Yeah?" Dark eyes brightened and the man tried a tentative smile. "So . . . you're staying in town then? For a while?"

Hmmm. "Yes. She told you her plan, obviously."

"Toldja we go back awhile. Sure, she told me her idea. But you don't look banged up or anything."

"No, all the brickbats were verbal."

A puzzled blink at that, but Roger remained on point. "I'm kinda glad to see you agreed to stick around. Your mom'll really like it. I didn't think—it didn't sound like the kind of thing you'd go for. No offense to you personally. I don't think hardly anyone would go for it."

"Behold, the exception to the sensible rule." The White Rose of York was squirming, and when he put the small fuzzy black-and-white bundle down, she trotted around the corner, out of sight, and then he heard the unmistakable sound of litter being shuffled about in a litter box. "She's house-trained?" he asked, incredulous, all thoughts of his six-month sentence momentarily banished from his brain. "That's amazing! She's an infant!"

"Not a litter box. Too tall—look at those short legs; she'd never make it over." The thought made Blake burst into laughter and Roger grinned in response. "Yup, never woulda worked. A cookie sheet with litter in it. Don't worry," he confided, as if Blake had been about to roar in horrified protest. "That cookie sheet is only for the White Rose of York."

"I am relieved, as will be the other guests." *Refuse all offers of cookies, just to be safe.* "And I stand by my statement; that's amazing. My brother wasn't house-trained until he was four, because Rake is terrible. I, however, was trained before my second birthday." *I must stop bragging about this, if Roger's expression is anything to go by. It's an odd thing to take pride in.* "Speaking of terrible, did my mother mention the dire fate in store for my brother?"

"Some things are best left alone," was the solemn reply, ruined by Roger's shrill giggle. It was such an incongruous sound from the pig farmer that Blake laughed, too. The White Rose of York had finished excreting and trotted back to them, wiggling her curly tail until Blake relented (after less than two seconds) and picked her up again.

It had been an unpleasant week and an odd day, so it was ridiculous how happy he was at that moment. Perhaps he was coming down with something. And there was always the comforting thought that he could be bleeding out in a canyon somewhere, trapped under a pile of train cars.

Blake had no idea whether he was rooting for illness, a train-car pileup, or spending six months in Sweetheart.

Need more data.

Ten

Natalie Lane watched the rented truck cover the last half mile to Heartbreak and was not impressed. This would be the first of what promised to be weeks of awful days, and not for the first time she wondered why she didn't give up, give in, and get lost. Follow half the town *out* of town. Let Sweetheart die.

Not even if he stuck a gun in my ear. Because it wasn't the town, it was never the town, it was always the people. Well. Most of the people. Garrett Hobbes, for example, could fuck right off. The world needed more golf courses like a diabetic needed a glucose drip.

The truck passed the last gate and pulled up between the farmhouse and Barn Main. The engine quit and she could see him in the driver's seat, moving his hands, and was he . . . ? Was he patting the steering wheel? In a *well done, mighty steed* way? Yes. Yes he was.

Self-congratulation must run in that family, she mused. *Oh, and look at this. He remembered to kick out the ladder this time.*

Too bad. She'd have loved to see him on his ass in the dirt. Again.

"It's you!" he said as he hopped down, having the balls-out nerve to sound excited. Except where did she get off? Before she knew who he was, she'd have been happy to see him, too. If anything, she was more pissed *because* she had liked him on short acquaintance. What if he'd never seen her in her other life? When would she have found out his terrible truth? Their first date? Their first month–aversary? Their wedding night?

Wedding night? Jeez, Natalie, get a grip.

"Hello again." He stuck out his hand, which she definitely didn't notice was large and looked strong, especially in contrast to her own teeny paws. Nor did she notice he had big hands and, as a glance at his shoes told her, big feet, and she definitely didn't form a theory about his dick based solely on his sizeable mitts. She also didn't notice how his smile took years from his face, or how his pricey clothes beautifully set off those long legs and wide shoulders, that the color of his crisp button-down shirt was the same color as his dark blue eyes, that his tan slacks

(slacks? Seriously? Slacks?)

fit like they were made for him

(of course they were; guy's probably got a fleet of tailors stashed somewhere)

and that his swimmer's shoulders made his waist appreciably narrow in contrast.

He was still holding out his hand, and she gave it a brief listless shake, the limp kind with the bare tips of her fingers. "You're late."

His smile faded. "It's nine forty-seven."

"Work around here doesn't start five hours after sunup."

"But I had to finishing Skyping with one of the Oxford archivers."

God. Worse than she thought.

He seemed genuinely puzzled, which cranked her state of mind from Pissed Off to Assault a Distinct Possibility.

"We had to discuss volume six, *The Fifteenth Century,* by E. F. Jacob."

"Had to, huh?"

"Oh yes!" To her horror he mistook sarcasm for interest, and warmed to the topic. The boring, inappropriate topic she didn't give a shit about. "Jacobs' work was invaluable, but he was a misogynist—not rare in early-twentieth-century academia—and likely a plagiarist, which of course calls his entire body of work into question. And he was a terrible driver. Illegally awful. So it's all quite a mess."

Quite a mess. The perfect description.

"So clearly, leaving it until later doesn't make sense. Oh, sure, you're going to suggest Mackie's *The Earlier Tudors*—"

"I really wasn't."

"—but my area of interest is in what came before the Tudors, not the Tudors themselves."

"Will you please shut up now? I might— I might have to stab you with something if you don't." Ah, yes, Natalie Lane: the first Lane to lose Sweetheart and then go down for federal assault. Her ancestors would be so proud.

"You want me to shut up?" Dumbfounded incomprehension. "After I explained? I find that puzzling."

"You find what *I'm* doing puzzling?"

"It's almost as if you don't care about what time it is in Oxford," he huffed.

"It sure is. That's exactly right."

"I apologize," he said at once. "I get carried away with my work. You were kind to wait for me. It's lovely to see you again." Then he smiled, a slow grin that she felt everywhere. *Christ, they must just fall over with their legs open for this guy.* The thought pissed her off more, which she hadn't thought possible.

"Where's your stuff?"

He blinked. "Stuff?"

"Your things, your clothes and phone and stuff," she said, impatient. "Let's get them to your room and then we can get to work."

"We?"

"Do you always repeat random words back to whoever's talking to you?"

"No, actually." He tried another smile. God, the man's whole face should be outlawed. "It's just, I don't always understand you. Which is interesting and charming."

No. He didn't call me charming, and I didn't find that charming. No.

She sighed. "C'mon. Let's get your stuff."

Still he didn't move. Well, he didn't move his legs. He stuck his hand out again. "Blake Tarbell."

Oh. Right. Common courtesy. She didn't have the energy to be embarrassed, for herself or for him. "Sorry, I'm Natalie Lane."

"It's very nice to meet you. I was really hoping to see you again, and that was before I knew I'd be staying for a while." He endured another limp *I don't care about you and have no interest in making a good impression* handshake. "Ms. Lane, have I done something to offend you?"

Besides getting within five hundred miles of Sweetheart? Besides the knowledge that a guy in tailored clothes who Skypes the UK to talk about dead people is my best option? Besides knowing I need you if only to get some of the heat off me? And the fact that you walk and talk like sex personified just pisses me off more? Nope, not a thing.

"Not everything's about you, city guy." *Lie.* This was all kinds of about him. But telling him so resolved nothing. "C'mon," she said for what she hoped was the last time. "Let's get your stuff."

Eleven

It was never supposed to be like this. She was supposed to *save* them. And banking was supposed to be a noble profession, not a punch line. From Renaissance Italy to Sweetheart, North Dakota. From the Medicis to the Lanes. What was the saying? From the sublime to the ridiculous in one step? Yep.

Once, Sweetheart had been a bustling midwestern town of just under ten thousand souls. Yes, they were off the beaten path a bit, but the land was lush, the hills (the few there were) were rolling, the hills were alive with the sound of music, et cetera, et cetera.

Then the state highway came, four lanes at 65 mph, set the cruise for 72 if you hadn't had a recent speeding ticket, and all at once, or so it seemed, all roads did not lead to Sweetheart. Fewer visitors meant the local B and Bs had to work harder for fewer (and fewer) guests. Less money meant . . . well, less money. Add a few exceptionally bad droughts, and then the farmers—in a town where every third family was in the ag biz—were in a jam. Add a shit economic downturn lasting over a decade, and everyone was in a jam. Too many young people left

(like Shannah Banaan and call her Shannah Banana once. just one time. see what happens)

and birthrates weren't high enough to compensate.

Any one or two of those things were survivable, but the combination made for a Michael Crichton–type chain of events that led to economic disaster, which in many ways was worse than a plague of knob-turning velociraptors.

So now this. Now this *mess* that went on and on. She thought that was the worst part: Sweetheart wasn't even a ghost town. A ghost town had no one; it had been dead so long it was less than a skeleton, practically dust. Sweetheart was the still-warm corpse, and not all the vermin knew it was time to abandon ship.

(wow, nice, Nat! you should write children's books!)

Now here came Vegas Douche with his Skyping and his awesome dark blond hair and his Italian shoes and his dopey grin, and Natalie truly didn't know whether to laugh or cry. She was afraid if she indulged in either she wouldn't be able to stop.

"Do you work here?" Vegas Douche was asking. "In addition to the bed-and-breakfast?"

"How's that important?" she replied, in no way planning to answer the question.

"Well. Yesterday you were wearing a navy blue double-breasted suit with a cream-colored blouse and nude panty hose, dark-blue-and-white running shoes, no jewelry."

There were no words. So she kept feeling perplexed. Yep. Perplexed was working. She was sticking with perplexed.

"And now you're in jeans and a red T-shirt lettered with the puzzling warning 'One by one the penguins slowly steal my sanity.' The same running shoes as yesterday."

"That's . . . quite an eye for detail." *Ya big perv. Who memorizes tennis shoe colors? It's definitely not turning me on. It's not making me feel special at all.* "But farmers and their ilk do occasionally dress like grown-ups. It's not like the movies. We don't all wander around barns wearing filthy overalls and chewing straw."

"I met one yesterday and he wasn't filthy. Why," Blake kept on, clearly bewildered by the turn the conversation had taken, "would anyone chew straw?"

"I'm one of your foremen here, I'll be the one showing you what you've taken on

(so welcome to Hell, Vegas Douche);
that's all you need to worry about. So this is your room," she said, deciding to get back to the subject. "I'm sure it's not what you're used to."

"It's not."

She'd get a headache if she rolled her eyes much harder. "But times are tough, so we all have to—"

"It's better."

"—make sacrifices and you'll just have to what did you say?"

He had been wandering around the attic while she dodged his job questions and suit observations, looking at the furniture, testing the bed for firmness, peering out the windows. "I live in a Residence Inn in Las Vegas. It's nice. I have no complaints. But it's a Residence Inn."

"Oh, Vegas?" Natalie had to take a second to clear her

throat, going for nonchalance. "That's where you're from? I hadn't known that. Before." *Subtle!*

Vegas Douche will never trip me up. Nope. Not this girl, Vegas Douche! No idea where you're from, Vegas Douche, Chicago, maybe? Pierre? London?

"This is . . ." He had stopped wandering and was now staring out one of the south-facing windows. ". . . much much better."

She tried to see the attic from his perspective, with a stranger's eyes, but all she could come up with was, *This is the place I went when I couldn't bear to go home. This isn't my home and it will forever be my home. It has old parts and new parts, and pretty parts and unlovely parts. It's on the market for pennies on the dollar and it's priceless.* She couldn't look at it with stranger's eyes; she had never been one.

The original farmhouse had burned to the foundation the year Prohibition was appealed. During a deliriously drunken party to celebrate Americans' right to again get shit faced, a party guest got too enthusiastic while feeding a bonfire, a situation made worse when the bonfire was inadvertently moved inside. The drunken guests tried to fight the blaze with alcohol. *Good-bye, original farmhouse, we barely knew ye.*

The replacement farmhouse had gone up the year Roosevelt put the New Deal into effect. It had been modernized over the years (central air and heat, among other unnecessarily necessary things), but it was still a three-story forest green farmhouse with white trim and a wraparound porch. The attached garage, also green, was large enough for four cars; the farming equipment was kept in another building off Barn Main. Inside the farmhouse were spacious rooms in shades of tan and cream, a series of bedrooms and sunrooms and nooks, a size-able working kitchen with multiple refrigerators and freezers, three bathrooms, and all of it topped with an attic that ran the length and width of the house.

The attic, too, had been done in light neutrals and, since heat always insisted on rising (dammit, physics!), was warmer than the rest of the house, but not unbearably so. There were two ceiling fans and the windows were all screened and opened easily. Where the roof slanted so that standing upright was impossible there was a series of deep bookshelves. They were crammed with everything from *Good Housekeeping* issues from the fifties to the entire *Little House on the Prairie* series to C. S. Lewis to Mark Twain to how-to tomes to gardening to a Bible to books on Nichiren Buddhism to J. D. Robb to Jane Austen.

The floor was all blond planking, but several throw rugs were scattered about, cutting down on the splinter potential. At the far end was a double bed made up with pale yellow sheets and a wedding ring quilt, placed just under key, slanted windows that gave whoever was in bed an unimpeded view of the eastern sky. A rocking glider was placed beside one of the south-facing windows beside a small fridge for snacks. Natalie had made sure it was clean and plugged it in for him last night but drew the line at stocking it with snacks and/or booze. If anyone deserved a fridge full of booze where they slept, it was her, dammit.

It was comfy and welcoming and she couldn't help being a little (a *little*) glad he seemed pleased. Glad, and surprised. No room service here at the farm. No one to launder his delicates or bring him a midnight hot-fudge sundae. And if he wanted a copy of *USA Today* slipped beneath his door at dawn, he'd first have to hoof it five miles into town and hope the gas station was open, buy yesterday's paper, then come back and slip it under his own damned door. Maybe Vegas Douche hadn't thought of those drawbacks yet.

"This is . . ." *Huh*. He was still babbling about his home away from hotel home. ". . . *wonderful*."

"I . . . I didn't think you'd much care for it." *Counting on it, more like*, her spiteful side whispered. It was true, she'd been anticipating shrill bitching. And he'd foiled her—again!—by finding the whole thing enchanting. She should be more annoyed than she was. "It's probably not what you're used to."

"I didn't think I would care for it, either," he confessed gleefully, like a boy who'd been caught stealing cookies and, instead of being punished, got more cookies. "Now tell me, what is the piglet situation?"

"The what?"

"I don't see any cookie sheets filled with excretions from an infant pig."

"*What?*"

"Thus I'll surmise I'll be the only one sleeping up here." He looked around. "No piglets then, very well."

"You sound disappointed. Why are you disappointed? Why do you love the attic but are disappointed we don't keep pigs in it?" Unspoken: *What is wrong with you?* Las Vegas must be so much weirder than she imagined.

"And look!" he added, and actually flopped back onto the bed so he was staring up at the slanted window. "You can see the whole sky from here! Not literally, of course. Even if we were outside and had an unobstructed view—"

"Pretty easy, because North Dakota—" Natalie interrupted.

"—yes, although I passed quite a few hills in my Supertruck, even so at most we would only see fifty percent." Then, as if he was anticipating Natalie's furious rebuttal, he added, "But quite a nice view anyway."

"Wait till the sun rises at five thirty tomorrow morning; see if you love it then." She'd gone for bitchy, but it came out exasperated. At least it wasn't fond exasperation.

"Thank you for the warning; you are most kind," he replied, and though he was trying for solemn the giggle ruined it. And the sight of the big, neatly dressed man wriggling around on a double bed over a decade old so he could look out the window while laughing his ass off just slew her. She couldn't help it, she *tried* to help it, but she laughed, too. The mingled noise was . . . how'd he put it? *Wonderful.*

Oh, hell. I am not finding Vegas Douche charming. That shit ain't happening. Not. Happening.

Right?

Right.

Twelve

Natalie Lane was a would-be murderess, a fiend so vile she had the potential to give Elizabeth Báthory competition. She was clearly trying to kill him, and had an excellent chance of succeeding, but he had yet to fathom her motive. Inherent sociopathy, he assumed, was not a motive, or at least not enough of one.

Oh God, she's so beautiful and her hands are so small and I want to hold them, I want to hold them all the time—

He shook off the sentiment. He would die on this farm. This horrible, hateful, brutal fucking farm. Heartbreak Farm, ha! It ought to be renamed Myocardial Infarction Farm.

Oh my gaaaawd! Rake laughed in his head. *Drama queen is not a good look for you, big brother; it's worse than that time I dyed your hair orange in your sleep. Sure, everybody called you Mario Batali all summer, but you had some dignity, man.*

He had suspected nothing that first day. In fact, he had taken quite a liking to Heartbreak at first look, not least because Natalie Lane, of all people, worked there! And appeared to love it and everything about it: the work, the animals, the buildings, the house, the best ways to torture Blake . . . it filled the already lovely woman with zeal that left her dazzling.

Zeal that left her . . . my God, man. Get ahold of yourself.

Good advice. He tried.

Natalie had given him a tour of the house, the barn (called Main One for a reason she would not explain), the other outbuildings. She had introduced him to several sullen men and women, and if glances could decimate he would have been murdered half a dozen times before lunch. Also, lunch was not at lunchtime. He had missed lunchtime. By thirty-eight minutes.

"Breakfast at five, lunch at nine thirty, supper at four."

"What about second breakfast?"

Yes! A small smile. "God, I love Billy Boyd." He found that puzzling but didn't comment. (Hours later, as his griping stomach kept him awake, he Googled and saw that was the name of the actor who played Peregrin Took in a series of movies that were somewhat popular. And thank goodness. He'd been afraid she had referenced a boyfriend, and then been annoyed he'd been afraid.) "Almost as much as Peter Dinklage," she'd finished (it was fine; Google had explained Mr. Dinklage was another actor and thus their relationship was platonic at most).

Along the way he was educated on the difference between a ranch and a farm. "Heartbreak Ranch? Really? Have we somehow ended up in a nineteenth-century Western?"

"Not a ranch. It's a farm."

"Difference, please?"

"A farm raises mostly crops. A ranch raises mostly cattle. A farm can have loads of cows and still be a farm. A dairy farm that grows no crops is still a farm. All ranches are farms, but not all farms are ranches."

"That makes no logical sense," he protested, annoyed, as he often was, by imprecise explanations. "Is there a cutoff point? If you have so many acres for farming, and so many cows for milking and what have you, where are you on the spectrum that the addition of one more cow makes a farm of a ranch?"

She had *stared* at him and that was the first time he felt close to death by foreman beatdown. Then had bypassed the definitions and added, "And I can't imagine you care, but it's called Heartbreak *Farm* because in the early nineteen hundreds a townie from Sweetheart proposed to a farmer's daughter."

"A story," he said, leaning against his Supertruck. (After she had given him a tour of the house they had returned to the great outdoors.) "Excellent."

"She turned him down because she wanted her kids to grow up the way she had, working the land, and all he wanted to do was leave town and make his fortune and never come back. So he left town and made his fortune . . . and came back a decade later. He bought up all this land and started building." She gestured at the house, the barn, the fields. "The house first. And when that was done he asked her to marry him again, and she said no. So he built the garage. She said no. He bought more land. She said no. He built Main One."

"And then she said yes," Blake said, since the answer was self-evident.

"Well, no, by then she had died of a stroke."

"Unexpected."

"She was eighty-four by then."

"This is a terrible story."

Natalie shrugged. "He never built anything else. But for a long time he meant to. The barn was nicknamed Main One because lots of people heard him call it that. 'This barn is the main one, but I'll add on a silo.' 'This is the main one until I build more outbuildings.' Like that."

"Again: terrible story."

"He did eventually settle for someone else and married her and fathered his first child at age seventy-nine."

"He must have indulged heavily in powdered rhino horn. Which was a legal indulgence back then, so the only stigma was one of humiliation, not societal."

"Dunno about that, but he was your great-grandfather."

"Ah." Blake took a moment to process the new data. A beautiful woman had on short acquaintance told him more about his family than his mother ever had. "So this farm belongs to my mom now?"

"No. His kid sold it and it's been changing hands ever since."

"Ah." This, then, was the moral: things come full circle. His grandfather, of whom he knew nothing save that he turned his back on his daughter when she needed his counsel and comfort as she never would again, sold the farm, and three generations later Blake tried to sell and was now penalized. As far as life lessons went, it was obscure and unhelpful.

"Thank you for explaining." Then a dreadful thought hit him. "Are you one of the families my mom told me about? Have you done things you never wished to do in order to hold

on to your family's land, which has been in your family a
century or more?"

She was giving him an odd look, but at least it wasn't a
glare. "No. I'm not in one of those families."

"Excellent."

Later that same day, she had introduced him to the other
farm employees,

(field hands? was that PC?),

all of whom had rhyming names

("Harry, Larry, and Gary? Really?"

"Really.")

and were sullen and disinclined to be friendly. They made
themselves very busy whenever approached, whacking nails
into posts, using pitchforks to stir things around, starting up a
tractor and driving away . . . random farm chores he didn't
yet understand. What Blake found interesting was that they
didn't seem to care for Natalie, either. Perhaps she was a strict
part-time foreman.

He heard scattered mutterings from Harry,

(no, the redhead is Gary),

one of which was, puzzlingly, "douche" and the other "Degas."
He had no idea why a trio of male farmhands would be concerned about feminine hygiene, but such things were not his
business. Nor had he been aware those same employees had a
passion for the works of Edgar Degas

(was it Degas' uncanny ability to depict movement they found
worth commenting on, or his penchant for portraying human isola-
tion? must find out),

but it was heartening to know that there was at least one
topic they could all discourse on.

Well, more than one, but he was reluctant to chat about how they were nearly made jobless and homeless by his various dealings with the local bank, Sweetheart Trust. (Ah, the carefree days of three weeks earlier when he was in his comfortable Residence Inn residence, authorizing wires to Sweetheart Trust while indulging in a Cobb salad with extra bacon and pondering what not to buy Rake for their upcoming birthday, because Rake was terrible.)

Natalie knew of Blake's complicity (he wasn't sure how but assumed it was the grapevine, something small towns were prone to, or so Updike's *Rabbit, Run* and Lee's *To Kill a Mockingbird* indicated). Natalie could have found out who he was in any one of a dozen ways; how she knew his identity wasn't the puzzle.

Her continuing manner of strained but polite dislike made no sense. If she knew he had paid off the other mortgages and surrendered the titles to Garrett Hobbes, she must know that, days before the closing was to happen, Blake had left Heartbreak alone. She should be pleased with him, correct? Especially since he was there to try to save the farm by being worked to death. At least, that was what his mother's logic had indicated. So why the stiff, unpleasant manner with him, with only an occasional smile or laugh, and that given over most reluctantly? It was a conversation he wished for and dreaded in equal parts.

Bottom line: she no longer liked him, and it was driving him mad.

However things would play out, his first day at Heartbreak had been tiring, though he had done little more than explore the area and meet the employees, all of whom liked to discuss douching and Degas when they thought he was out of earshot.

Perhaps it was being out in the fresh air most of the day, or perhaps his brain was demanding it power down to process everything he'd learned thus far. Whatever the reason, he collapsed onto the attic bed with a grateful sigh, and darkness began to descend almost at once. Before it took him completely, he reminded himself tomorrow was a new day, a new start, a new chance.

If I turn out to be even a bit good at this, perhaps Natalie will smile more. And if I prove to have no knack for this, perhaps Mom will relent, which would make me *smile more. Either way, tomorrow is another beginning. Not a new beginning; everyone says that, which is odd, because by definition all beginnings are new, so they're merely indulging in redundancy, which is a waste of nnnnnzzzzzzzzzzz . . .*

Thirteen

Myocardial Infarction Farm was like the apple Queen Grimhilde presented to Snow White: lovely on the outside while hiding the excruciating death within.

Blake realized this when he attempted to get out of bed and at least 400 of his body's 642 muscles seized in protest. His usual disorientation upon waking in a strange place

(ow everything hurts did I work out in my sleep? or get run over? in my sleep?)

kicked in and it took him a few seconds to recall where he was. Sweetheart, North Dakota. The farm. The attic, facedown on the bed. Fully clothed, shoes on. Natalie had delicately suggested he invest in a pair of cowboy boots

("You're not dressed right; you're not shod right; you look like a cruise ship tourist in those tennis shoes, God, why am I putting up with any of this?")

and his verbatim reply had been equally courteous

("Never! I would literally, literally and not figuratively, literally die before investing in cowboy boots. And where do you keep the Band-Aids?"),

if also vehement.

Sweating, because the sun had been shining on him for hours (in Natalie's defense, she had warned him of the perils of east-facing windows when one lives on a planet that rotates in that direction). Right hand clutching a tube of BENGAY like a smoker clutched a pack of cigarettes. Left hand clutching his cell phone, as he had been in the middle of texting Rake his threat du jour, because Rake was terrible. Blake cracked one eye open and squinted at the last text he sent.

The deepest darkest depths of Hell await you, little brommmmmmmmmmmmmmmmmmmmmmmmmmmmmmmmmmmmm Text sent 7:45 P.M.

He slooowly began allowing his muscles to obey his brain's command to cease their complaining and get to work and calmed himself by pondering his position.

Must have collapsed on the bed and sank into sleep like I was sucking down ether.

He wasn't dying. He hadn't been in a coma. He hadn't been in a horrific accident (probably; he hadn't quite abandoned the cherished daydream that this was all a train wreck–induced delusion). He had worked harder than he ever had in his life, and that included the summer he spent assisting the University of Leicester unearth Richard III's skeleton from its parking lot prison.

Working Heartbreak Farm was more difficult than digging up a dead body. But his muscles would adapt, making it easier to get through days like yesterday.

"Oh God," he groaned, stumbling to his feet like a drunken

octogenarian with two sprained ankles. "My muscles will adapt! That might be the worst news of my week. I'll get used to this." The thought was as staggering as it was horrifying.

He hobbled into the small bathroom just off the stairs, hands pressed to the small of his back

(so this is why the elderly often walk this way! it's the only way to curtail the agony. that and an IV full of morphine),

and groaned at his reflection

(kill it! kill it with fire! and make it brush its hair)

and found even the muscles in his fingers had been affected. It took over a minute to finesse the cap off the toothpaste and another before he was brushing his teeth. Muffled groans bubbled from his lips along with toothpaste, making it look like he was in the final stages of rabies.

He changed into inappropriate work clothes (according to Natalie Lane, but he hadn't had a chance to upgrade, or would that be downgrade? he'd only packed three outfits in the first place) and limped down the stairs into the kitchen. He was in agony, yes, but at least he could look forward to a hearty breakfast, since he could smell bacon and other wondrous things and oh no no no no!

"What time is it?" he demanded, and it didn't sound like a whimper *at all*, dammit.

"Time to miss breakfast," Gary chortled, slooowly finishing the last piece of bacon, because even on short acquaintance it was obvious he was a heartless bastard.

"I'm ravenous."

"Prob'ly should've gotten up in time to eat, then." Gary was—was he? He was! He was positively savoring the bacon, which, Blake could not help but notice, was cooked perfectly to his taste. It stood stiffly in Gary's grip, crisp and dark, and shrank with each chomp. It looked so delicious Blake was giving serious thought to yanking Gary's plate away and then licking it. .

"That is *it*." Blake wondered at the thump, then realized he had stamped his foot like a child having a tantrum. "Fission has been reached."

"Eh?"

"I'm getting a hot plate. Or a microwave. Or a fireplace. Something with which I can cook in the attic so I don't have to suffer breakfast before dawn, lunch before ten, and supper at four."

His outburst seemed to amuse Gary to no end, and the man let out a blatant chuckle as Blake limped to the refrigerator to extract orange juice and pour himself a glass the size of a flower vase. To think there was a time when he eschewed all fruit juice because of the unnecessary glucose high. Now an unnecessary glucose high was the only thing keeping him from constructive manslaughter.

A short man, red haired and freckled (and how his job wasn't murder on the man's complexion Blake did not understand), tanned and lean, Gary was wearing Natalie Lane–approved work clothes: ancient jeans, a clean but faded red-and-black plaid shirt, broken-in boots, a grimy baseball cap. As he chewed bacon his jaws moved laterally, like a bovine's.

"Prob'ly you should just hang it up already." Grind, grind. "Head on back to Vegas."

Blake paused in mid-gulp. Orange juice had never tasted more glorious. He could almost hear his starving cells groan their gratitude. "How do you know where I'm from?"

Shrug. "Ever'body knows."

Hmm. I feel so . . . what's the opposite of comforted? "I'm not hanging it up." *Yet.* "It hasn't even been three days." *Yet.*

"Don't worry." Gary stood, bussed his own plates, cutlery, and coffee cup to the sink, then stretched, yawned, and ambled to the door. "It gets worse. Gotta get to work. You, too, I guess. Or, dunno, have more juice or something. Either way, like I said, it'll get worse."

Don't you threaten me, Gary! I could buy and sell you a thousand times over if my mommy hadn't frozen my accounts. As a manly threat, it left much to be desired. Perhaps something like *when my mommy hears you've been mean she'll make you sorry!* Perhaps not.

Blake sucked down another vase of orange juice, liberated some bread from the pantry, ate two slices in twenty seconds, then shuffled out to face another day of Dante's Inferno.

Fourteen

Are you one of the families my mom told me about? Have you done things you never wished to do in order to hold on to your family's land, which has been in your family a century or more?

Well, no. Not at all. Natalie Lane knew exactly who she was: the town boogeyman.

She had known Blake would have no idea who belonged on Heartbreak and who didn't. And because she wanted a closer look, she presented herself as his part-time foreman. It wasn't as though she couldn't make the time; the bank had already cut her hours to fifteen a week. And it's not like Gary, Harry, or Larry would care enough to notice, never mind rat her out. They'd be saving most of their ire for Vegas Douche, and thank goodness.

Okay, so he's here and you're here and your sinister disguise has fooled him completely and now what?

She had to make Blake see the folly of his check-writing

ways. Which meant she had to make him love Heartbreak. Love it for itself, not the golf course it was in danger of becoming. Which was impossible. But Sweetheart was in the state it was in because too many people gave up. She was in it to win it, if "win it" meant "eventually slink away in defeat."

Insanity: doing the same thing over and over again and expecting different results. Einstein was right about that, even if he'd never gotten the hang of teaching.

Regardless: time on Heartbreak made for a nice change from foreclosing on people's homesteads. Which was the inherent irony of her position: The bank didn't want farms. The bank wanted—*needed*—money. There was a reason foreclosure was the second-to-last stop. What would Sweetheart Trust do with a bunch of farms not being farmed? There were only three options, and they all sucked.

1) Keep the farms and rot along with the rest of the vanishing town. No.

2) Let Garrett Hobbes finish the job he started, which would lead to strangers in hideous outfits stomping around in cleats whacking small white balls over land her ancestors lived for and bled for. *Hell* no.

3) Felony murder. Good short-term plan, bad long-term plan. *Nuh-uh.*

Oh, and here he came, limping out the door, then pausing on the porch and blinking up at the sun like he didn't know what the big yellow thing in the sky was. He slowly gazed around the dooryard, taking in the barn, the other buildings, the sky, the ground. Then he shuddered, honest to God shivered all over, then limped toward her. It was, she had to acknowledge, a purposeful limp.

Gotta give him some credit, he knows what we all know. Knows he's not cut out for this. Hasn't quit. The fact that it had only been a few days didn't tamp her admiration; she'd seen people quit Heartbreak after two hours, never to be seen again.

And what was she doing, admiring Vegas Douche? Cripes. She didn't admire his stubbornness, the inevitable genetic trait of any Banaan offspring. And she definitely didn't feel sorry for him as he painfully made his way across the yard to her. No, she was cold; she was an ice queen; nothing touched her; nothing mattered but her mission, she was unmoved by the gentler emotions.

So she greeted him with, "Unmoved!" and then wanted to slap herself in the face. A lot.

"Good morning." Dammit, why did his voice have to be so pleasingly deep? He didn't talk; he rumbled. He'd probably sound like a gravel truck during sex. Which shouldn't have sounded hot—gravel didn't do anything for her, sexually—but was.

During sex? Lane! Get your shit together! Don't make me come down there!

Good advice, brain.

"Morning." An improvement over unmoved, at least.

"There are two bees on your head."

"Why are you counting the bees on my head?" She reached up, slowly pulled off her hat, and blew softly at the fat striped things, who buzzed at her in a *we'll let this go because we're in a good mood, but we could fuck you up if we liked,* and flew away. They were all over this time of year; Natalie didn't mind. It was the idiots who shrieked and jumped and flapped at bees, scaring them, who got stung. Bees were picky; they didn't want to eviscerate themselves unless they thought it was worth the cost. She could relate. "Sleep well?"

"Comatose well." He stood before her and braced himself. "What are you doing at Heartbreak today?"

You. Not we. Bastard. Like that, she was annoyed all over again. Annoyed by his silly clothes, his silly voice, his silly face. She'd been saving the worst chore to give the big jerk time to settle in but at once abandoned that plan. "Yeah, c'mon, there's one more thing that's going to be your responsibility. Too many people have quit, and I don't have to tell you this farm doesn't have near enough employees. There's three times the jobs for not near enough people."

"You certainly don't have to tell me," he agreed, falling into step beside her. "And yet you *did* tell me."

"Foreman prerogative!" she snapped back, and was surprised when he laughed.

"Agreed. I await my list of labors with giddy anticipation and what the hell is that thing?"

They had stopped at the small corral behind Main One, a small fenced-off area about forty feet in diameter. Inside, a stocky, shaggy pony was standing in the middle of the corral, glaring at them. Her coat was the exact color of dust, her tail and mane the exact color of shit. Her head was proportionately large to her body, and the legs were sturdy and looked capable of any task the animal might demand from them. Small ears, big eyes. Most animals with large dark liquid eyes looked adorable; the pony's eyes appeared to be filled with rage, or at least scorn.

Blake, standing beside Natalie a prudent distance back from the corral, tried to speak, coughed, tried again. "What is *that*?"

"Six Two Six Nine Nine Three."

Another dry bark of a cough. "That's her name?"

"That's her PIT tag number." At his look, Natalie elaborated. "Passive Integrated Transponder."

"So when she runs amok on a blood-soaked rampage, you can track her down and blow her up? Christ, she looks like a barrel with legs. A large barrel."

"She has to be; she's a breed of pony—"

"That thing was a pony before she ate a barrel? Where did she even get a barrel?"

Natalie giggled and managed to finish. "—that can carry adults."

"Pity the adult."

Exactly, Vegas Douche.

"And see her glare at us!" Blake seemed unable to look away from the game of chicken stare 626993 had initiated. "She's all by herself, too, back here." Blake looked past the corral at the great field of grass spread out behind Main One, which took up the better part of an acre before disappearing into the far tree line. It was peaceful back here, yeah, but he was right: lonely, too. "Why even buy the thing in the first place?"

"Because at the time, 'the thing' was to have plenty of company." Natalie managed, barely, not to kick him in the shin. "She's the last, and her purchase made sense at the time. Ponies eat a lot less hay than horses, and often don't need grain at all; they're much cheaper to keep. And pound for pound, they're strong for their size."

"Ah. An economical equine."

"Not bad," Natalie said, and snickered. To give Vegas Douche his due, he bounced back pretty quick and had a way with words. If anyone else had talked in that stuck-up way of his, they'd be laughed at. Vegas Douche pulled it off, somehow. God, if she wasn't careful she'd start to like him, which would screw things so completely it didn't bear examining.

Don't worry, Nat. He'll say something douchey any minute, and you can go back to being annoyed. The thought was honest, but she couldn't miss the inherent bitchiness in it. *Is that the kind of woman I am? Or does Vegas Douche just bring that out in me?* She decided it was the former. She hated it when people blamed their behavior on other people.

They both watched the ill-tempered pony trot away from them after baring her teeth in what Blake probably assumed was a friendly smile but what Natalie knew was a *I've got no problem biting if you give me shit, and even if you don't,* display.

"What does Six Two Six Nine Nine Three have to do with me? If the thing is so much trouble and the last pony? Do you— Oh God." He reached out and clutched at a post to steady himself. "You don't— Do you require me to kill it? I did not sign on for slaughterhouse duty. Come to think of it, technically I didn't sign on for anything Heartbreak related."

"Would you even know how to put Six Two Six Nine Nine Three down?" she asked, honestly curious.

"Not remotely," came the reply. "I have no idea how to murder a pony; what a failure of a human being I've become." Pause while his brow furrowed in thought, and she swallowed a chuckle. "Just for curiosity's sake, what would be the traditional method? Firearms? Poison? Making her listen to hours of Strauss waltzes until she commits suicide in despair? What is the etiquette here?"

"You've got an inventive and disturbing mind," Natalie

said, not without admiration. "You're not gonna kill her; you're going to take care of her and break her. Well, not break—she's saddle broken, but stubborn. Your job will be to remind Six Two Six Nine Nine Three that she's supposed to take riders now and again."

"Ah." Blake's dark blond brows arched like alarmed caterpillars. "So you want to kill *me*. Surely there are ways you could do that without a coroner putting 'deservedly stomped to death' on my death certificate."

Dammit! Now she liked him again. "Nothing's coming to mind," she replied cheerfully. "Once you break her by reminding—"

"I object to everything in that sentence fragment."

"—we can sell her and use the money in any number of ways. See, it's all interconnected." She made her fingers do the *here's the church, here's the steeple, open the doors, look at all the people* wiggle, emphasizing the *people* part of the wiggle.

"What in the world are you doing with your hands? That's not American Sign Language."

"Hush up, ya idjit. Pay attention. One part of the farm finances another part, which finances another. That's bad in times of economic downturn, but it also means that when things start improving, they improve across the board. See?"

"Hanging the financial hope of Heartbreak Farm on my ability to tame a feral equine will only end in disappointment for you and death by stomping for me."

"Could be." She hadn't been this happy in ages; his transparent horror was cheering her up. And she knew without understanding how she knew that he wouldn't quit. At least not anytime soon. "I'm willing to risk it."

"I feel safer already." They watched 626993 amble back and forth. "I'll need to do some online research."

"Oh, sure. The Internet is a big help when it comes to jobs you just need to jump in and start. Google 'how to ride a bike' while you're at it."

He held up his hands like she'd pulled a gun on him. Which she hadn't ruled out. "All right, fair point. I'll again admit I don't know what I'm doing. You're the expert; where do you advise I start?"

"Why d'you just assume I'm an expert?" Suspicion bloomed in her chest like nightshade. "Are you assuming that because I'm part Native American I have some kind of secret ancient mystical Indian way with horses?"

"Are you?" He tore his gaze from 626993 and looked at Natalie. "Do you?"

"Uh, no." *Easy, girl. He assumed you were an expert because he thinks you're the foreman because that's the lie you told him. He didn't assume you were an expert because you've got your mother's cheekbones, who got them from her mother, and her from hers, and so on back a few centuries.* "You didn't— I assumed you assumed." She tried a smile. "Probably says something about assuming."

"I had no idea what your lineage was," came the mild reply. "None of my business, really."

Natalie waited, expecting the usual white platitude, *It's okay; I'm one-sixteenth Cherokee myself,* or perhaps a dose of American Indian Princess Syndrome, or an acknowledgment of the glut of Pretendians of late. Or her personal favorite: *Hey, I'm cool with your heritage; you can tell me your real name.*

She decided to anticipate, not assume. There was a difference! Wasn't there? "My name really is Natalie Lane, y'know. It's not She-Who-Pees-in-Woods or anything like that."

"People *ask* you that?"

His horror—for once, not aimed at himself or his situation—cheered her. "Oh, sure. It's always people from—" Las Vegas. New York. Boston. And, weirdly, Pierre, South Dakota. "Um, it's out-of-towners, usually."

"City folk," he mock-drawled.

"Yep. They fall all over themselves trying to show me how totally not racist they are, then they want to know which of my ancestors was raped by the white man. They also apologize. A lot. 'It's terrible what my people did to yours; I'm so sorry.'"

His eyes narrowed, which she didn't find thrilling *at all*. "That's appalling. Do you shoot the well-meaning idiots with the bow and arrows handed down from your ancestors while they baste themselves in a sweat lodge?"

It took a second for her to get he was joking and then she started laughing so hard she had to steady herself against his shoulder so she wouldn't fall. It wasn't especially funny, but it *was* from an unexpected source. And the deadpan delivery had been perfect. "I'm saving it for Smack a Pretendian Day," she wheezed at last. "The tribe looks forward to that all year."

"Of course they do." He returned his attention to 626993. "Perhaps I could start by trying to stroke her." As if she understood his intent, 626993 stopped in mid-amble, glared, and her ears went flat. "Would you recommend that?"

"Nope."

"Right."

At his sigh, Natalie gave him a pseudo-manly clap on the back. "I'm sure you two will be very happy together."

Another sigh, and then he came out with something that made no sense. "Did you know trains crash so infrequently, you're more likely to be injured during the car ride to the station? It's true. My train probably didn't crash."

"Okay." *Cracking up already, poor idiot.* "I'm sorry? I guess?"

"Thank you." Then he straightened his shoulders and headed back to Main One, and she definitely didn't watch his ass as he walked away.

Fifteen

Up at dawn. Four slices of toast, courtesy of his new toaster, made from the bag of dry goods he kept stashed in the attic to delay death by starvation. He refilled his old plastic bottle with water from the bathroom tap, which got agreeably cold or agreeably hot, depending on his needs.

Pulled on his Thursday clothes: jeans reinforced at the knees

(I can add handling a needle and thread to skills I never knew I would need and now regret the necessity of knowing),
a gray twill shirt, clean but fading with all the washings and turning lighter gray, so that was all right. Hiking boots, slooowly bending to his body's will and growing more comfortable by the day. Thick white socks, also turning gray with repeated washing.

A hat was vital. Not just to avoid the discomfort of the sun in his eyes but also to protect him against melanoma by keeping the murderous rays off his head, face, neck.

(Natalie said I'm getting a farmer's suntan she said it like it was a compliment it likely was not a compliment I will pretend it was a compliment.)

Gloves were just as vital, and he was amazed to see how quickly they wore out. On his third trip to town he'd bought a dozen pairs, and he had gone through four. He grabbed a new pair and stuffed them into the back pocket of his jeans, grabbing his phone and Supertruck keys off the nearest bookshelf.

He checked his phone to see if Rake had replied to his latest hate-fueled text, which his brother refused to take seriously by referring to them as hexts, even nagging him when he was too tired to send one, because Rake was terrible.

No, nothing since Blake's last outgoing hext—*text, dammit: My vengeance will be epic and permanent, little brother.* Not so much as a *bring it, dickwad* or *I can't believe your robot overlords let you stay up this late.* He let out a small sigh and tucked his phone away, then realized the extent of his P.O.W. conditioning: He *missed* his *brother.* Too much to bear. *Don't think about it now.*

He took a last glance at himself in the mirror, hardly recognizing the lanky snob with tired eyes and blistered hands. The blisters would heal, would protect themselves by hardening into calluses over time. Possibly a metaphor there. He was too tired to think of one. *Don't think about it now.*

Appropriate clothing, he had learned by the end of the first week, was vital, and everything he bought in Heartbreak had to pass the Lane Decree: tough, but comfortable. *(O Natalie Lane I dream of the day I do everything right and you're generous with those gorgeous smiles and your bright eyes gleam with mirth.)*

Child of the most populated city in a desert state, citizen of a considerable financial center, he'd had no idea how rough the mere surface of the planet could be on everything at Heartbreak: equipment, people, clothing, animals, people, buildings, people. His clothes, new just days earlier, looked like he lived *and* slept in them (which, if it had been an especially grueling day, he did). He'd never showered so often in his life, and showers had never felt so luxuriously satisfying. At least he didn't have to deal with constant reapplication of N,N-Diethyl-meta-toluamide as the others did. Odd thing to be proud of, but then, he had so little to be proud of these days, and so he grinned as he remembered yesterday's encounter.

"I love everything about this time of year—" *Slap!* "Except the bugs." *Smack!* Natalie had scowled at the squashed mosquito and blood blotch on the underside of her arm. Her forearms were tough and tanned, but the undersides were pale and chubby and he wanted to kiss the bug bite and make it better and she would likely execute him on the spot and it would be worth it.

"I feel like I spend every hour of daylight putting on more bug spray. God knows what all that DEET is doing to me, or the environment. *Blech.* Never get used to it."

"Of course you do."

That had earned him twin raised eyebrows. He loved it when she did that; it made her eyes seem to sparkle at him. *For* him. Which they of course were not. But more fodder for his mental folder (filed under *Natalie Lane: Things That Will Never Happen* in his subcortical network or, as Rake would call it, Blake's Spank Bank) was always welcome.

Her eyes and eyebrows were still doing that thing Blake

loved. "What'd you just say? You're agreeing that of course I have to keep gooping this stuff on?"

"It—it comes with the job. Right?" he added, hearing the note of uncertainty but unsure how to proceed. He'd almost blurted something ridiculous, like *The bugs cannot resist you; they want to be on you and taste you; you can't blame them.*

"Right! The job. *My* job." She had scratched furiously and looked anxious, for some reason. "Yeah, you'd think I'd be used to it by now, since this is my job and all. If I don't do it, these things eat me alive."

I empathize. I've occasionally considered doing that myself. Ohhh, boy, did he. He hadn't needed to take himself in hand so often since he was seventeen.

But that was yesterday and today was today. *Today was today? Ugh. Need more sleep.*

Munching toast, he took the stairs to the kitchen, nodded at Harry and Larry (Gary had been getting difficult to track down, problem #62 on Blake's list of things he did not know how to deal with but must), and headed outside. Another day, another dollar. Possibly less than a dollar; he had no idea what his salary was. He had $14,321.98 in his personal checking account the day Mom had frozen all the other accounts, the ones she controlled. His expenses were low; all he'd bought so far were clothes and periodicals, and he had changed paperwork with the car rental agency, opting for a long-term contract to get better rates for the Supertruck. He'd offered to pitch in for groceries, and had been politely turned down. He had no idea who paid the bills at Heartbreak—they might have been ready for foreclosure, but people still lived and worked there, and those people needed running water and electricity and food.

But none of his, for which he should be grateful. At such a rate, his money would last for months.

Oh God. Last for months! It didn't bear considering, so he didn't. And speaking of money, at what point would his mom decide he had been sufficiently punished? *Perhaps the problem is you still see it as punishment. You're here to learn empathy, to understand that not everything can be solved with multiple green pieces of paper. You're here to appreciate the hard work that goes into feeding the world, and why unceremoniously forking over perfectly good farms to the bank spit in the eye of all of it.*

Or perhaps she's waiting for you to grow up.

Unfortunate. He had no plans to change his worldview, he *did* appreciate the hard work it took to feed the world, trying to help his mother was not a bad thing, and if not enjoying manual labor meant he hadn't grown up . . . well . . .

He hadn't.

And wouldn't.

So there.

Sixteen

"I have studied your ways, *Equus ferus caballus,* and I am to be your master now," he told 626993 in a stern tone. He schooled his body language to project serene dominance. *I know I'm in charge, so I need not flaunt it, and my not flaunting it will soothe you and you will accept me as the alpha pony.* "It's an uneven relationship that I cannot help, and I assure you I am, if anything, less enamored of this than you are. The best way to endure this, and survive this, is if we cooperate."

Six Two Six Nine Nine Three cocked her tail and let loose with what looked like a thousand brown crab apples. Her body language, Blake could not help but notice, projected, *Fuck you, puny pink monkey-human.*

Blake told himself there were worse beginnings. The maiden voyage of the *Titanic.* Filling the *Hindenburg* with hydrogen. *Plessy v. Ferguson.* The Donner Party's shortcut. His conception.

He fished out his phone, took a picture of 626993's retort, and sent it with a hext to Rake, because Rake was terrible.

"This isn't over," Blake warned 626993 in what he hoped was a suitably threatening tone, and then walked away, because for the morning it *was* over.

PLAN B

"We must bond. It's a matter of survival, yours as well as mine. No, wait! Come back. I don't like it any more than you do, Six Two Six Nine Nine Three, but the quicker we endure and get this done, the quicker I can return home and you can do whatever it is you do when you're not pondering my demise by squashing."

Six Two Six Nine Nine Three, as was her wont, let loose with dozens of poop-shaped, poop-scented golf balls. He preferred to think of them that way. *I know it's shit,* he'd explained to a bemused Natalie. *Let me have this illusion, dammit! It may be my only way to survive this.*

Poop-scented golf balls, it's perfect, she'd replied, which made no sense, and then she dashed back to Main One, giggling, and left him to 626993's rebuttal. He could actually hear Rake's voice in his head: *Rebuttal, get it? See what I did there?*

Blake stopped thinking about Natalie's lovely giggles and Rake's unlovely sense of humor and instead focused on the unlovely, unhumorous

(that is not a word I am in so far over my head I am losing my grasp on my native tongue)

specimen glaring at him. "As part of the bonding process, according to several online sources, it is vital that I give you a name. Naming you will bring us closer as a couple. Yes," he added hastily when she cocked her tail in warning, "I know how that sounds, but consider the logic of it. It's hard to feel as if you belong, or are among people you can trust, if you're merely a number to them. Well, Six Two Six Nine Nine Three, henceforth, your name is Margaret of Anjou. I have named you for a woman who has gone down in history as the She-Wolf of France, remembered for being vengeful and blinded by her own importance. I trust I don't have to explain why."

A snort. Margaret of Anjou tossed her head, trotted toward him, and when he stretched out a hand

(it'll be fine if she chomps, it's not my dominant hand)

she promptly turned and scooted the other way.

He sighed at the feminine rejection, something as humbling as it was rare. "Very well. Margaret of Anjou earned her disrespectful moniker through several actions viewed unfeminine and disloyal for the times, 'the times' being the fifteenth century."

He checked Margaret of Anjou's water. Fine and fresh.

"Bad enough she was French," Blake continued. "Nothing inherently wrong in that, but England and France had a long, bloody history of loathing each other. Bad enough she was entitled and arrogant—but such things often come from a royal rearing. Bad enough her husband, Henry the sixth, suffered from then-undiagnosed schizophrenia and was frequently unresponsive to stimuli. He once went over a year without speaking, or moving under his own power. (Do not get me started on his religious delusions.) And bad enough that her husband shared her bed so infrequently, even when in his right mind, that most believed her son was a bastard, possibly by Edmund Beaufort or James Butler."

Blake checked Margaret's feed—too low. He trotted to

Main One, helped himself to a scoop, trotted back. The corral didn't have a gate, but the bars were wide enough so he could bend at the waist, insert himself vertically, then straighten and be inside with Margaret of Anjou. Who, true to her namesake, ignored him as she would anyone not her better. She never ate unless he was several feet away.

"Any one of these could be overlooked, if not condoned," he continued, running his fingers through the feed to check for insect life or irregularities. "But she had the gall to want to rule *for* her husband, not meekly hand over the regency to the Duke of York. Essentially, her actions were a domino effect that sparked off a thirty-year civil war and cost tens of thousands of lives. She paid a heavy price for her pride: in the end, she died alone, penniless, widowed and childless and hated.

"Something to think about, eh, Margaret of Anjou?"

The pony switched up her rebuttal this time, presenting a mighty squirt of urine to express her disdain.

"Yes, well." Blake sighed and was glad, not for the first time, that she kept at least five feet between them at all times. He had wondered if she'd been abused, which amused Natalie to no end.

Sorry, there's no dilemma-causing backstory for you to rescue her from. This is not The Pony Whisperer. *Sometimes ponies are jerks. You know you've got shit on your chin, right?*

Odd how I always want to scratch my face while mucking out stalls, had been his chagrined reply. Now, back in the present, he returned his attention to Margaret of Anjou. "Pride was her undoing as well. You should take care." *I am threatening a pony. This is how low I have sunk.* "She never quit, though. You have to respect that if you can respect anything."

Come to think of it, Margaret of Anjou had something in common with several significant females in his life: the pony, Natalie Lane, his mother, the nuclear option.

His mother. *Hmm.* It had been several days; he was still here; Heartbreak remained unforeclosed upon. Perhaps it was time he acquainted her with new facts and sought her counsel. And perhaps her checkbook.

Seventeen

PLAN C

"'Music hath charms to soothe a savage breast, though most people assume 'beast,'" Blake explained, carefully setting up his phone on one of the posts, then activating the Margaret of Anjou playlist. " 'To soften rocks, or bend a knotted oak.' Did you know that is one of the most misquoted sayings of all time? And that the people who misquote it think William Shakespeare wrote it? Insanity. Now then. Pay attention." He hummed a little and pressed play. The lilting strains of "Ode to Joy" filled the paddock, followed by the lilting thuds as Margaret of Anjou kicked the post so hard his phone flew thirteen feet.

Music Margaret of Anjou Does Not Like

  1. "Ode to Joy"
  2. Brahms' Double Concerto

3. Mozart's Clarinet Quintet
4. Everything by Rachmaninov
5. Tchaikovsky's Concert Fantasy for Piano and Orchestra
6. Strauss' "Festival Prelude"
7. Louis Armstrong's "What a Wonderful World"
8. Bing Crosby's "Swinging on a Star"
9. The Angels' "My Boyfriend's Back"
10. Lesley Gore's "It's My Party"
11. Lesley Gore's "You Don't Own Me"
12. Dusty Springfield's "You Don't Own Me"
13. Joan Jett's "You Don't Own Me"
14. Everything else by Joan Jett
15. The Beatles' "I Want to Hold Your Hand"
16. Muddy Waters' "You're Gonna Miss Me (When I'm Dead and Gone)"
17. The Rolling Stones' "It's All Over Now"
18. Aerosmith's "Cryin'"
19. Tom Petty's "Breakdown"
20. David Bowie's "Loving the Alien"
21. INXS's "Devil Inside"
22. Def Leppard's "Love Bites"
23. The theme from *M*A*S*H*
24. The theme from *Psych*
25. The theme from *Rocky*
26. The theme from *The Simpsons*

Eighteen

PLAN D

"How?" he shouted, rolling to his feet and smacking the dust off his rear end. "How are you able to get *any* of your devil hooves off the ground enough to throw me? You're so fat! Yes! I'm fat shaming you! That's what your demon-pony antics have reduced me to! Margaret of Anjou, you are morbidly obese! I am switching you from hay to rice cakes *at once.*"

PLAN E

"If I put you back on hay and bring back your salt lick, will you stop shitting everywhere? My research on whether or not they make diapers for ponies has thus far proved inconclusive."

Nineteen

"Son of a *bitch*."

Whispers became rumors became common knowledge became fact. Garrett Hobbes, self-proclaimed man of action, decided enough time had passed. Time to visit one of Shannah's bastards and find out what was going on. Blake or Rake or Jake or whatever the hell; trust Shannah to not only *not* be embarrassed at being caught out as a slut in front of the whole town but then also give the bastards cutesy names. Like spreading her legs hadn't gotten her bounced from Sweetheart! The whole town had seen *that* coming and the schadenfreude had flowed like wine. The Banaan family of quitters quit on Shannah Banana. *Ha!*

He left his office and eyeballed his shark gray Fiat convertible, parked haphazardly to the left of the crip space. No scratches or dents from errant car doors this time, excellent. The local fucks were all jealous, and knowing that made it worth the occasional trip to the auto-body shop. Sure, visibility was shit and the car handled with all the maneuverability of a pumpkin, but still: convertible!

I know you're all mad about being losers, but leave the car out of it, chrissakes.

He climbed in, started it, and waited a long moment to give the jealous fucks on the street a chance to see the difference between his future and theirs. The only people he could see were that crone Bev Harmon and her gross gay grandson, Cameron. Bev ran Sweetheart Sew and made a decent living doing alterations. She and her husband liked to flaunt their great love affair by tearing each other's clothes. Fucking ripping her blouse like an animal! Bev mended so much of her own crap that she soon started doing it for neighbors. Her queer son was probably primed to take over the business.

Oh, well. Maybe Cameron would mention it while he was repairing ripped bodices or braiding his hair or whatever the hell gay guys did. Not for the first time, Garrett breathed thanks he was a man's man. *No, not like* that. *A real man.* That's what he meant. Besides, the one time he'd asked Benjie to the movies, the guy had the fucking gall to point out Garrett's 1) homophobia, 2) shit taste in movies, and 3) contempt for the Harmon clan.

When did everybody start keeping track of every innocent little comment to come out of his mouth? He was surrounded by people who couldn't appreciate him, never mind catch on to his subtle sense of humor. And they all had minds like fucking tape recorders, always braying back things he'd said like he didn't have layers or something. He had plenty of layers, dammit! And a convertible!

He had to drive through town to get out to Heartbreak,

and was treated—as always—to a reluctant *This Is Your Life* slide show as he drove past businesses and people familiar from his earliest childhood.

Here was the Dipsy Diner, where he'd knocked a tray of entrées out of the waitress' hands for a joke nobody got, including the basketball players in the booth behind him. They'd expressed their displeasure by holding him down and squirting mustard up his nose. His luck to prank the one waitress working while her son, a center on the varsity squad, was three feet away. Fucking jocks, no sense of humor. He'd sneezed mustard for three days. Ruined his taste for the stuff; now he was strictly a ketchup man.

Here was Sweet Gas, where he'd shoplifted half a dozen Hershey bars and a two-liter bottle of Coke with no one noticing. It was winter, he was in his parka, he was supposed to look bulky, it was working, dammit!

His foolproof plan disintegrated when he tripped and fell against the counter, which made the bottle of Coke blow up. He'd looked like he was streaming Coke from every orifice, plus it turned out he'd snatched Hershey's dark, not milk. He hated dark. And the old fuck running the station made him mop the floor *and* reimburse him for the Coke (no biggie) and the dark chocolate (which sucked), and he had to do it all without changing his clothes, so every step was a sticky squish.

Here was Sweet Soft-Serv, where, after being ditched for prom, he'd eaten seven vanilla ice-cream cones in a row, then promptly thrown them up with a *glurt!* His barf had still been cold; that's how quick it had come back up. He remembered watching it drip off his shoes and thinking, *Jeez, tell one or two nigger jokes and Myra Dedman gets violently politically correct.*

Fifteen bucks for a box of condoms going right down the tubes with the puke.

Here was Heartbreak Farm, onetime cool-kid hangout/ cow-tipping HQ. For whatever reason, people liked the place. Didn't matter if they were from a neighboring farm or sold used cars on the other side of town, the fucking idiots were drawn here. The unromantic origin story struck a chord with just about everybody, and once they saw the place for themselves they kept coming back. It was weird and baffling.

Jonathan Banaan's monument to his lost love, what a joke. What had been going through his mind, obviously gone to Swiss cheese after so many years of unrequited nooky? *Welp, she said no to the house and no to the garage, but she sure won't say no to the barn!* Fucking moron. People ate it up, though. It had been the social center of the town—a good trick for a farm ten miles outside the city limits—and people had been gathering there for a hundred years, seemed like. Heartbreak had hosted fireworks and barn dances and (*weird*) christenings and (*weirder*) funerals. *Funerals! Of people who didn't own or work on the farm! What. The. Fuck?*

He was glad he'd outgrown the place even before he was forbidden to return because people have no fucking sense of humor. The horse was barely singed when the cherry bomb went off. You'd think the whole town had been brainwashed by PETA fucks.

And it didn't matter. It was over and it didn't matter, and sometimes he could forget the misunderstandings, and sometimes he couldn't; sometimes they seemed so fresh they were like big bruises all over his chest. And it didn't matter! Sweetheart was dying, and Garrett was almost free, and everything was going to work the way it should, and Blake Tarbell, who'd so obligingly bought up the deeds, who essentially traded deeds for a ticket to Garrett's very rich, very exciting future, was somehow in this awful fucking town and somehow working as a fucking plow hand at fucking Heartbreak Farm, for fuck's sake.

And there he was! Striding from the house to the barn like he knew where he was going. Like he knew where things were, even. Which was so ridiculous it was funny. Where'd he even get blue jeans that not only fit him but looked like he'd been working in them for days? The guy had probably been born in a three-piece suit; who was he trying to fool?

Garrett pulled up right next to the barn and climbed out, giving Vegas Douche a long look at his car. Blake might want to know where he could get one himself. Garrett would be happy to tell him—he wouldn't even have the car if not for Blake Tarbell.

"Hey."

Blake had paused, pitchfork over one shoulder, and nodded back. Then continued into the barn to do God-knew-what. A pitchfork? The fuck?

Garrett raised his voice and tried again. "Hey, how are you?"

"I'm fine," came the cheerful reply. Tarbell had a helluva phone voice, all deep and rumbly, which translated well in person. Garrett had heard the old joke about the fat guy on the radio who sounded thin, or whatever the fuck, and had expected someone not at all exceptional. So of course the guy was tall and broad shouldered and blond and good-looking. *Fucking* of course. He was streaked with dust and sweat, was tanned in some spots and burned in others, and looked like he'd keel over

and die if someone even glared at him, and *of course* he somehow made all that work. "Everything is fine."

"It is?" *Fucking better not be.* Sweetheart was going and
Heartbreak was gonna be gone soon, too. Well, not so much
gone as made into a much better thing. A much much *much*
better thing. "Everything is fine" was *not* the goal here.

Tarbell waved an arm to indicate the general area. "This
isn't here, you know. I'm not here, either."

"Uh, what?" It was warm, temps in the high seventies, but
not that warm. Garrett, mindful of where he was stepping

fucking shit,

followed Blake into the barn. "Sorry, I didn't get that."

"I'm bleeding out at the bottom of a train wreck." Blake
grabbed a wheelbarrow, plunked the pitchfork into it, pushed
it to the stall at the far end, then opened the stall and started
forking the soiled straw into it.

"What. The. Fuck?" It was the only thing Garrett could
think to say. Crissakes, it was true. Blake Tarbell, millionaire
douche, was living on Heartbreak and working the place. Of
his own free will, apparently. Or maybe not; maybe there was
a bad guy around who had stuck the barrel of a gun in Shannah Banaan's mouth (which could only be an improvement)
and said . . . what? *Muck out stalls or the old lady gets it?*

"None of this is happening," Blake explained with puzzling
good humor. "You're not real."

"I am too real!"

"Sorry. You are not." Both men heard an agitated whinny
from just outside and Blake at once turned to yell in that direction. "You will get your apple pieces after I have cleaned up
all eighty pounds of your shit, Margaret of Anjou! So it will be

some time, as I'm certain you are aware! Plus I have to cut the fruit into tiny pieces because it would be a terrible loss to the world if you were to choke and die!" He turned back to Garrett. "She has recently allowed me to groom her, but I suspect it's because she enjoys the humiliation I feel when I have to brush her gigantic belly."

Garrett couldn't manage words, could only feel incredibly puzzled and freaked out. He finally found his voice and went with the obvious question. "Why are you here?"

"The stall, alas, is not going to muck itself out. Also, my mommy has taken away my allowance."

Garrett stood, watery brown eyes

(fucking allergies)

watering from the dust

(fucking dust),

and recalled reason eight thousand why he fucking hated fucking barns. Buildings built, literally, to house dirt and filth and smelly animals. The fucking things were dusty and smelly in February, crissakes, which this wasn't; it was late spring and there was as much mud as grass. "But why are you *here?*"

"Have we met? I think not, stranger who has come to a farm to take an unsanctioned poll, apparently. My name is Blake Tarbell," he said with exaggerated formality. He stripped off a glove and extended a hand filthy despite the glove. Garrett looked at it, appalled, until Blake shrugged and put the glove back on.

"Christ, your hand! What have you been doing? Punching cactuses?"

"Cacti. And no." He examined his hands and added, "Margaret of Anjou did not take kindly to her new bridle. The good news is, the pain lessens when I pass out. And you are?"

Garrett shook himself like a cat pissed off after a bath. Or a land developer after getting disturbing news about what was supposed to be a sure thing. "Sorry, we've only spoken on the phone. . . . Garrett Hobbes."

"Ah." A nod. "Yes, I recall the name."

"Just wanted to swing by, say hi."

Blake cocked an eyebrow, which would have been all debonair and everything except he was slinging shit at the time. "Just to meet and greet? No curiosity as to what I'm doing here? I commend your restraint."

"What *are* you doing here?"

"Farewell, restraint. And that." He paused and forked up more shit. Dumped it into the wheelbarrow. "Is the question."

"Yeah, I know. Are you maybe gonna answer it?"

"I am here to make amends. And possibly become a better person. And try to form a love for a specific patch of land, because some parts of the planet have greater sentimental value than others. News to me," he added with a shrug. "I live in a desert."

"But all the other farms have been taken over." *Love for a specific patch of land? Become a better person? What. The. Fuck?* "It's just Heartbreak left now, and Putt N'Go needs it for the water table."

"Poop-scented golf balls," Blake muttered, because the fucker was clearly losing his mind. "Now I get why she found that so amusing."

He ignored the mumble and stayed focused. Like a laser! "Without this farm, Putt N'Go can't build." *Without this farm, I'm trapped.*

"I sympathize," Blake replied with an utter lack of sympathy, "but the goals of the Putt N'Go corporation are irrelevant to me."

"But not to me! Look, a lot of people are counting on this going through!"

"Excuse me," came the polite reply, "but it's been brought to my attention that the opposite is true."

Garrett restrained the urge to kick the nearest stall. *Probably get splinters and tetanus and fucking die right there. Get a grip, Hobbes. Just because Grandpa and Great-Grandpa died on farms—and they weren't farmers!—doesn't mean you will.* "All right, *I'm* counting on it going through."

"And I am not, nor is my mother, nor is most of the town. Which raises the question: Why would you broker a deal if you didn't control all the property you were offering the buyer?"

"And let one of the farmers steal my deal? Once people heard about the golf course they'd have dug in and the whole thing would get way out of hand or—worse!—scrapped altogether. And because they gave me a car *and* an advance, you stupid shit!"

"And that . . ." With a nod toward the dooryard, where Garrett's awesome fucking car was parked. ". . . should have been your first clue that you were in cahoots with soulless corporate denizens who seek nothing but despair. That is the most unfortunate-looking convertible I've ever seen."

"The car's great and the deal's great!"

"Do you shout often? You've done almost nothing else since you parked your awful car in the drive. You'll hurt your throat if you keep it up."

"What are you *talking* about?" he screamed.

"A helpful tip, Mr. Hobbes: wait until after you've gone to bed, then scream into your pillow. Not only does it release stress;

you'll sleep like a baby." He flexed his gloved hands, grimacing. "Works for me."

A crazy man. That's what he was dealing with. Vegas Douche was crazy. Maybe always; maybe Sweetheart had done it to him. Didn't matter if the result was the same: a crazy man was slinging shit on Heartbreak and fucking up his future awesome life.

Hobbes tried to come up with a reasoned rebuttal, but all he could think was that the deal would be saved by whatever means necessary and Vegas Douche would have to be killed, or at least run over.

"Listen up." Sure, Blake was big and dirty and looked capable of shoving Garrett's teeth into his nostrils, but Garrett knew how to play rough, too. "I've been trapped in this fucking town for four fucking generations. I hate the town. Relatives who weren't farmers have died on farms in this town. I hate farms. Not only will this deal get me the fuck out of Sweetheart and into the heart of Manhattan, which is the *opposite* of a farm; I'll leave rich."

Vegas Douche was now leaning on the pitchfork and staring at him like *Garrett* was the freak weirdo covered in shit, with scratched hands. "Why in the world would you tell me any of this?"

"To *explain.* You were on board *before.*"

"Stop that." He'd finished mucking out the stall and was now carrying bags of feed from one end of the barn to the other, for some idiotic fucking reason. "Stop talking in italics."

"What the *fuck* are you talking about? Are you gonna keep your word or not?"

"Of course I'll keep my word."

"Oh." Sweet relief flooded him. Garrett almost sagged against the filthy wall. "Good."

"Oh. Not to you. My word to my mother." Then, like Garrett would actually give a fuck, Blake added, "I owe her, you know. And I didn't give you my word about anything. We shared a few business transactions."

Garrett did *not* want to talk about Shannah Banaan right now. "Yeah, but you'll get it if I assumed that once you sold me the *other* farms you'd also sell me the *last* farm!"

"And you'll get it if I remind you that erroneously representing yourself as the controller in land speculation was likely going to be problematic." A demanding whinny and Vegas Douche turned to the sound like a flower to sunshine, or something equally fucking poetic and weird. "All right, Margaret of Anjou. I have finished cleaning up your leavings, and I have your apples right here."

Vegas Douche grabbed a small brown paper bag and walked out the back. Garrett followed, because anywhere in the world was better than the inside of a barn.

Outside smelled better at least, though, since they were downwind, not much better. At least he'd gotten Roger Harris' pig farm on the chopping block, or it'd *really* stink. Word was losing his family farm sent ole Roger right into Crazy Fuck Land. That he was living at the B and B with his last pig, no less!

Here was a small corral, all white bars and no gate, and inside the corral was the fattest, butt-ugliest pony Garrett had seen outside of horse porn.* The closer he and Vegas Douche

---

* Horse porn, as I discovered while researching this book, is a thing. I am so sorry to be the one to tell you that.

got, the more the pony extended her thick neck and shook her head and showed her big square teeth.

"Jesus *fuck*."

Vegas Douche frowned while rummaging in the bag. "That's 'Jesus Fuck, Your Majesty.'"

Sure, pal. Hold your breath and wait for that *to happen.*

Unlike any other pony Garrett had seen, this one retreated from food. Vegas Douche set three slices of apple on one of the posts and took a careful step back.

"Look, you gotta see reason on this one, Veg—uh, Mr. Tarbell."

"Oh, after enduring your vulgar rants I feel you should call me Blake."

"Blake. It's not just me, it's *Christ!*"

The pony had come close, sniffed the apple, then let loose with a kick and booted the apple right off the pole. Garrett had to make a conscious effort not to cringe back and run like the wind. Couldn't show fear in front of Vegas Douche. Who was, if anything, pretty calm given that the reason the bitchy pony was so fat was because she probably devoured her handlers in the night.

"I am aware it's not to your exact liking, Margaret of Anjou!" he snapped, getting way more upset at the pony than he was at Garrett's deal getting fucked. "I didn't have time to sprinkle cinnamon sugar on them. It's naked apple slices or nothing."

The pony thought that sucked, if the squeals and snorts and kicks and gnashing of teeth were any indication. Vegas Douche sighed and closed the bag Garrett assumed was stuffed with naked apple slices. "Well, I'm certainly not giving you a treat now. You'll have to stay in your corral and think about what

you've done." Then he turned and walked back to the barn.
"Tough love," he muttered to Garrett, like he gave a ripe fuck.

"I don't give a ripe fuck!" At Vegas Douche's snort, he fell
back on what was, to him, the simplest most obvious argu-
ment to get the guy back in line: "You were on board before."

"Yes, well." He put the bag back and started rolling hose.
Garrett only then realized the floor was as clean as barn floors
ever get. Which meant Vegas Douche had quit Vegas to shovel
shit and hose down barns. He felt like his brain was getting a
cramp; it was all too strange to wrap his head around. "I was
an asshole before. I am trying to atone."

"I could care less!"

Blake flinched. *Ha!* Garrett straightened and smirked. *Got
him on the run, mess with the bull and get the horns, probably not
used to anyone actually giving him the business.*

"No, Mr. Hobbes. You stated you could care less when in
fact you meant the opposite: you could *not* care less. I loathe
when people do that. It tops my list of grammatical pet peeves,
along with 'nauseous' getting mixed up with 'nauseated.'"

"I don't know what the fuck you're talking about."

"'Nauseous' is when you make other people feel nauseated.
If you say, 'I'm nauseous,' what you mean is that there is something about you that makes other people feel nauseated."

What. The. Fuck? Garrett nearly bit his tongue in half. "We
had a deal!"

"In fact, you and I did not. You may have had a deal with,
er, who was it? Golf and Barf?"

"Putt N'Go, you forgetful fuck!"

"You were much nicer on the phone." Vegas Douche had
the nerve to sound fucking *wistful*.

"You were giving me what I wanted over the phone!" *Ugh.* Probably should rephrase, if Blake's snicker was any indication.

"Ah, if only my twin was here. He'd drown you in a chorus of jokes heavy with sexual innuendo."

Oh, fuck. There were two of them; he kept forgetting. No one had seen either of Shannah's crazy brats before now. Her parents hadn't even kept pics of them.

"Our deal"—*how fucking annoying, the douche was still yapping*—"was for the farms in foreclosure. Heartbreak wasn't in foreclosure just then—"

"It would have been!"

"—and, as must be obvious to you by now, it's off the market, hopefully for good."

"You know we need them!"

"In fact, I did not know that. No surprise, given your policy of dealing everyone out."

"There's no deal without Heartbreak!"

That," Blake replied, pausing to take a deep swig from a water bottle that looked like a pony had stomped on it, and Garrett bet he knew which pony, "is not my concern."

"You're gonna be a fucking migrant worker for fucking Heartbreak instead of living in Las fucking Vegas?"

"Apparently."

"What the fuck?"

"Was your father a minister?"

"Fertilizer salesman," Garrett replied shortly. "Dead now."

Blake blinked like an owl, Garrett had noticed. Slowly. Next the guy's head would swivel around and he'd hoot at the treetops. "I had that same thought: *What the fuck indeed.* It's

not what I was expecting at all when I Martianed my mother."
At Garrett's bulging eyes (which indicated not just confusion
but killing fury) he added, "It's a Tarbell thing from a book
our mom read. It means being overbearing and sexist while
convincing the lady in question your overbearing sexism was
for her own good." He turned in the direction of the town and
shook a gloved fist. "Are you happy now, Mom? When will
you release me from this hellhole?"

Hellhole? Yes! Garrett could work with *hellhole.* For the first
time that day, he and Vegas Douche were on the same page.
Vegas Douche hated the work and hated the farm and wanted
out but was too chickenguts to stand up to his mommy. Garrett could fix *everything* with some phone calls and paperwork.
"You can release yourself, y'know."

The hose had been rolled and put away. "It's not that simple,
Garrett."

"Wrong, Vegas D— wrong, Blake!" He was almost hyper-
ventilating with relief. "Took me a minute to catch up—"

"Only a minute?"

"That you need help. You're stuck and you don't know how
to get out— Blake, I *invented* that!" Maybe he'd shake Blake's
hand on the way out. He'd do a lot of stupid social things to
see Heartbreak back on the chopping block. "We can get
through the paperwork in a day."

"No."

"All right, two days, but only because the only notary's a
bitch and she'll find ways to stall, so we have to go one town
over." If there was anyone he loathed more than the Banaan
clan, it was Natalie "my shit don't stink" Lane. Who'd also, if
the rumors were true, been hanging around Heartbreak a lot.

But she'd always had a soft spot for the shithole. And it wasn't like the bank was going to need her much longer. "You'll get out, I'll get out, Heartbreak will get flooded and then buried in golf balls, and Sweetheart Fertilizer can finally *die*."

"Sweetheart Fertilizer?"

Garrett gritted his teeth. Hadn't meant to let that slip to the one guy in two hundred miles who *didn't* know what he did for a living. "Family business."

Yes. His family had been in the business of peddling shit (natural as well as man-made) for generations. The company motto ("We'll Take Your Crap!") was cross-stitched on pillows all over his parents' house. They lived and breathed fertilizer, which was as horrible as it sounded. The business had killed his grandfather; a Sweetheart Fertilizer truck sideswiped his bicycle. Ironically, he was on a bike after losing his driver's license for too many DUIs.

"There's much more to fertilizer than what most people assume," Vegas Douche was telling him, like Garrett didn't know shit about shit. "It's not just animal waste; it's peat and sewage sludge, not to mention—"

"I know!"

"And the craze for all things organic could only help that side of your business."

"I don't care!"

Thank God his father had finally croaked. The geezer would never have allowed any of this. Garrett's mom didn't like it, either, but fuck her—most days she had pudding for brains anyway. Fucking Alzheimer's: it made the patients a zillion times more irritating while taking years to actually kill them.

Garrett sucked in a breath to calm himself. Out of the shower less than an hour and he could feel his shirt getting soaked under the arms. This meet 'n' greet hadn't gone at all the way he'd thought it would. *Happy place, where the fuck is my happy place?*

Anywhere but here, that's where. "Listen. Listen to me, Blake. Sweetheart fucking sucks. You know this. I know this. Everyone except the farmers knows this, and they don't know shit because all they can smell is shit."

"This is fascinating, and somewhat obscene."

"No, listen. You and me, we're exactly the same."

"You and I."

"Right! I've been trapped on this prairie for generations and I'm not taking over the family biz. I always knew I was gonna do better, and I am. I'm the guy who set this whole farm foreclosure/death of Sweetheart in motion. And *thank God*! Hay season aggravates my allergies, I fucking hate livestock of any kind, horses are useless except in New York City for those stupid handsome cab ride things for tourists—"

"Hansoms."

"—I hate driving forty-five minutes to get a gallon of milk, everything in the 'Heart closes at nine P.M., and I'd rather barf; yeah, that's right, I'd rather fucking *barf* than keep the family biz going one more generation.

"There's more out there than Sweetheart, Blake, and you're maybe the one other guy in town who gets it. And I'm ready, I'm *more* than ready, to go. I could go to Hollywood!"

"You would flourish in Hollywood."

"Thank you! I could go to—to the Riviera!" *That was a rich-guy thing, right?* Blake would know what the fuck he was talking about. "I could start a chain of strip clubs! I could design my own line of toilet paper! What*ever* I do, it's because a classy life is waiting for me and the sooner the 'Heart turns into the area's biggest and best mini-golf course, the better!" He paused and forced a long, steadying breath, then finished: "My point is, we're the same."

"Ah . . . no."

"We can get the fuck out and never look back."

"Oh. You're assuming that because I said— Ah!" The guy looked relieved for some reason. Why now? The time to look relieved was when Garrett first explained how much the same they were. "You misunderstood. I meant I can't sell Heartbreak Farm as in *can not* sell Heartbreak."

Garrett blinked. He'd been falling into a fantasy involving the Victoria's Secret fashion show and a tray of cream puffs. "Can't? Listen, you don't want Shannah Banaan sticking her nose in our business; who could blame you? But I can help you quit all this in a way where the blame wouldn't fall on you; it'd just hit me. Which I'm used to, believe me. Like I said, I'm the guy who set this whole thing in motion. You can leave town with your conscience totally fine."

"Ah." Blake was frowning, which put grooves in the dirt on his forehead. "I apologize; I was imprecise. I *won't* sell Heartbreak, though technically I can, is that better?"

"Nope." Lately even looking at the population sign (*Hello, Sweetheart! Pop: 9,339*) was enough to give Garrett a rage-induced nosebleed. Nine thousand three hundred thirty-eight people all complicit in his great-grandfather's determination that every Garrett generation would sell shit forever, amen. "It's not."

"Unfortunate. Well, thank you for stopping by, but it seems I must go back to the house and put cinnamon on several apple slices. Not that I'll be thanked for it!" he added at a shout, glaring past Garrett in the direction of the fat, mean pony.

"No!" Before he could stop himself, he'd seized handfuls of Vegas Douche's shirt and was practically shaking the man. "Let me Martian this for you!"

"Remove your hands," came the chilly response, "or I'll break your wrists."

He probably could, too. Garrett could barely get his fingers around the guy's blocky wrists. He was too lost to care; if anything, he just clung harder. "Let me be your fucking Martian, you crazy fuck!"

"Um . . ."

They both looked over at the interruption. Natalie fucking Lane was standing in the far doorway, looking as surprised as Garrett had ever seen her. And no wonder. He and Vegas Douche were nose to nose and there had been shouting. A lot of shouting. And threats of violence. She probably thought they were going to start fighting. Or fucking.

"I can come back, if you want . . . ? Yeah." She started to turn, her expression frozen in a grimace of startled shock. "Sorry to interrupt. I didn't see anything. I don't know anything."

"For God's sake," Vegas Douche muttered. Garrett concurred, and let go of the guy's shirt. Natalie fucking Lane catching him groping another man. *Day couldn't get any worse, though, right?*

Right?

Twenty

Natalie fucking Lane couldn't believe what
(no, idiot, that's his nickname for you; it's not actually your name)
Natalie Lane couldn't believe what she was seeing. Of all
the days to telecommute for the bank! She'd been in the office
when whatever was happening started happening. Unsettling
enough to hear the snarling boom of Garrett's convertible
(whoever heard of a guy in his twenties having a midlife crisis?
it's the only thing he was ahead of the curve on),
weird to see it parked outside Main One with Garrett nowhere
in sight by the time she made it outside, weird to hear shouting
that wasn't Gary yelling for a fire extinguisher or Blake prom-
ising a grisly death for Margaret of Anjou
(God, now he's got all of us calling her that ridiculous name),
but then to come upon them and see they were chest to chest.
Kissing close. And the worst part, the most emotionally shattering weirdest most inappropriate part . . .
    She'd been jealous.

Of Garrett Hobbes.

Almost as bad: Garrett knew she didn't work for Heart-break. He wouldn't know *what* she was doing, exactly (she was no longer sure herself), but he knew enough. He could out her in five seconds. And then . . . and then . . .

Well, what? Why did that thought make her so anxious? Why had she been having trouble getting to sleep when she pictured someone blowing her secret? What was she afraid of? Blake would storm off because she hadn't come clean about working for the bank? He couldn't storm off. He'd accuse her of having a secret agenda? She did, but it wouldn't change their working relationship.

No, the reason she didn't want Blake to know she prevari-cated was simple and staggering: she didn't want to disappoint him. She'd been riding his ass for days

(not even in a good way . . . sigh . . . when was the last time I got laid, anyway? there was snow on the ground, and it wasn't last winter)

about his morality, his pretension, his arrogance. His smug white-guy entitlement. About how if Heartbreak died it would be, if not entirely his fault, then a lot his fault. How being honest and forthright was a damned sight better than being rich and distant.

Meanwhile she worked for the bank that was profiting off Garrett's deal with the devil.

Problematic.

"What the fuck are *you* doing here?" Garrett had released Blake and was glaring at her like *she* was the asshole interloper.

"None of your concern. This is still private property, so blow."

"What the fuck is it with people who have no business working this farm suddenly working this farm?"

"There is no need to speak to Natalie like that." Blake said it calmly, but he sure didn't look calm. At least he'd assumed Garrett was speaking to her *about* Blake, rather than lumping her *and* Blake in the same category. (And in fairness to the scumbag, it was actually a pretty good question.) "You've worn out your welcome, not that one was ever extended in the first place. Run along, Garrett."

"Fucking right I will." He took a couple of steps toward Natalie, who took a compensating few steps away because *ugh*, Garrett Hobbes. "Natalie, why in the fuck d'you even care? What's the big deal about this fucking place? You never lived here."

"You'll never get it, Garrett," she replied kindly enough. She'd feel sorry for him if he weren't such a contemptible ass. And he could be the nicest guy in the state (except that was Roger Harris, owner of the White Rose of York) and she still couldn't put it into words. It was one of those places that felt like home even if it was never your home. Heartbreak was hot chocolate on a cold day, fireworks and potato salad, weddings and funerals. People were born and died and moved on and came back and Heartbreak was always, always there. You didn't have to own it to feel you belonged. "There's no point in me trying."

"I don't— Oh."

"What, oh?" She was suspicious; Garrett had a familiar look on his face, the one that presaged him saying something horrible. Worse: he was actually trying to make it come out *not* horrible, which was why he now looked like the "before" picture in a hemorrhoid ad. He had never, to Natalie's knowledge, succeeded in lessening his awfulness.

"Are you invested in this whole 'the land of my ancestors is sacred' thing because, uh, because of your, uh, heritage? Because we'll put a casino here. Don't worry about that."

Blake, who had collapsed on a nearby straw bale to rest and take a swig of water, paused in mid-gulp. Then he unfolded and climbed to his feet. It was leisurely and careful. His face was utterly calm and Natalie had never been so afraid for an idiot than she was at that moment for Garrett. She crossed the barn to get between them and wasn't leisurely or careful about it. "Nope! Nope nope nope! Please don't, Blake. He can't help it; he's stupid."

"Hey!"

"Shut up, Garrett. I'm trying to save you. Just *shut up* and stay stupid."

"Look, all's I was saying is I get it!" He held up both hands, placating her or Blake, she wasn't sure. His palms were disturbingly shiny; he liked running his hands through his thinning hair but used too much conditioner, so it was often greasy. "My people did terrible things to yours and you want compensation. It's fine. I get it. We've got you covered."

"Give me a break, Great White Fathead! Your 'people' didn't even *get* to America until long after my 'people' had been shunted off to reservations. No one I'm related to was ever repressed by anyone you were related to."

"Okay!" The idiot blew out a relieved breath. His relieved breath smelled like chili. "So you admit you've got no reason to hate me or the land deal."

"I hate the land deal and it's got nothing to do with being part Native American!" The barn swallows, who hadn't minded

Garrett's yelling, were taking flight at hers, probably because of the shrill factor. Her father, who'd been a flight scientist before retirement, had the theory that the madder Natalie got, the more supersonic her rant. "I hate it because there are too many golf courses already! I hate it because your plan to re-place all this with that awful disaster putt-putt course is stu-pid! I'm allowed to be revolted by things that are revolting, get it? I don't have to show my Official Indian Reservation I.D. card to prove it's okay for me to be annoyed."

"Do you guys really have those?" Garrett nodded and man-aged to look grim *and* smug. "I knew it."

"Go. Away." *Gah*, she was so steamed she could feel her pulse in her temples. "Kill. You. If you don't. *Argh*."

"Fine, but just know your angry-squaw routine doesn't scare me."

"Did you know it's possible to scream so loudly the blood vessels in your throat rupture?" Blake had maneuvered around Natalie and was once again nose to nose with Garrett. "Imag-ine the kind of pain that would induce that. Throat-rupturing screaming. It's the kind of pain that is agonizing, but not quite enough to make you pass out. The worst kind of pain, I think."

"You don't scare me." This from the driver's side of his car, as he'd wasted no time getting fleeing distance from Blake. Nata-lie was impressed against her will; she'd had no idea Garrett Hobbes could move that fast. "Nothing about you is scary!"

"He's scaring the shit out of me," Natalie admitted, then smirked as Garrett's rebuttal was swallowed by the shriek of his engine as he roared out of the driveway in reverse. There was a crunch—

Blake winced. "Was that the stump?"

—and the sound of tearing metal—

The wince turned into a grin. "My, he's certainly hung up on it, isn't he?"

—followed by the car stalling, only to start up almost immediately and keep going, the engine making a *blat-blat-blatttt* sound that grew steadily distant.

"Too bad he had to leave so soon." Blake sighed in mock regret. "I felt a certain kinship with the man."

"Never in a hundred years are you anything like that jackass. When we were fourteen, he grabbed my ass when he was supposed to be spotting me in gym for the rope climb."

Blake's grin disappeared like he'd been punched. "His address, please. Work *and* home."

"No, no." She waved away his misplaced adorable unnecessary machismo. "Took care of it myself. Let's just say he never again neglected to wear a cup when we had class together. Any class: Phy Ed, Algebra, Home Ec, Spanish . . ."

"I found him to be somewhat loathsome," Blake admitted. "He struck me as one of those unfortunates who blame everything and everyone for their own dreadful decisions. From what I gathered, everything that has gone wrong in his life—"

"And *so much* has gone wrong," Natalie interrupted with a grin.

"—is somehow the fault of . . . this town? And apparently fertilizer? Or at least his family's long, proud history selling it?" He shook his head and looked adorably befuddled. "Perhaps I'm not one to pass judgment. Our mother never spoke of Sweetheart, never discussed her roots—"

Don't say anything. He's opening up and he's being the opposite of a Vegas Douche. Of course, compared to Garrett, anyone would seem the opposite of a Vegas Douche. But this was no time to explain exactly why Shannah Banaan had not one damned thing to brag about, remember fondly, or look forward to. She couldn't imagine a family less excited about bastard grandchildren. She was just surprised their fate took almost three decades to catch up with them.

"We never had a sense of history to live up to—or to live down." *Ah. Still babbling about the family history he knew nothing about.* "When our father passed, we were instantly wealthy. So I can't relate to Mr. Hobbes' dilemma."

"He's a douche. That's his dilemma."

"He *was* unpleasant," Blake agreed. "And that was before his unfortunate assumptions about you."

She groaned. It was all still so vivid. She'd need a lot of booze to start repressing the afternoon. "Is there anything more annoying than a well-meaning racist?"

"A comic-book villain, perhaps? He was so over-the-top. It wasn't unlike watching a play. I kept waiting for him to twirl his moustache while tying a widow to train tracks because she wouldn't sell the family farm."

Natalie felt her eyes widen and shouted before she could suck it back. "Hey!"

He flinched and looked around as if for an attacker. "What? What?"

She calmed herself; poor guy had no idea.

(poor guy? he was Vegas Douche not so long ago, ya big softie)

"Blake, I'm sorry to yell, but you can't go around saying stuff like that."

"I've offended you?"

"No, but . . . look, just . . . don't talk about Garrett's great-grandfather like that. It's not just because he's still upset about it; it's just generally regarded as not cool to bring up. Guy's got enough problems without having to live down what his ancestor did."

"Wait. What?" Blake sat back on the bales as if worried his legs would quit. "Are you— That *happened*?"

"Of course it happened. Where do you think villain stereotypes come from?"

"No, come on." She could see him struggling with the concept. "His great-grandfather was Snidely Whiplash?"

"Shhh. And yes. That's why even when they were trendy, no one in his family would ever wear a cape or a top hat, or grow a moustache."

"When were capes and top—"

She kept going; it was important that Blake internalized this. "That's like the Holocaust to his family. Which is ironic, because they're all Holocaust deniers. But it's the one aspect of his awfulness that's not to be made fun of."

"I'm never going to understand this place, am I?"

She shrugged. "That's up to you."

"I'm not sure it is."

She shrugged again—*what to say to that, really?*—then handed him the small bottle she'd grabbed on her way out the door . . . *when? Ten minutes ago? Felt like longer.* Blake glanced down at it, puzzled, then looked up at her and smiled. *God, that smile. Nnfff.*

"I know Margaret of Anjou likes cinnamon on her apples. Thought I'd save you a trip."

"You're very kind," was his careful reply, but that *smile*. Like she'd just done the smartest, coolest thing ever. Like she wasn't a lying, deceitful sneak.

"I'm not. I'm not kind, Blake." And she dreaded the day he'd find out, and hated the dread.

Twenty-one

Over an hour after she'd called it a day (twenty-first century or not, there was only so much work you could do on a farm once the sun was down) she was spreading butter and brown sugar over a piece of *lefsa*,* then rolling it into something resembling a delicious cigar and wolfing half of it in one bite. *Oh, lefsa. You take so little, and give so much.* It needed cinnamon, which was too bad because—

Oh. Blake. As if reading her mind, Larry and Harry, who were sitting at the kitchen table playing poker (online, not with each other, fallout from the Deuces Wild Incident of 2013), were discussing him, unless Vegas Douche was the nickname of yet another wealthy, jaded stranger from Vegas who hung around Heartbreak for reasons known only to him and maybe two others.

---

*Traditional soft Norwegian flatbread popular in North Dakota and Minnesota. Also delicious. Very, very delicious.

"Vegas Douche hasn't quit."

Larry scratched his chin. He hardly ever had stubble, only freckles that went with his pale skin and carrot-colored hair, but he never gave up trying. "Nope. He hasn't."

"Might not."

"Yep."

"Might die."

"Risk I'm willing to take." Larry rose, then looked up to see Natalie's gaze on him. "What? I didn't say I wouldn't feel bad for the guy. I would. A little. Jeez, I've known him less than a month. I don't haveta give the eulogy."

"He's not dead yet!" she almost shouted. *This.* This was what happened when she stopped going to the bank and went to Heartbreak instead. She ended up liking a city guy and snapping at someone she'd known since third grade.

"Yeah, but when he *does* die! Someone else will have to do the eulogy!"

Harry, still playing poker on his phone, called his opponent's bluff, then looked up and rejoined the conversation. "Any idea how long he's sticking around?"

"If he knew," Natalie replied, absently wondering where Blake even was, "we'd know."

"He knows the town's going belly-up, right? So why hang around?"

"To help it maybe not go belly-up?"

"How the hell's he gonna do that between mucking stalls?"

Natalie said nothing. Blake's wealth was a well-kept secret in town. She only knew because she'd seen the property paperwork in Shannah's name and the foreclosure paperwork with Blake's name. It was making Natalie nuts, knowing Blake could write a check at any time and . . . and—

Go on. Say it. Even if you know saying it out loud would taste like shit in your mouth.

—save them. But Vegas Douche saving them only solved the immediate problem. One or two checks couldn't fix two decades of an economic crapshoot. It was likely too late to stop Garrett's land deal, but even if they could somehow put the brakes on it, the original problem remained: What next?

So what? What?

"They giving you shit down at the bank?" Harry asked. "Heard the boss is a real bitch."

She snorted. She was the boss at Sweetheart Trust, which he well knew. Everyone but Blake knew. "Fun-*nee*."

"All this because Shannah inherited those farms?" Larry asked. "She shows up; then a few weeks later Vegas Douche comes calling. And neither of them have left."

"Weird," Harry agreed. "Like the plot of a book or something, where at the end all the seemingly unrelated incidents end up being totally related."

"A stupid book," Natalie grumped. This wasn't fiction, dammit. It was her life. All their lives.

"It'd almost be interesting," Larry allowed with a nod, "if interesting things happened in Sweetheart."

Harry fiddled with his phone, indicating he needed two more cards from his online opponents. "This is all Jonathan Banaan's fault. He built Heartbreak, didn't quit, then had more Banaans. What a bastard!"

"He *was* a bastard, remember? His mom was the town li-

brarian and she never got married after the Sam's Delicious
Meats guy knocked her up."

"Starting Heartbreak's long tradition of hot slutty librarians."

It was true. Employees of the Heartbreak Public Library
were absurdly hot. You practically had to clip a head shot to
your résumé to get an interview over there.

"We're lucky we're not hip deep in Banaans," Harry continued. "Raise. So there's that to be thankful for, I guess."

*Not being hip deep in them, it could be argued, is a huuuge part
of the problem.* But no point in discussing it at this late date.

"Guess so," Larry agreed while Natalie nodded. If only
Shannah's family had died, none of this would be happening.
But they hadn't died. It was a lot worse than that.

"Call," Harry said.

"Ha!" Larry was squeezing his phone so hard his knuckles
were white. "Got this guy on the run." Natalie glanced at his
hand, then walked around the table to check Gary's.

"Um . . ."

"What?" Harry snapped.

"Guys, I think—"

"Go away, Nat," Larry ordered. "I'm about to sink this jagoff for trying to buy the pot."

"I am not!" Gary snapped back. "I don't— Wait."

Natalie started for the back door. She hadn't been present
for the Deuces Wild Incident of 2013, but it had become legend within hours. She had no interest in witnessing the next
iteration.

"Wait, what's your hand?"

"Three threes."

"Goddammit! I'm playing you online, aren't I?"

"Are you CowboyBaby Number One? Because if you are, then yeah."

"My sister is CowboyBaby Number One and you know damned well I'm playing for her while she gets over the C-section for the twins! She's had a really tough time since the sheriff got amnesia!"

"It's retrograde amnesia, not anterograde! He'll be fine! And I knew you were playing, but how the hell would I know *her* online poker handle? Sweetheart isn't *that* small."

"Sweetheart is incredibly small and you know it, you fourth-generation son of a bitch!"

She let the screen door swing shut, relieved to be on the other side. Let Gary and Larry work out (or not) their weird online poker flirting thing that everyone knew meant they wanted to bang but needed to fight the urge for at least eighteen more months, because *Brokeback Mountain*. She could not would not get involved; she had a nonexistent love life to fret over and a city guy to find.

Why d'you even care, Nat? You're not his keeper. He's probably sleeping or went to town or done any one of half a dozen things that aren't your concern.

She told her inner self to get bent, and pretended she wasn't getting a little worried about Vegas Douche.

Twenty-two

She found him absentmindedly slapping mosquitoes while reading to Margaret of Anjou. Warm light spilled from Main One, lending dim light to the corral. It was cloudless and the moon was nearly full, and distracted as she was, Natalie once again thanked God for the sight. There were places where you couldn't see the stars for all the artificial light. Blake had spent every night his first week walking around and gaping up at the sky. Twice she'd found him snoring in the tall grass near the tree line. Was that when she'd started finding him almost adorable?

He was leaning on one of the posts, reading something from his tablet the bugs found mighty interesting (though it could have been just the light). Margaret of Anjou was a dim, puffy shape at the far end of the corral.

"'We are unique individuals with unique experiences,'* that's what it says here. "God knows you're unique, I'm reasonably

---

* John Gray, *Men Are from Mars, Women Are from Venus,* 1992.

certain, though you are my first pony. According to Gary, who can be helpful when he isn't tripping me with a rake handle or washing my Supertruck with the windows open, you are one of the most unpleasant creatures he has ever encountered. And a rather unpleasant creature like Gary would know."

Natalie wanted to say something while hating to intrude, so hovered just out of his sight line, waiting for her moment.

"Which makes you a unique individual, to be sure. I wonder what happened to you? Were you made evil, or born evil? It raises the inevitable question of nature or nurture." He paused to bat bugs away from the small glowing screen. "And I have to say, as unscientific as my opinion is, it *must* be nature. Because I am who I am, and Rake is who he is. If it were nurture, we would both be terrible. But it's nature, because only Rake is terrible."

"What are you doing?" She blurted it without thinking and, startled, he dropped his tablet. *Oh, boy.* It was so dark out, she really hoped he hadn't dropped it in a pile of—

"Son of a *bitch*."

"Maybe it's just mud?"

Blake groaned and stooped to pick up his tablet. "It hasn't rained for a week."

"I'm sorry; I didn't mean to startle you."

"And I didn't mean to be startled." He sighed and used part of his shirtsleeve to rub it-wasn't-mud off the screen, which had of course fallen screen-side down.

"We were wondering where you were."

"No." He had turned his back on Margaret of Anjou to give Natalie his full attention, which was startling and far too thrilling. "*You* wondered. Why?"

Because I think of you all the time. And not like how I used to think about running you down with the tractor. I mean, I still think that, but lately you've been naked in that fantasy.

She ignored the question. "Come into the house. Harry made that thing you like."

"Haricots verts with poached eggs and tarragon vinaigrette?"

"The other thing you like."

"Bacon and Swiss chard pasta?"

"No, the other—for God's sake," she said, laughing a little. "Of course you're a foodie."

"Harry," he replied, putting a hand over his heart while looking reverent, which made her laugh harder, "is a phenomenal cook. He told me he wept when they quit publishing *Gourmet*. And I believed him."

"Yep. He did. On and off for a week." She smirked, remembering. "His wife was confused and pissed, which is why she's now his ex-wife."

"And you have a wonderful laugh."

Pleased, she thanked him.

"It comes perilously close to being shrill, but it's redeemed by how your eyes get crinkly when you giggle."

"Dammit! You just can't let a compliment be a compliment, can you?"

"You and my mother," he sighed, "are of like mind."

"Yeah, yeah." *Weird. The thought of having something in common with Shannah Banaan. Disturbing.* "Time to quit. Let's go in."

He'd been squinting at Natalie in the low light but nodded and came with her willingly enough. Halfway back to the house he cleared his throat.

"I am aware that on short acquaintance you dislike me," he began, then paused. "Ah. Thank you for not disagreeing."

"I'm warming up to you a bit," she couldn't help pointing out. "I don't spit on your shadow anymore."

He looked wry. "From such small things dynasties spring. Regardless, I'd like to take you out to dinner."

"Why?"

He nodded as if expecting her question. Like tall, broad-shouldered rich studs asked her to dinner all the time and what made *him* so special? She had to swallow a snort; what a world that would be. "So we can discuss—"

"Because you're in it every day, I gotta give it to you. We were just talking about it. But it's only been— What? Two and a half weeks?"

"Seventeen days, thirteen hours."

She groaned. "See, that's the sort of thing that pisses me off. This isn't a prison sentence, you big goober." When he didn't reply, she added, "It's not! Okay, maybe you can't help thinking of it like that. But that's the thinking that got you stuck here in the first place, right? So what's there to discuss?"

"Anything. Everything."

Flattery was being replaced by glum anger. Slumming. That's what this was. He knew he wouldn't be here forever. He knew *she* knew that. But hey, make time with a local, maybe get some NoDak nooky, while away the hours until it was time to run back to Vegas.

"We can discuss anything you like," he was saying, and then she lost it.

"Discuss what?" She was dumb enough to again be warmed by his interest, and stomped the warmth until it went away.

"Your big plans for the farm you don't give a shit about? How you don't want to be here, but Mommy's making you? How the second you and your mom make up you're on the next flight to Vegas?"

"Actually, I'd take the train again; it was quite nice," he replied absently. Then: "I'm confused."

She snorted. "Got *that* right."

"Are you angry because—"

"Oh, boy, I hope you cleared your afternoon. Because I've got a list."

He shuddered a little. "No doubt." They were at the kitchen door. The windows were open; it had been a mild day in the low seventies, no need for the air conditioner. The relative silence made for an excellent warning system: they could hear shouting and chairs being shoved around.

"Deuces *aren't* wild! They're never wild! I made that rule in 2009, for God's sake!"

"Except when we're doing Texas Hold 'Em! I made *that* rule in 2007!"

"Dear God, no," Blake gasped, freezing in place even as he reached for the screen door handle. "Not the addendum to the Deuces Wild Incident of 2013?"

"They were playing each other online," she sighed, "and only realized it about five minutes ago."

He nodded once, decisive. "We'll flee." Without discussing it, they started to circle around to the front porch. "We were discussing the reason for your dislike."

"We were discussing the fact that it's a huge long list and you're not the only one on it."

"Oh, I don't doubt it." He chuckled. "Though how anyone

besides me would be foolish enough to get on your bad side I cannot comprehend."

"Aww. That's sweet." It was!

"You could so easily end any of us where we stand. If you were a boa constrictor, your jaw would already be unhinged in preparation."

She swallowed a groan. "Did you really just compare me to a goddamn snake?"

"It's an apex predator," he replied, sounding *wounded* of all things. She squashed the urge to apologize, and was beginning to realize that was his thing. He'd make an absent comment that was the nicest thing ever, then immediately follow it up with something annoying.

"Do you dislike me because I'm not from here—"

"Maybe I dislike you because you compare me to predatory snakes!"

"No, I only just did that, and your animosity has been directed toward me for several days. So is it because I'm not from Sweetheart? Or North Dakota?"

"Naw. The gal who runs the bait shop/singles center—"

"Bait Mate?"

"That's the one." Things that worked in other places weren't always suited to Sweetheart singles. Wine tastings were considered a waste of time when both town bars had adequate selections. There wasn't a sports bar, because the North Dakota Wizards left for Santa Cruz in 2012, they didn't have a team in the NHL, and nobody gave a shit about curling. Movie dates? Nobody wanted to drive an hour and forty-five minutes to see the latest *Transformers* explode-a-thon. And Starbucks had been run out of town within six months, nine out of ten residents refusing to pay eight dollars for a cup of coffee, no matter how dramatically sweetened or mixed or whipped or frozen.

But there were lots of fishermen/women in town, and a lot of them hooked up at the bait shop (pardon *le pun*). You could pick up a bag of smelt and get a date for the fishing opener at the same place.

"Yeah, her—she was from Atlanta and everyone liked her. Except Garrett Hobbes, but you know: Garrett."

"Then is it because I don't wish to be here?"

"Don't flatter yourself. Kevin Sumner showed up to survey the place when they were figuring out where the new highway would go, and he never did get around to leaving. And everyone liked him, too—you should have seen all the locals at his funeral!"

Blake doggedly continued; she had to admire it. Or be terrified of it. "Or because my mother has frozen my assets?"

"Leave your mother out— Wait, what?" *This* was news. "You're not rich?"

"No. Nor is my brother; our mother controls the family's wealth."

"But . . . you . . . I heard your father—" *Wait. Wait. Calm down. There's an explanation. If he didn't have money, he couldn't have signed off on the paperwork I saw. Ergo, he has money.*

"Yes, the money is from my father's side, but he died when my brother and I were minors."

"Sorry." A knee-jerk social platitude, she knew, but it was true; she was sorry. She couldn't imagine her life if her father had died when she was a kid. Her earliest memory was of helping her father with one of his many experiments; their kitchen had as many Erlenmeyer flasks as forks. He still lived in the house where she'd grown up, and there were pictures of her late mother in every room, including the bathroom and basement laundry room. "That must have sucked." She instantly cursed herself for channeling a seventeen-year-old girl. *Must have sucked? Really, Nat?*

"The sucking was not as encompassing as you might assume." Blake shrugged. "I never knew the man, though I understand he's a lot like Rake, so I don't actually mind not knowing him, because Rake is terrible."

"Yeah, yeah." Blake was almost pathologically obsessed with his brother's terribleness. It was at least as troubling as men who were obsessed with their mothers. Which Blake might also be. "Talk about the money more, please."

They had reached the front by then, and he held the door for her as they went inside. "My grandmother didn't know about us until the reading of his will, and sought us out to both make our acquaintance as well as inform my mother she would be the trustee of his estate."

"Okay." Deep breath in, deep breath out. *There's money. Somewhere, anyway.* "So. Then?"

"Mom has always been generous until, ahem, recent events. She'd never tried to control how or what we spent, but legally she always had the option. She is now exercising it." This last on a note so dry it could have smoked trout.

Natalie rubbed her forehead, willing back the instant headache. Nothing. This had all been for nothing. She'd been trying to figure out how to make Vegas Douche save Heartbreak when she "should have been working on Shannah Banana."

"Shannah who?"

Horrified, Natalie looked up into his dark blue eyes, now wide with stunned surprise. "Oh my God. That was out loud? I'm so sorry. I was thinking too hard."

"Nonsense, you were thinking just right."

She groaned and clutched at his forearm. He stiffened but didn't pull away. "Please *please* don't tell Ms. Banaan I ever *ever* called her that. She hates it; the whole family hates it; she put Garrett in the hospital over it; now let us never speak of this again."

"Nonsense!" He was as happy as she'd ever seen him, and it completely changed his face. *God, what a smile.* "It's brilliant; you're a genius. And henceforth Mom shall be known to me only as Shannah Banana."

"No!"

"Don't worry; it will remain our dirty secret." His grin was getting downright predatory, which was doing delicious and unwelcome things to her midsection. *Imagine him naked. Looking at you like that. Like he could eat . . . you . . . up . . . ummm . . .*

"If you do this," she said, trying for stern but whining instead, "then you're the terrible one. Not your brother."

The grin fell away as if slapped off. "Do *not* say something you can't take back, Natalie," he warned. And why was that *hotter*, for God's sake? "Now where is my phone? The taunting must start at once."

No! What have I done? Time to leave town. Never thought I'd go unless someone stuck a shotgun barrel between my shoulder blades, but the alternative is a peeved Banaan.

Blake had by now darted up the stairs to the loft, Natalie plodding behind him. He all but lunged at his phone, nearly dropping it in his haste. "Oh, Natalie, lovely Natalie," he said cheerfully, waiting for the call to connect. "I shall buy you a new pair of gloves and perhaps also a collinear hoe."

"Thanks, but I got one for my birthday." Impressed in spite of her blossoming terror, Natalie reminded herself that two weeks ago Blake wouldn't have known a collinear hoe from a hula hoe, like some loser. "You've been paying attention."

"Of course, I pay attention to everything you—damn. Voice mail. This is too good to leave on a soulless recording. I'll save it. Yes. Excellent."

Then he scampered—scampered!—across the loft and swept her up in an exuberant hug, spinning her around and giving her a noseful of sunshine and cotton and dirt, all underlaid with the clean sweat of exertion.

She almost kissed him.

Days later, dialing for the ambulance she knew wouldn't make it, she wished she had.

Twenty-three

Finally, *finally* Rake began responding to his hexts and voice mails. Blake had dropped off to sleep savoring two wonderful memories: his mother's nickname and getting Natalie Lane in his arms for seven seconds. Given how alarmed she looked when he'd hugged her, it would likely be the last time he did, and he planned to treasure the memory. *Probably for the rest of my life. The farm foreman who got away.* His mother's nickname, on the other hand, he would use again and again, and he planned to treasure that as well.

He had also made up his mind about the nuclear option and decided it was past time to turn his key. He disliked the holding pattern he was in, and the nuclear option, while extreme, promised to put an end to it. Just as well Rake chose today to get back to him; he would need to be warned. As annoying as Rake was, even he didn't deserve to go into such a situation blind.

Blake's last thought as he dropped off was, *Natalie's hair smells like cherry blossoms, which is impossible. I wonder where she buys her shampzzzzzzzzz . . .*

Thirty seconds later, his phone buzzed, making everything on the beside table tremble, and he groped for it. A squint at the time told him it had been eight hours, not thirty seconds. He'd never slept so well or so long in his life. For the sixty million Americans who suffered from insomnia, Heartbreak was the certain cure. Side effects: sore muscles, blisters, suntans, pony sitting, unrequited crushes.

Christ Blake I thought my phone was going to blow up what's going on with you I mean jeez?

Blake snorted. Of course. He should have realized. *Did you lose another phone, idiot?*

No! I know right where it is, it's still at the bottom of the canal, so now who's the idiot?

Canal? Never mind. Thank you for eventually acknowledging my dozens of communiqués.

Only your phone auto-corrects communications. See? Mine didn't. Where are you?

If you'd listened to any of your voice mails, you'd know.

And if you had a Facebook page like a real live boy, I'd also know. Where?

The fifth circle of Hell.

You're back in Vegas?

No. The real Hell. Actual Hell.

What are you doing in L.A.?

Having an incredibly irritating text chat with my twin.

Because I'm terrible? People have told me you think I'm terrible. Personally I don't see it.

Enough of this. Blake stopped texting and called.

"Dude!" Rake picked up immediately, in mid-yawn from the sound of it. "Do you know what time it is here?"

"No," was Blake's truthful answer.

"Damn. Was hoping you did, because I'd kinda like to know. I can't tell if the new phone is right and when I use the hotel phone the guy on the other end won't speak English."

"I cannot help you." Rake could be anywhere. Staten Island. Rome. London. Walmart. "And you're a grown man who's nearly thirty; stop using 'dude.' Where are you?"

"Venice, I'm pretty sure."

Blake rolled out of bed and stretched, watching the sun come up while clutching the phone in his other hand. He instantly loosened his grip; his hands were sore. "Pretty sure? Even for you, that's odd."

"Venice is the one with canals instead of streets, right? And people speak Italian? And the Italian food is really good? And there's gelato all over the place?"

"Yes, you dolt. Italy is seven hours ahead of the Central Time Zone, so that should help you narrow it down." He shuffled over to the toaster, stifling a yawn. He had carefully cleared one of the bookshelves of the Little House series and several Carl Hiaasen novels and kept his dry goods there. Now he popped two pieces of bread in the toaster. "You are in Venice."

"That's a relief. It sucked, not knowing where I was."

"Wait, you weren't making another tiresome joke? You just *woke up* in Venice?"

"See? You're not the only person having a weird month. Not to belittle your woos or anything—"

"Woes."

"—but I'm neck deep in my own shit; I promise."

"Your shit is not as all-encompassing as my shit, I assure you."

"Wanna bet? I'm stranded on the other side of the planet with no money in a country where I don't speak the language, and I don't know where my pants are. Doesn't that make you feel better?"*

"It does," Blake admitted. "What's her name?"

"There are four of them, I think."

"Good God."

"Now I just have to figure out which one is responsible for my being here. And what I have to do in order to get the hell out of here and get back home."

"Rake, I know exactly how you feel." Blake could not recall sympathizing more. "Wait. You said you're stranded with no money. You didn't return my call to find out what trouble I'm in; you called for a loan so I could get you out of the trouble *you're* in."

"Anything sounds bad," Rake whined, "when you put it like that."

"You are terrible. And it gives me genuine joy to tell you I have no money, either." He stepped into the bathroom to brush his teeth while Rake muttered various epithets on the other end. After spitting and rinsing, Blake added, "Like me, you've brought this on yourself."

"You know I hate listening to you spit."

"There are far worse places to be stranded than Venice."

---

* To find out what poor Rake's been plunged into, check out *USA Dead Ahead!*

"This is true." Rake sounded cheerful again and Blake approved of his brother's effervescence, though he rarely shared it. You could knock Rake down, but he never stayed prone for long. "So your messages said you're in Mom's hometown? And you're working on a farm?"

"Are you asking me? If that's what my messages said? Because you're using an upward inflection at the end of your sentences? Like this?"

"God, I hate you . . . *yes.* I'm asking if it's true."

"I am incarcerated in Sweetheart."

"Ha!"

"And I am working on a farm. Not one our mother inherited."

"Uh, that's good, I guess? Not really sure what you're wanting to hear from me on this one . . ."

"Our great-great-grandfather built it."

"He did?"

"Or was it our great-grandfather?"

"Are you serious with this shit?" Rake sounded incredulous. Blake could relate.

"Completely. My toast is ready."

"Did you just say your toast is ready?"

"Is it a bad connection or are you tracking more poorly than usual? Yes. My toast beckons. And after that I might have time to steal some bacon if I can somehow lure Gary from the table. Then I must feed my pony, the terrible Margaret of Anjou, and foil whatever Plan B Garrett Hobbes may be putting into motion so his fertilizing company goes under and he's free to open a chain of strip clubs in Hollywood. Or possibly design toilet paper."

There was a long silence, which Blake enjoyed as he munched dry toast. Finally, a tentative Rake asked, "You use the word 'terrible' a lot. They gave you a horse?"

Leave it to Rake to seize on the least important part of that list. "They cursed me," Blake corrected, "with Margaret of Anjou, the foulest, cruelest, most vile pony in the history of equines. And perhaps she isn't terrible."

"Sorry, did you say it *wasn't* terrible?"

He sigh-groaned. "*She* is just one more problem I can't solve on a list of problems I can't solve. If you're drowning, you don't especially care if someone pours a bucket of water over your head."

"You need to get laid," Rake said, his go-to answer for every problem Blake discussed with him. "Clear your pipes."

"Vulgar."

"And effective! Tell the truth, you haven't gotten any farm tail, have you?"

"You are terrible."

"Old news, big brother, and answer the question."

Blake paused, swallowing the last of the toast, then admitted, "I don't deny having infrequent intercourse of late."

Rake's crow of delight came through as though he were standing beside Blake. "Knew it! That's Blake-ese for 'major dry spell.'"

"By choice!" he protested. Which wasn't the whole truth. Ava had broken it off, and he'd been unable to take the other women up on their generous offers of sex, since they were in Vegas and he wasn't. "I've been trapped on the desolate prairie, and the opportunities for intercourse have been rare." Except not really. On his trips into town he'd run across several men and women who made it clear Blake could come over and play farmhand whenever he wished. And at any other time, he would have taken at least two of the ladies up on their blunt, friendly offers.

But it wasn't any other time. He'd seen Natalie Lane on his first day here, and that was that. He wanted Natalie Lane, he would never have Natalie Lane, he wouldn't settle for someone who wasn't Natalie Lane, the end; ad infinitum. Rake was terrible, but Blake was a fool.

"Okay, first thing," Rake was yammering, "maybe you'd have more frequent intercourse if you stopped referring to it as intercourse. Just a thought."

"It's accurate," he protested. *And distinctly unromantic,* his brain supplied. Terrible Rake, making the occasional good point.

"Hmmm."

"Stop that." Rake's *hmmm* usually meant he was stumbling over a truth Blake had no intention of discussing, or even confronting.

"There's a girl, isn't there?"

"Of course not." Natalie Lane was not a *girl.* She was a woman, an extraordinary, complex, puzzling, lovely woman who smelled like cherry blossoms hundreds of miles from the nearest cherry tree.

"Ugh, fine, a woman, there's a woman stuck on the prairie with you."

"There are several." *Evade, evade!*

"Good for you, Slutty McSkank."

"Of course I'm not interested in all of them, just Natalie Lane." *God* dammit. Blake knew he was smarter than Rake, but the bastard was able to do this nearly every time! It must be his native cunning. Jackals could occasionally outwit lions, after all.

"You're sooooo easy," Rake chortled. "So talk about Natalie Lame."

"Lane, you imbecile." It was always tricky at first, speaking through gritted teeth, but Blake eventually remembered the technique. "And she's wonderful. Smart and driven and fierce."

"Uh-huh, and what's the body situation? Is it wonderful to watch her arrive, or watch her leave? Or is it more about the face?"

"You are a pig." And it was wonderful to watch her arrive *and* leave. "And she has a lovely face. She's Irish and Native American and has wonderful blue eyes and gorgeous cheekbones."

"Nice." Rake actually sounded impressed, but he could have been referring to the room service menu.

"She's kind," Blake agreed, "but she doesn't think she's kind. And she loathes me, of course."

"What, 'of course'? She hasn't known you enough to loathe you, so where's she get off? Hey, if she doesn't get what a great catch a history-obsessed, technology-loathing glum slutty stick-in-the-mud like you is, screw her."

"Thank you." Blake meant it, because he knew Rake was, in his own way, being kind. Rake could be, uh, not sweet, exactly, but loyalty was something the Tarbells had in common. Rake and Blake kept their distance from each other, but that didn't translate to indifference. "She sees me as an apathetic interloper who has contempt for her way of life, and she's not entirely wrong."

"You're too hard on yourself," came the instant response. Blake waited, and Rake did not disappoint: "That's *my* job, you apathetic, interloping jagoff. Ask her out!"

"To what end? She won't leave Sweetheart under her own power, and I won't stay."

"Um, I dunno, because you like her? And she'd like you if you unclenched long enough? And it'll make your prairie sentence go a little faster? You don't have to marry her, for God's sake."

If only. He sighed. "Thank you for the advice. I'll consider what you've said."

"Uh-huh, Blake-ese for 'You're full of shit, but I'm way too classy to tell you.'"

"Yes."

"So let's talk about something we *can* agree on, namely, how we can get back control of our money."

"Excellent question. And it's fortunate you chose this week to acknowledge my messages—"

"I *woke up* in another *country*, you self-absorbed jerkass! Without pants!"

"—because you need to understand: I have employed the nuclear option."

Another long silence broken by Rake's whispered, "Don't even joke about that, Bro."

"I would never, because I agree. It's not a thing to joke about."

"You didn't. Right? Blake? Come on, man; you're winding me up. You didn't really do that. Right? Blake? You didn't, right?"

"Rake, our mother left me with few alternatives."

From the phone, a tinny, hollow groan: "Oh, *God*."

"And if nothing else, it will be a way to get some answers out of Shannah Banana."

"Who? Listen, tell the truth. I won't be mad; it's a good joke." Rake managed to croak a fake laugh into the phone. "Really good, but you didn't really do it, right? The nuclear option? You've eloped with Natalie Lame instead—"

"Lane."

"—and this is just a weird way for you to break it to me gently. It's fine. I'm not mad. You really got me on that one, Bro, good one."

Rake's inability to focus on anything other than the nuclear option, including the wonderful nickname for their mother that she hated, spelled out in precise detail the level of his terror, and Blake's determination.

"I did, Rake. This is not a drill. I called her last night. She's coming."

"You arrogant ass," Rake breathed. "You've killed us all!"

"The line," Blake said, because he had long memorized the dialogue from one of the finest movies in the history of cinema, "is 'You arrogant ass, you've killed *us*.'* And in fact Tupolev's arrogance did doom his crew, although technically the explosion when the torpedo impacted the hull killed them and, if not that, then the water pressure, or they drowned. Whatever the official cause of death, it was, in fact, his arrogance that doomed them all."

"Seek help, Blake. Not just for being stupid and crazy

---

* Tom Clancy, *The Hunt for Red October*.

enough to call Nonna Tarbell, but just in general. You're completely nuts."

"Could be." Blake was surprised at how calm he was, how sanguine. *Once you have done the unthinkable, there is nothing left to fear.* "But watch yourself, little brother. It's probably genetic."

"Great. Just keep my name out of *everything*. I'll figure out my own mess on this side of the world, and you and Nonna stay over there on your side, and we'll meet up at Christmas or something and, I dunno, shake hands or hug or something, and that'll be fine until our birthday. Assuming you even survive."

"Yes, there's every chance this will get me killed, and that's only if I'm not dying at the bottom of a canyon."

"Blake. Seriously. Call someone. You've lost it, dude."

"Don't call me dude. *Godere Venezia.*"

"Sorry, what?"

"It's 'Enjoy Venice' in Italian."

"Oh, shut up. Fucking show-off." And Rake was gone.

There were worse ways to start the day, Blake decided, and celebrated his steady hands in the face of nuclear immolation with another piece of toast.

Twenty-four

He thought and thought and finally swallowed hard, and when Natalie came close to check the condition of the stall he said, "I'm meeting my grandmother for lunch. I have yet to see you take a day off and you work harder than I do. Would you like to join me?"

Except Margaret of Anjou, who had stubbornly resisted exiting the stall for the corral, chose that moment to lean against him to scratch an itch. So what came out was, "I'm meeting my graaaaggghhhh off off *get off you are killing me!*" He groaned and threw his elbow into the pony's side (repeatedly), desperate to get her off his ribs, which she interpreted as the smallest brush from a random mosquito for all the attention she paid. "Cursed equine!"

"Oh, you, get over here." Natalie, praise all the gods, had found the snack sack chock-full o' sliced apples sprinkled with cinnamon. She shook it at Margaret of Anjou, who eyed it, then leisurely wandered to Natalie to haughtily accept . . . No, she was retreating to the far end of the stall, ears flattened against her head and several square teeth showing. She'd only wandered over as part of her never-ending campaign to screw with bipeds.

Fortunately, Blake had taken advantage of those few seconds of not being squashed into oblivion and scurried from the stall. He leaned on the door and carefully felt his ribs, groaning under his breath. *Vile beast.*

"You, um, okay?" Natalie was trying, and failing, to suppress a grin.

"Oh, of course, never better, my shattered ribs are mere flesh wounds. Stop that!" he snapped as she collapsed into giggles.

"Sorry. I am, I promise— Look, I've had that happen to me. Rookie mistake, letting her get you between her and the wall, and I warned you, Blake; you know I did. I know exactly how it feels, and it's not funny, it isn't; it's just— Your expression—you're usually so cool and collected—"

"Usually my breathing is unimpeded by several hundred pounds of smelly equine!"

At that, the lady lost it and reached for him, clutching his arms to steady herself, and Blake instantly recovered from his snit. Even at 7:00 A.M. she looked wonderful, the rising sun bathing her in golden light as she berated him for not putting the tractor away. But she also looked wonderful at 7:00 P.M., when she was dusty from eyebrows to heels and berating him for hiding Margaret of Anjou's salt lick.

Once he could breathe without bursting into tears, he asked Natalie to lunch again, she accepted between giggles (to his astonished pleasure), and the morning flew. He was in such good humor he only peripherally noticed his throbbing hands. They were the last part of him to acclimate to his new work schedule, the only part, he thought, left of the old Blake, lonely single Anglophile (though only Anglos from the fifteenth and sixteenth centuries) and history nerd. Pre-Heartbreak, his greatest physical exertion had been using the hotel's treadmill at 2:30 A.M., often with a copy of *Lancaster and York: The Wars of the Roses and the Foundation of Modern Britain* on the display screen in front of him.

In what was objectively three hours and twenty-seven minutes, and subjectively eight seconds, they'd left Heartbreak and were seated on the B and B's south-facing porch. There were several small tables set with crisp linen and spotless pale blue china, and frosty pitchers of booze-ade (according to their hostess) beading with condensation were kept brimming.

"Careful," Natalie counseled. "You can't taste the booze, which is problematic because it's basically all booze. Easy to end up on your ass."

"Noted." Blake shrugged off the warning. He was a large man and had excellent tolerance. Las Vegas practically had bars in church, and he'd been holding his liquor since he was nineteen.

"Not sure if you knew; this is the only B and B in town now," Natalie explained, refilling both their glasses, "but the good news is, it's excellent."

"I haven't been back since I started at Heartbreak." He thought of the Blake of nearly a month ago with a combination of fondness and contempt. *Poor idiot never had a chance. His fate was sealed the moment he didn't die in a train crash.* "It's charming." He sipped his booze-ade and managed to not smack his lips. It was delightful, lemon juice, sugar syrup that had been steeped in rosemary sprigs, sparkling water, something else he couldn't identify. Thirst quenching and so refreshing! "My mother likes it here quite a lot." And Nonna had better, since her only other lodging option was the Sleep Inn just out of town on Highway 19. The good news was, he had prevaricated about his arrival time, wanting some time alone with Natalie before they were nuked.

"Back in the day, it won awards. And somebody wrote to *Bon Appétit* for one of their recipes. Their muesli, I think."

Blake grimaced. "I never cultivated a taste for cold, raw oatmeal."

"Savage." She snickered. "Have something else, then. Last call isn't for a few hours."

"That's amazing."

Natalie stared at him. She'd taken a quick shower back at the farmhouse and her hair was a damp helmet that clung to her finely shaped skull, tendrils curling here and there. "The weirdest things impress you. What's amazing about last call?"

"Las Vegas, remember? New York is not the only city that never sleeps. I was twenty-three before I ever heard the phrase 'last call' in a bar. My brother and I always assumed it was one of those things people say in movies that no one says in real life."

She shook her head, smiling. "You're so easy to impress sometimes."

"In fact, I'm not. It's just . . ." *You.* ". . . this place." *And you, in this place.*

Blake ordered the special; Natalie had the gazpacho, which came with a small loaf of the potato bread the B and B was famous for. Natalie made him try the heel and it was excellent, with a crisp crust and pillowy texture. He asked to try her soup and was surprised and pleased when she scooped some into her spoon and fed it to him. He made a determined effort

Her mouth was on this! And now the thing that was in her mouth is in my mouth! The thing that was in her mouth is in my mouth! Which should not be arousing but is! Oh my God oh my God ohmyGod!

and the first sip of ripe tomatoes and cucumbers and peppers and garlic tasted like summer. He blurted, "Sweetheart might not be the doomed enterprise you fear," and returned to trying not to wolf his entrée, aware that his table manners had deteriorated due to near-constant hunger.

"Okay, that came out of nowhere."

"It did not, because it's the main issue of contention in this town. It's why I'm here; it's why you're *still* here. Everyone talks about Garrett's dreadful golf course like it's a fait accompli, but that's inaccurate."

"Okay, I'm listening." She was giving him most of her attention, which, given that he knew how delicious the soup was, was terribly flattering. "You've got a point; if it really was a lost cause, what's any of it for?"

"Sweetheart can come back from this."

Her eyebrows arched in skepticism as she helped herself to more bread, which she would dunk in the soup and slurp down, soup sometimes dribbling down her chin. On anyone else, it would not have been enchanting.

"It can be done," Blake insisted as if she'd argued. "There are historical accounts of abandoned towns—ghost towns, places in much worse shape than Sweetheart—reviving and even flourishing."

"Okaaaay . . ."

"Alexandria!"

"The one in Minnesota?"

"No."

"Okay, well, I'm gonna need more than that."

He lowered his voice, realizing he'd shouted. It was getting warm on the porch, and he needed more booze-ade to rehydrate. "Once, it was the second-largest city in Egypt. It hit a sizeable decline during the Middle Ages but surged back in the eighteen-hundreds and millions live there now."

"Okay, first off, Heartbreak being stone dead for centuries before surging back doesn't help the people here now. And I don't want millions of people. None of us do; fifteen thousand or so would be plenty. Ten, even."

"And in a perfect world? If nine thousand people showed up tomorrow? Is it enough?"

She was nodding again even before he'd finished speaking; she had considered this more than once. "If Garrett's deal bit the big one and the Nazis at Putt N'Go sold the farms back, if once we got them back we could hang on to them, we just need one good growing season. *One*. It wouldn't be an instant fix—there's no instant fix—but the cash from the crops would be a major foot in the door; if we can get that much done we've got a chance to bring it all the way back."

He nodded. "Yes, I remember the spreadsheets." They were many and varied, and there were nights he fell asleep on them (he only had time to read them in bed).

"Right, we don't need a balance sheet—not for this part, anyway—because that only indicates one moment in time. We've got to think in terms of a P and L statement, since that covers a period of time—months, quarters, years, whatever."

"You know quite a lot about finance." Was there anything Natalie couldn't do? When she wasn't giving the tractor an oil change she was holed up in the house crunching numbers. When she wasn't showing him the quickest, easiest way to muck out a stall she was shooing deer out of the kitchen garden. (Deer, he had discovered, were plentiful and stupid in this part of the world. He was beginning to suspect God wanted them all to die, as they had no protective instincts Blake could discern. He practically had to elbow them out of his way some mornings.) "You could teach a course in such things."

"Yeah, uh, sure, what, you're surprised?" Rattled for some reason, Natalie had quit drinking the booze-ade and switched to water, which she now guzzled. She put the glass down and panted, "All farmhands know that stuff. Practically a job requirement up here."

"I was unaware."

She let out an inelegant, lovely snort. "I'll bet."

He held up his hands as if being arrested. "I'm not belittling you. I think you're wonderful." *Idiot!* "Um. The spreadsheets, the proposals. Those are the things that are wonderful. Which is what I meant when I said they were wonderful. The spreadsheets. Not you." *Christ. Why not just pull her pigtail and run away, you jackass?*

Luck was with him and she was distracted, because she gasped and grabbed his wrists, then yanked them toward her.

His chest socked against the edge of the table and he stifled a grunt as she glared at his palms. "Jesus, Blake! What have you been doing?"

"Er . . ." *Not like her to ask questions when she knew the answers.* "Working?"

"Right, dumb question. Listen, you've got to take better care of these. Cripes, you've got blisters on top of blisters."

"Well. I have a lot to do."

"You don't want to leave Sweetheart with hooks instead of hands."

I'm starting to lean toward not leaving at all. Wait. Where had that come from?

"You need to wash these out," she continued, "and then go heavy on the antibacterial cream. Several times a day if necessary, okay? Jeez, why didn't you say anything? Never mind. I know why you didn't." She hadn't let go of him, just kept scowling at his hands. "I'm sorry; I should have told you."

"You did." He hadn't believed her, then.

"More than once, I mean. How were you supposed to know?"

"Thank you, I—"

"Look who it is!"

They both glanced up; Blake had been so enchanted with Natalie's hands in his he hadn't noticed Roger coming up to them. Even better, even more wonderful, Roger had the White Rose of York on a small pink leash. Not just pink, he realized after a closer look. The leash had a pink-and-black background; the foreground was decorated with little pink skulls.

"Hello." Natalie had let go of him

(sigh)

and he turned to her. "Natalie, this is Roger—" She smiled a little and Blake realized he was introducing people who had likely known each other for years. *Idiot.* "Never mind."

"Hi, Rog."

"Natty."

She sighed. "Not since I was ten, Rog."

Blake was beaming, delighted. "Natt—"

"Stop now if you want to live to see the sun go down," she warned, and he cut himself off. "You've got great manners, but I don't need you to introduce me to anyone living in this town, because oh what the hell?" She had, Blake realized, belatedly noticed the White Rose of York. If he had been blessed (cursed?) with Rake's ego, Blake could convince himself Natalie was so interested in him, or his ugly hands, she failed to notice a leashed piglet in the vicinity. But no. Impossible. Perhaps even Rake's ego wasn't that strong.

"Sorry, I was remiss." Blake again managed not to snicker. "This is Roger's pig, the White Rose of York."

"Oh come on!" she moaned, covering her eyes. "What is the deal with weird names since you got to town?"

Roger, meanwhile, was beaming while the piglet trotted close to Blake, who reached down and scratched behind her ears. The piglet let loose with a blissful *unf unf unffff* and the small curly tail wiggled in delight.

"Shannah thought it up; she's a smart gal. Shannah, I mean, not the White Rose of York." Roger paused and scratched his fringe. He was dressed in jeans, a long-sleeved red shirt, running shoes. His hat was in his hand; Roger had snatched it off his head when he'd spotted Natalie. "Though she's not dumb or anything, either."

"She's almost twice as big as last time!" Blake was amazed. Was the White Rose of York some sort of porcine mutant?

Natalie was smiling at him. "She likes you."

"They are social creatures. And quite intelligent, and inquisitive as well. Did you know they—" Blake stopped when he realized he was explaining pigs to a farmhand and a pig farmer.

Natalie didn't seemed irked, thank heavens. "They're great; we all thought it was hilarious when they were the trendy pet in Hollywood for a while. Not sure if your research covered this, but pigs convert food to mass faster than almost anything. She'll be huge. Which is fine, because, you know: pig. Just . . . don't get attached."

"No?"

"Blake, this isn't a petting zoo."

"There must be some middle ground between petting zoo and wholesale slaughter."

Natalie started rubbing her forehead. "Oh, boy."

"You haven't gone to all this trouble—protecting her from her siblings and teaching her how to use a litter box—simply to kill and devour the White Rose of York, right? Roger? I'm right?"

There was a long pause, which was answer enough. "But this is nonsense. And it's awful to think about."

"Maybe don't think about it then?" Roger asked.

"Never! That way lies tyranny." Natalie groaned; Blake ignored her and pressed harder.

"The White Rose of York is very high on the adorability scale, and she's quite intelligent, too. How can you even think of consuming a creature so charming and lively?"

Roger cleared his throat. "You do realize you're eating lamb chops while we're talking about this, right?"

"Dammit!" He glared down at the succulent chops, the lunch special. "Lamb lollipops," they were called, because of how the bone was dressed. "Apples and oranges." Even as he said it, he knew it wouldn't fly. "Please consider what I've said, Roger."

"I will. The time for that—if it ever comes—is a long way off."

Natalie broke in. "Heard this was your last one?"

"Last litter," he corrected her.

"Oh, okay. Garrett's been babbling around town that you're down to one, so I just . . ."

"That poor idiot." Roger shook his head. "The worst thing that could happen to that boy is for him to get what he wants. A turd with money is still a turd."

Wait. Is that some sort of veiled insult? Not to Garrett, but . . .

"They're letting me keep the rest of 'em on the farm until the bulldozers show."

At "bulldozers," Blake felt his stomach drop. Was Roger a casualty of Blake's "money solves everything" blunder? Noooo. No. Consider the evidence: Roger had known who Blake was at their first meeting and been nothing but pleasant. No one in this town had hesitated to express their displeasure with him; he doubted Roger was the exception. There were other reasons why bulldozers were en route to Roger's pig farm, reasons that had nothing to do with Blake.

You're just paranoid. Right? Right. You're ground zero at the site of a future nuclear explosion. You're seeing monsters everywhere.

As if reading his mind, Roger smiled. "It's fine."

"It is?"

"Losing the farm."

Shit! "It *is*?"

"Oh, I hated the idea at first, but letting the farm go means I can retire a few years early. Now I can do more traveling, work on my . . . my hobby. Which is good. I've never had the chance—it's good."

Uncertain why the man had suddenly gone reticent, as if he were almost ashamed of whatever his hobby was, Blake was nonetheless grateful for the man's benevolence. "Roger, I apologize. When I helped Garrett with the property deal, I didn't understand the consequences. I'm—" He couldn't help glancing at a frowning Natalie. "I'm trying to make up for that now."

"Sure you are," was the easy, pleasant reply. "I know. And Shannah's mighty glad to have you in town, too. We have dinner most nights and she talks about you a lot."

My mother is dating a pig farmer? That thought—Blake had no idea how to feel about it, mostly because his mother hadn't been on a date for years—was followed by, *That's why he was so pleasant and nonconfrontational when we first met. And why he's still that way. He knew why I'd come before I knew why I'd come. Hoped I'd see what I had done and come to regret it. Decided there was no point in a confrontation since Heartbreak would punish me worse than anything he could do.*

I am a shit.

"That's all very nice to say, Blake," Natalie began, her mouth screwing into a small twist, "but these are people's lives and their homes, which you didn't give a shit about before your mom—"

"Excuse me, young lady," Roger interrupted politely, "but you're not allowed to be more upset at the fate of my farm than I am."

To Blake's surprise, because he thought Natalie could be upset about whatever she wanted to be upset about, she blushed, dark pink staining her cheeks beneath the tan. "Of course. I apologize." To his astonishment, she added, "To you, too, Blake. I don't mean to give you constant shit. I think— I think by now it's more reflex than anything else. Which doesn't make it right. It's pretty good, having you at Heartbreak." To Roger: "You should see this guy work. You should see his hands!"

I . . . I . . . am I going to faint? No, it's just the heat. And the wonderful thing Natalie didn't have to say but did. I haven't been this pleased since . . . since . . . idiot, they're waiting for your response.

"What a kind thing to say," Blake replied, and that made her blush harder for some reason.

"It's not kind." She shook her head, staring down at her soup bowl. "I'm not kind. You've gotta get over that idea of me."

Roger cleared his throat. "Your mama know you're here?"

"God, no." He wouldn't have been able to speak with Shannah Banana without giving the game away. The nuclear option was most effective and devastating when no one knew it was coming. His grandmother would be pulling into the driveway within minutes, and *that's* when his mother would realize what he'd done, and not a nanosecond before.

If Roger was puzzled as to why Blake would have lunch with a local girl where his mother was staying without telling her, he didn't comment. Instead he twitched the leash, carefully pulling the White Rose of York away from their table.

"Gotta get this gal squared away before I head out."

"I'll watch her," Blake interjected so quickly he startled himself. "I mean, ah, it's no trouble to supervise her. For a little while. If you like. I don't mind." He glanced at Natalie, who was gaping at him. *Does my fondness for the White Rose of York make me more acceptable to her, or less? Not enough data.* "Natalie doesn't mind." *I hope.*

"Naw, I'll be gone for a couple hours."

"Don't you have enough on your plate with Margaret of Anjou?" Natalie teased, and laughed outright at Blake's shudder.

"Welp, if you'll excuse me, I gotta go tickle trout."

"Sorry?" *Please don't be a euphemism for masturbating; please don't be a euphemism for masturbating. Unlikely; he wouldn't say such a thing in front of Natalie. Would he?*

Natalie took pity at Blake's clear confusion. "It's fishing, ya idjit."

"Oh." He paused. *Idjit?* "That doesn't help me at all. I'm still mystified."

"You in a nutshell." *A strange thing, she'd sounded almost . . . fond?*

"It's how we old-timers like to do it. You just"—Roger bent at the waist and wiggled his fingers over an imaginary trout in an imaginary stream—"do like this. It puts 'em in a trance and then . . ." He mimed gently seizing the entranced trout and heaving it up onto the imaginary riverbank. "Supper!"

"That is genius. I think." *Was it? On the one hand, it would take time. On the other hand, no equipment necessary. He might have to do some research.* "It might be self-defeating, I'm not sure."

"I'm goin' with genius," was the cheerful reply as Roger moved past their table into the house, the White Rose of York trotting in his wake. She let out a squeak as she passed Natalie. "See you kids later."

When the porch door had closed, Natalie leaned forward and almost whispered, "Isn't he the biggest sweetie? One of the nicest guys in town maybe."

Her mouth has never been so close to my face. "Maybe?" he managed.

"Did you hear him stumble when he was talking about his hobby?"

"Yes, that was odd."

"He takes these long mysterious vacations that he never talks about." She was still leaning close to him, still speaking in a low, intimate voice that Blake could hear with his groin. He'd had no idea he could hear with his groin; working on a farm was wreaking changes all over his body. "He doesn't bring it up, ever—and you know how boring people can get about their vacations. He never has pictures. Not that he's shown anybody, I mean. It's all pretty weird. The latest theories are he's a spy brought out of retirement for one more job— which has happened about eight times—and he has a man-whore kink and goes to a big anonymous city to rent his body to tourists and the occasional skeevey local."

Blake snorted so hard he nearly aspirated his booze-ade. "I won't thank you for putting that mental picture in my head."

She laughed, delighted. "Think I want it in *my* head? I don't want to picture *any* of that stuff on my own. Why shouldn't you have to suffer, too?"

Her head was so close to his! He wished he had a wonderful secret to tell her. Something titillating but nonthreatening. *I had a nightmare I ran down Margaret of Anjou with the tractor and woke up laughing.* Ah, no. *I am considering my brother's advice but have no idea how to go about seducing you.* Pass. *Your shampoo is mysterious and it's the wrong time of the year to smell of cherry blossoms.* He liked her confiding in him. He wished he could be overt about smelling her damp hair. "It's not long," he blurted, and then wanted to smack himself.

"What isn't?" She followed his gaze and touched her hair. "This? No. Not practical for my work. And I have to keep my bangs short, and if I wear it too long it makes my face disappear. I have a fat face!"

"You do not." He was almost mortally offended. "You have a wonderful face."

"I noticed you didn't say thin."

"Broad," he said firmly, "is not fat."

"Why so interested in my coiffure? D'you want me to break out the braids, maybe stick an eagle feather in my hair?"

"No, only warriors, chiefs, and braves had that privilege," he replied without thinking, "and that only after a brave deed done and then told to the tribe."

"Been reading up on me?" she teased, and at once it was difficult to hold her gaze. *Idiot! Must you always show off?* He mumbled something about indigenous people and matters of intellectual curiosity and could see she was trying not to laugh. A good sign, he hoped.

"It's fine. I'm flattered. I promise there won't be a quiz."

A quiz I could handle. It's being in close proximity with you that I find difficult and distracting.

"I would never assume that after reading a Wikipedia entry

about Lakota and Dakota tribes I would know all there was to know about you." *Alas.* He didn't and never would know all there was to know about her.

"Are you sure?" At least she was still teasing; he hadn't offended her with his clumsiness. "Most people think what Wiki tells them to think. And how'd you know I was Dakota?"

"Process of elimination," he replied promptly. "Strictly going by the numbers, your ancestors were likely Sioux or Chippewa. After researching the area, it seemed likely you were—" *Stop. Just stop.* "Lucky guess?"

"Never in your life," was the kind reply, much more than he deserved.

Okay. She's not annoyed; you haven't made an irredeemable ass of yourself, on this topic anyway. Move on. Talk about the weather. Talk about the White Rose of York. Natalie is not your own personal font of Native American trivia.

"I . . . I—"

"Yeah? You okay? You look weird. Weird*er*," she clarified. *Why is it so hot out here?* "Nothing."

"You sure? I don't mind if you've got questions. It's nice to see someone going to the source, frankly. Not that I'm much of one, I identify equally with my mom's and my dad's cultures."

"I'm fine. I am. I have no questions. I seek no knowledge." She leaned in again. "Are you suuure?"

"It's just I found the government hierarchy to be fascinating with the subdivisions being divided into tribes as they are—"

"Ha! Knew you'd crack."

"—and you would think their autonomous nature would make governing difficult, but it seems to work, which raises several more questions, and though the U.S. and Canadian governments acknowledge your citizenship they also consider you dual citizens, which must be quite advantageous . . ." He took a breath. ". . . and although some tribes were patriarchal in nature I found their encouragement of girls to hunt and fight to be not only indicative of an open mind but in fact putting them ahead of their time, which I think was a factor of the leaders—the *itancans*—no longer being exclusively male."

"Wow."

He wanted to hide. "I'm sorry."

"How come? You made some good points and you never once offered me the chance to smoke a peace pipe." At Blake's horrified groan, her smile widened. "That was— Your curiosity about things, it just eats at you sometimes, doesn't it?"

"Yes. That's exactly what it does." She understood, miracle of miracles. He'd half expected a faceful of booze-ade.

"My grandpa was our *itancan* for years."

"He was? Really?" *Was.* Dammit. No longer a source. *Yes, like she would allow you to corner her grandfather and fire questions at him while resisting the urge to kiss his granddaughter.*

"And ahead of his time—which means your relatives and mine have things in common."

He wasn't hearing right. Was he? "Really?"

"Of course, really. Look, your family was never especially loved around here, but they did big things and they left their mark on the place. No one can deny that."

"They certainly left their mark on my mom," he replied grimly. "She coped as best she could."

Natalie was nodding. "Yeah, and that's something else we have in common. No matter how strongly I identify as a Native

American—or don't identify—I promise you, someone always thinks I'm not doing enough. Or that I'm doing too much. Or that I'm hiding. Or that I'm flaunting. You can't win, and there's no point in trying to please everyone all the time. It's—It's family stuff; it's complicated and even crippling for some people. And none of it's easy, even when you love them and want to be with them."

"I think you're fortunate, knowing where you came from. Crichton said if you don't know where you came from, you're a leaf that doesn't know it's part of a tree." When Blake had invited her to lunch, he never would have dreamed of this, an earnest and honest discussion of families and their fallout. It was all he could do not to seize her and hug her and tell her however she identified or didn't was exactly right for her and no one else's damned business. Not wanting to ruin the most pleasant lunch he'd enjoyed in years, he resisted the urge. "My mom never spoke of Sweetheart or her family. We learned early on not to ask about them."

Very early on. It wasn't that their mom would shout or get hysterical or that she forbade discussion of the subject or would refuse to answer. She would get very quietly, very visibly upset and he and Rake would feel terrible for raising the subject.

No other subject was off-limits: she would answer questions about sex, money, politics, racism, religion, or any combination thereof. But she had little to say on the subject of where she came from. Eventually Blake came to understand it was a defense mechanism, one that kept her sane but made her take refuge in pride. For years, pride and her sons were all she had. Blake suspected all three held equal value in her eyes. In this, they were alike.

Whoever they were and whatever they had done, his mother had raised the twins on her own. That was all Blake needed to know, and he stopped asking about her family before his eighth birthday. Rake made up his own mind and stopped asking six months later.

"If they hadn't died and left her the property headache, we wouldn't be out here—Mom and me, I mean; Rake isn't here because Rake is terrible—and I still have more questions than answers. How can I spend close to a month in my mother's hometown and still not know anything?" The habit of not pressing, it seemed, ran deep.

"Died?" Natalie had pulled back with an expression of surprise. "I'm not getting you. They didn't—"

"Blake!"

They looked up; Shannah had stepped out on the porch with a glass of iced tea and her Kindle. No matter how often Blake persisted in buying her hardcover books, she persisted in riding the tech river. He had nothing against technological advancement, but there was nothing like the feel of a solid book in your hand. Bytes were no substitute for pages.

He rose to his feet. "Mom."

"Natalie Lane?"

"Are you asking her if that's who she is?" he asked dryly. For her part, Natalie seemed flustered.

"Uh . . . hi, Shannah. I thought—" She looked at Blake, helpless. "I thought we were having lunch with your—"

"Roger is tickling trout, if you're looking for him." It wouldn't do to have Natalie give the game away. And he must have misunderstood Natalie's expression. *Natalie Lane doesn't* do *helpless; I must be misinterpreting. And it's too damned hot out here!*

He guzzled more booze-ade and squashed an evil chuckle at the havoc about to be wreaked.

Shannah was smiling at them both, dressed in her weekday outfit of dark slacks and a cream-colored blouse so simply designed it was almost stark. She had a navy blue cashmere sweater draped over one arm and her reading glasses on the end of her nose. She seemed so delighted to see him the first niggle of guilt slipped into his brain.

"This is a surprise, my boy. I'm so—"

"Holy *shit.*" At the rare epithet from Natalie, both Tarbells glanced at her, startled, then at what she was speaking of: the black stretch limousine at the far end of the driveway, just pulling in.

His mother's eyes went round as she put two and two together. One could argue that anyone could have commandeered a limousine from the airport and ordered the driver to take them three hundred miles into the Dakota prairie. Except not *anyone* would. *Someone* would, though, and his mom would know who. Fascinated (and not a little terrified), Blake realized he could almost see her working it out. *Blake + Heartbreak ÷ his resentment × insatiable curiosity = Dammit, Blake!*

When she shouted, he was surprised the porch windows didn't shatter on impact.

"Blake Tarbell!"

Blake almost dropped his glass, recovered, toasted his mom, then turned to Natalie. "You should be running."

Twenty-five

This is the most amazing thing I've ever seen, and that counts the time Blake was hosing down Margaret of Anjou with one hand and reading her Shakespeare's Henry VI, Part 3, *with the other.*

Natalie knew it was wrong to feel such excitement, knew she shouldn't be a witness to this. She felt like a spectator at a tennis match where the players had guns instead of rackets and the prize was murder. But Blake was fascinating and his mom was fascinating and his *grandmother*! *Holy God!*

"You activated the nuclear option," Shannah was saying, arms folded across her chest. "Touché, my son."

"You left me little choice, Mom. Hello, Nonna. Booze-ade?"

An older woman right out of central casting for Well-Off Caucasian Grandmother, Blake's grandma

(the nuclear option?)

had left the limo before the driver had even unbuckled his seat belt, and was now standing before them on the porch. Natalie saw at once that she and Blake had the same eyes, that wonderful riveting deep blue, and the same coloring, pale skin and dark blond hair. Hers was streaked with silver and pulled back in a neat chignon. She was wearing an old-fashioned tweed skirt, a cream-colored blouse with a bow, sensible black low heels, a black cardigan (in the country! it was seventy-four degrees!), a small string of pearls, and an honest-to-God faux fur snugged around her throat.

"I came as soon as you called." She accepted Blake's offer and took a glass. "Well, as soon as you called, plus several hours for travel. I woke up," she added with a wistful look at the horizon, "in Boston. But this is nice, too."

"Thank you, Nonna. This is my employer, Natalie Lane."

Shannah's brow wrinkled into a frown, but Blake's grandma interrupted before she could comment. "This is delightful! Fresh lemon juice . . . um . . . sugar syrup? And rosemary? And something else I can't quite put a name to . . ."

"Vodka," Natalie said helpfully. "Lots."

"Yes, thank you, dear." Natalie felt the near burn of the woman's examination and saw Blake shared more than her coloring. "My grandson spoke of you when he wasn't pleading for rescue."

"Nonna . . ."

"He said you work hard and resolutely refuse to take crap from any source."

"Oh. That's, um, yeah." *Smooth, Nat.* "That was nice of him."

"Mrs. Tarbell, I'll thank you not to interfere in this matter between my sons and me."

"Oh, is Rake here, too?" she asked, the picture of innocence. "And for heaven's sakes, Shannah, I've been asking you to call me Ruth for decades."

This time it was Blake's turn to pipe up with a helpful comment. "Rake is in Venice. Against his will, apparently."

News to Natalie. But not to Shannah, she noticed, because the woman didn't blink. "We're not here to discuss Rake."

Because Rake is terrible, Natalie mouthed at Blake, who, to her delight, stifled a chuckle.

"Quite right. I'm here to have lunch with Blake and his friend Natalie. Oh, thank you." Trish Miller, who helped run the B and B with her sister and brother-in-law, had appeared with another place setting. She winked at Natalie and headed back to the kitchen. To her relief, the other diners had left and they had the long three-season porch to themselves.

Blake's Nonna adjusted her faux

(the woman screams money might not be faux fur might be actual *fur),*

seated herself, then turned and waved at the limo. The driver started the engine and began backing out of the driveway.

"Don't worry," she told Natalie, who wasn't worried at all. "He'll come back for me tomorrow. Oh yes. More of this please." Natalie obligingly filled the older woman's glass. "Tell me about your farm. Heartache?"

"Heart*break.* It's not really my farm, I'm just—" She had to be careful. Shannah knew Natalie didn't work there. "—just helping while we figure out . . . while we try to—" *What?* She didn't know anymore. And Blake had never known, through no fault of his own. What was any of this *for?*

"Well, it's kind of you—"

"I'm not kind."

"—to put up with my grandson." A light, almost brittle laugh. "I can't imagine how much work he is."

"He's not work. He *does* work." *Wow. Here thirty seconds and Shannah's freaked and Blake looks like someone clipped him with a brick. Nuclear option indeed.*

"No need to exaggerate, dear. My grandson knows a little bit about almost everything. Not enough to be satisfying. Just enough to drive you to distraction. 'Keep this up and you'll give me an aneurysm.' 'Actually, at your age a heart attack is more likely, Nonna.' 'Shut up, darling.' 'Very well, Nonna.'"

Natalie giggled. "Sorry, Blake, but she's got you dead to life."

"Now, about your farm, I'm sure *he* thinks it's work, going on and on about the endless minutiae of, say, how farming goes back to the ancient Greeks—"

"Neolothic era, actually," Blake said quietly.

"—while the people around him are the ones getting their hands dirty."

"You don't know what you're talking about, Ms. Tarbell. He gets his hands dirty." Natalie reached for his wrists—they'd shuffled seats to accommodate the nuclear option, so Natalie was now sitting beside Blake. "Look! He works harder than anyone. He's putting farmhands to shame." *Well, Gary.* Which wasn't much of a trick, actually. "See?"

"It has been decades, actual decades, since someone told me I didn't know what I was talking about." She leaned forward, inspecting Blake's palms, and looked back up at her with one of the sweetest smiles Natalie had ever seen. "And in this, you're right. I didn't know. Thank you."

A test, Natalie realized when the older woman instantly

dropped the snobbish affectation and patted Blake's hands. *She was testing me. What a bat.*

"Your poor hands, darling, you have to take better care." Then, to Natalie: "Isn't he marvelous?" Blake's loving grandma was looking at him like—well, like a loving grandma. "My son's looks," she added fervently, almost like a prayer, "and Shannah's brains. An outstanding combination."

Natalie agreed, and couldn't help notice the look of surprise on Shannah's face. *Compliments from Miz Tarbell aren't something she's used to, maybe.* But without knowing how she knew, Natalie at once sensed it was more than that. Shannah's family history would have made it impossible to open up to a stranger. She would have never, could have never, let anyone in, especially Blake's grandmother. She would have known by then of the Banaan family curse.

Blake cleared his throat. "The reason I called you, Nonna—"

"You want your money back. Well. My son's money, God rest his silly soul." The smile dropped off as if plucked, and the woman's blue eyes went dark with sorrow. "A fool, but my fool, and my fault. The money—my money—it ruined him."

Blake sighed. "Apples and oranges, Nonna. I am nothing like my father. There's no need to punish me for the things he's done. Money hasn't ruined my life. It didn't ruin his."

"Wrong, and wrong, and it's not punishment, dear."

"No? Have you asked my mother?"

"Atonement isn't punishment."

Shannah looked ready to bolt, and Natalie didn't blame her.

"I am almost thirty years old," Blake said through gritted teeth. "It is inappropriate for you to sit in judgment of me and

levy fines on what you perceive as my bad behavior. Your arbi-
trary actions have forced me to go over your head."

"You squealed on me," was Shannah's flat reply.

"Well, yes. And now you must reap the whirl—"

"I'm not giving you any money, Blake," his grandma put in.

"What?"

"I didn't give your mother control of the trust to second-
guess her. She did a fine job of raising my son's children; I won't
cast doubt on her judgment now, for all you're grown men."

"*What?*"

"My son chose your mother, Blake. I have to respect his
choice. He wouldn't want me to undermine her the minute
things aren't going your way."

"Chose?" Blake shoved his chair back, doubtless to leave,
then checked himself and stayed put. To rant, apparently,
because he followed up with, "Can we please stop romanticizing
their one-night stand? They barely knew each other! They married when Rake and I were born because you would have cut him
off otherwise. It was a shotgun wedding and you were holding
the eight gauge."

"Twelve gauge," Natalie mumbled. God, he was so cute
when he tried to sound like a local yokel. And his voice, already deliciously deep, seemed to drop into the basement as he
gave way to fury.

"They never lived together! They barely spoke in the years
before he died. It's time to face the truth of his marriage,
Nonna: Your son lost interest in my mother about eight seconds after he filled the condom *ouch!*"

He clutched his face and glared. Natalie, raised by hunters,
hadn't even seen Miz Tarbell's arm move. *I could learn from this*

woman. Natalie traded glances with Shannah. *Never in life did I think anyone could intimidate Shannah Banana. This is fascinating agony. Don't panic, don't panic.*

"Do not lie." Blake's sweet li'l old lady grandma was sitting tall and straight, her back not touching the chair and sunlight flashing on her pearls. "You know the idiot didn't use a condom."

"Actually, I didn't. Rake put it down to 'birth control fail' and I agreed."

"I should g—"

Blake's hand shot out and grabbed Natalie's wrist as she started to rise. "Her version has gotten ever more saccharine over the years, Natalie. Would you like to know how it truly was?"

She sat. Couldn't help herself. These people were insane, and fascinating, and insane.

Twenty-six

"Dead?" Rake stared at the older woman who had been waiting, along with their mother, in the kitchen when he and Blake got home from school thirty seconds ago. The kettle had boiled; there were two cups of tea on the card table along with the plastic sugar bowl and spoons.

"Our father's dead?"

"I'm afraid so, boy." Their mother was gripping the back of the folding kitchen chair and he could see how white her knuckles were. "This is your grandmother, Ruth Tarbell. Ruth, this is—"

"My son's seed!"

Rake actually flinched back. "Oh, man. Please don't call us that." He would have said more, because even at thirteen Rake was terrible, but Ruth Tarbell had crossed the faded kitchen tile and hauled both boys into a hug that smelled like lemon and felt like tweed. "Thank God, oh thank God. Look at you, so handsome. I haven't seen you since you were babies when I made your idiot father—when I was at the wedding."

"Thank you," Blake managed. "It's nice to meet you."

"Oh, man," Rake muttered. "I'm missing b-ball practice for this."

After a decade, their lemon-scented tweed-clad grandmother released them from the prison of her embrace. "You're surprised," she observed.

"People aren't usually this happy to meet us," Blake admitted. "Rake is terrible."

"Blow it out your butt sideways, Blake. Um, Mom, are you . . . ?" Rake trailed off, went to their mother, and slipped an arm around her waist. And not to show off how tall he was getting, for a change. "Um, I know you guys were technically married, but it's okay to be sad. And it's okay to not be sad. Right, Blake? That's okay?" He looked over at his brother with a hopeful expression.

"Of course." The exchange, Blake noted, had not been lost on their grandmother. *And that's our family dynamic in a nutshell: Mom is nominally in charge; Rake is the rebel but checks with me on issues of acceptable behavior; I'm somehow the arbiter of when to mourn. Or not mourn.*

"See, Mom? Blake's all 'it's cool.' So if you're sad—"

"I am fine, Rake." She patted the hand he had around her waist. "Thank you. Mrs. Tarbell—"

"Ruth, darling."

"—was telling me about your father's will. It seems— It seems he left us some money."

"Oh. That's good, right, Mom?" Blake balanced her checkbook and knew any amount of money would be an improvement. No one worked harder than his mother, who had flatly forbidden him to get a job; his job, she explained, was to study and get good grades; *she* would worry about the rest of it. He would, of course, get a job anyway. Never mind waiting until he was sixteen, either. There were advantages to being the genetic double of a criminal mind with poor impulse control. Rake would know who could forge him a new birth certificate.

In the meantime, perhaps their dissolute father had left as much as four or five thousand dollars. School had only just started and already he and Rake needed money for athletic fees, school supplies, book covers, and terrible mass-produced lunches. Their jeans were getting too short again, too, and the ones they were wearing were less than four months old.

"Look, you don't expect us to cry or anything, right? I mean, we get how you'd be upset, but we're kind of not." Rake hadn't budged from their mother's side, and his grandmother's expression was inscrutable. "Because he never visited. We didn't know him. I mean, we're sorry for *you*, Mrs. Tar—"

"Please don't call me that. Ruth, if you like. Nonna, if you want to know my preference."

"Italian for 'Grandmother,'" Blake spoke up.

Ruth Tarbell turned the full force of her gorgeous smile on him for the first time. "Clever, clever boy."

"Oh, gross," Rake groaned.

"God, you're both his very image." It seemed for a moment that tears would threaten, but she willed them back. Her smile never slipped. "I'm told you have your mother's brains. Thank the Lord."

"Yep, praise Jesus and all that, so what'd he leave us?"

"Rake." Their mother said it quietly enough, but Rake

snapped his mouth closed so fast Blake heard teeth click. He indulged the rare impulse to side with his brother.

"It's a fair question, Mom. Nonna wouldn't have come all this way for no good reason."

"Everything," was the simple reply. "He left you everything."

Twenty-seven

"You whirled into our lives like a tsunami of tweed and tea, at once heartbroken and overjoyed." Good *God*, it was hot out here! "And you changed our lives for the better, but you've always watched and waited for the fall you feel is inevitable. You think blood will out, and you've spent years expecting us to expire in some sex-related shenanigans, but we're not our father." His grandmother, it must be said, was getting on in years. That must be why her whole face was a blur; all he could make out were piercing eyes, rose pink lipstick, and face powder.

"Are you all right?" Natalie murmured.

He blinked down at her, surprised. "Fine, yes."

"Because you're screaming."

"Oh. Sorry." He made a visible effort to calm himself. He noticed he was standing. *When did that happen?* "Better?"

"Much."

God, she was so beautiful. And concerned! Possibly about

him! Or just horribly embarrassed to be there, like any right-thinking person would be.

"If you two don't mind," his mother said with raised eyebrows, "you were ranting about—"

"It's not just about me, Mom. The quarterly payments on the shelters are coming due."

"Shelters?"

"My grandson used part of his fortune—"

"That's right, *my* fortune," he emphasized. Sometimes there was no point to subtlety.

"—to set up shelters for single mothers all across the country."

"Shelters that aren't free. Well, for the residents they are, but they cost money."

"Yes, I see."

"Money I don't have."

"We get it, Blake."

"Because unlike Rake, I am not entirely a layabout lazy playboy reprobate. I'm only partly a layabout lazy playboy reprobate! Yes, my relationships are all shallow and meaningless, but at least I'm helping people when I'm not indulging in meaningless sex!"

Wow.

He peered down at Natalie, swaying ever so slightly. "Am I shouting again?"

"Little bit, yeah."

"Don't worry about the shelters," his mother began, and Blake turned on her quick as thought.

"Are you fucking kidding me?"

"Blake!" A trio of feminine reprimands. Reprimands in stereo.

"Well, are you? It's the only explanation. The whole reason

I'm marooned here is because you think I'm not taking responsibility for my actions! So when I point out my other responsibilities the response is 'don't worry about it'? This is what is known as a mixed message, Mom! And what about the York Loans?"

"Like the White Rose of York, that York?" Natalie asked, which was adorable.

"Yes. I also provide loans to single mothers for low-income housing in the Vegas area. Loans I can no longer make good on. 'Dear Miss Smith, you and your baby will have to keep living in your cockroach-laden studio apartment because I'm grounded.' I'm not signing those letters, Mother! *You* sign them."

"For cripes sake," Shannah muttered. It hadn't taken her long to revert to the local patois, Blake noted. Before last month, he'd never heard "cripes" out of her mouth. "And don't call me Mother."

"Maybe sit down while you rant," Natalie suggested, and he obeyed at once and got a smile for his trouble. Oh, she was a goddess.

"So you see," he said, and it was hard to say that for some reason. All those *s* words. He was slurring

(another s *word! curses!)*

for some reason. Well, he was tired. He'd been exhausted for a month. " 'Snot just my dissolute lifestyle on the line. You really think I was mad because you took my allowance away? Okay, I was, but not just because of that. I'm mad—angry, I mean; 'mad' is British English for 'crazy,' which I'm not. Probably not. Nonna, Mother, while you're busy breaking me of habits you indulged for years, innocent families will lose their homes. But that's all fine, because I'll have learned my lesson, won't I?"

When there was no answer forthcoming, he tried again. "This! This is why I had to turn the key on the nuclear option!"

"The what?" Nonna asked.

"I got the idea from you!"

"You two intimidate each other by threatening to invite me to visit?" Ruth considered for a moment. "That is genius."

"My mom is unmoved by the plight of single mothers, which is absurd, as she is one! Was one, I mean. Although technically you still are, even though we're grown men. *Grown men*, Mom! 'Swhy I hadda bring out the big guns: the tweed tsunami! You have only yourself to blame. And you! Nonna! I get you all the way out here and then you've got the nerve to back my mother! You don' fool me; you think I'm a mess, too."

"At the moment, yes." Ruth turned to Natalie. "How much vodka would you say is in these—"

"A liter."

"Ah."

"Maybe two?"

"Oh."

He shrugged it off. Natalie had muttered something earlier about alcoholic punch, but that didn't apply to him.

Christ, he was tired. And when had he stood? Again?

His occasionally telepathic mother rose, took his hand, and gently eased him back into his chair. "You're tired, Blake; I know."

"I am not! Don't you *dare* send me to my room. Which is across town anyway."

"I should go. I'm finished eating anyway." No! Natalie the Wondrous was leaving! It wasn't to be borne.

"No, stay. I like you so much. It's awful without you, I don't want you to go home; please stay." And why were all the women staring at him?

Natalie colored, which deepened her natural tan and gave it rich rose undertones. "Blake, I like you, too—"

"You do?" *Gasp!* "Really?"

"—but I think you've had too much to drink. Being tired and working hard has kind of trashed your tolerance, so I think—"

"She's the best foreman in the world," he told his grandmother, who was looking at him with an expression he couldn't identify. "She knows everything about farms because she's a wonderful farmhand foreman."

"She's not a farmhand."

"And she knows more about financing and mortgages than any farmhand I've ever met. And I've met three!"

"She's not a farmhand."

His mother's voice seemed to be coming from a tunnel. What the hell was the aggravating woman doing in a tunnel? And braying nonsense? "Of course she is. She's the one who taught me everything I still don't know."

"Um . . . Blake . . ."

"Shush, Natalie. I must tell Mom more things about your wonderfulness. Wondrousness?"

"Son, she runs Sweetheart Trust. The bank in town."

He laughed and waited for Natalie to join in, or calmly refute his mother's senile implication. When Natalie didn't say anything, he beamed.

"See, Mom; see, Nonna? This is how wonderful she is: She won't even correct your doddering nonsense though she knows you're wrong, wrong, wrong."

"Stupid," Natalie was muttering. "So stupid."

Eh?

"I was stupid. My own fault. Lunch with your grandma seemed safe, dammit! She wouldn't know who I was. But I completely discounted the simple fact that everyone else *would* know who I was."

"Wait." The room had begun to tilt lazily. *Someone should check the porch foundation.* "It's true? You work for the bank?"

"I couldn't resist your invitation to lunch, okay? I wanted to hang out with you, and not as a function of our work."

"*My* work," he corrected.

"I knew it'd bite me in the ass and I *still* couldn't say yes fast enough." She was shaking her head, her nearly dry hair curling under with lingering moisture. He caught more of her sweet scent, which was an unwelcome diversion.

"Then why were you even out there? I— I don't understand." He couldn't bear to look at his mother, who had known, or his grandmother, who likely thought he'd gone crazy on the prairie.

"I—I didn't trust you. I didn't know why you were really here. It sounded like some kind of contrived plot—you have to spend the night in this haunted house to get your inheritance; you have to work on this farm to save it . . . like that. It just sounded like a load of shit. I wanted to see you up close."

"The whole time—" The porch had gone from a slow tilt to a lazy spin. He could barely look at her, literally and figuratively. "You watched me work and you just—" *Laughed. Mocked. Judged. Laughed more.* "An' that's not even awful enough. The worst part is, a fake farmhand is still a hundred times better at it than I was."

"I'm not a fake!" Natalie had gone from mortified to angry, which was hilarious. She was on her feet . . . and so was he. Again. *Still?* He couldn't remember. *Why do I keep standing only to sit right after? No wonder I'm dizzy.* "I practically grew up on that ranch! I worked there every summer when my mom got sick and she had to quit *her* job. After she died I kept working to earn money for college. We had the funeral there and *you don't care! About anything!*"

"I cared about you, you deceitful shrew! I've been killing myself on Heartbreak in an attempt to earn the respect of a *banker.*"

"I'm not the villain in this piece, pal." Probably. That was Garrett, right? *Right?* "If you keep on like this, pretty soon I won't be able to stand the sight of you!"

"And pretty soon I will *adore* the sight of you!" he snapped back.

"Don't you dare adore me! You take that back!"

"Never! I *will* adore you and you can't stop me!"

"Blake—"

"Son—"

He cut them off with a rough chop through the air. "Enough. I have no interest in discussing this any farmer. Further, I mean. That was a farming slip. *Freudian* slip. I've got nothing to say to either of you farmers. Ladies. What–the fuck–ever." He rounded on Natalie. "Or you! I am no longer speaking to you or spending time with you! You are dead to me, Natalie Lame. Yes! That's what Rake calls you because he is *not* terrible—"

"Don't say things you don't mean," Blake's mother had the gall to warn.

He ignored her, which he should have done starting about five minutes after exiting the womb. "Rake was wise! He knew the truth even though he had no idea what the truth was. I will not see you or speak to you or touch you again, Natalie Lane. Now come with me." He seized her hand, ignoring her startled squawk, seized his mother's sweater from the back of her chair, and rushed from the porch into the main house.

"Blake, first off, why did you just mug your mom? Second, this is the opposite of not seeing me, and third, what are we—"

"Here." He dug in his pocket and handed her the keys to his Supertruck. "My condition may be detrimental to driving."

"On account of how shit faced you are? Good call. What are we doing?"

He'd pulled her through the parlor, the hallway, and found the room with all the fainting couches. And . . .

"Ah-ha!"

The White Rose of York, who had been stretched out snoozing in the afternoon sun, twitched, rolled over, saw him, trotted up to them. He wrapped her up in the sweater and she squeaked a greeting.

"Blake!" Natalie hissed. "That's cashmere! And a pig that doesn't belong to you. What do you think you're doing?"

"Not letting her be slaughtered and devoured. The scene of my humiliation is now the scene of the piglet's rescue. Take us back to Heartbreak."

"Then what?" Natalie stood in his way, clutching his keys in her small fist while he hugged the White Rose of York to his chest.

"Then I don't care what you do. And drive carefully. Do not startle her. A pig's scream can hit one hundred and fifteen decibels."

"I *know*, Blake!"

"Ah, yes, I forgot how bankers are required to take animal husbandry courses." She opened her mouth, then closed it at his cold stare. "Time to go."

Twenty-eight

She let a day go by before she dared approach him. The Amazon delivery gave her the opportunity she had been waiting for, and dreading.

Shannah and Ruth had come out twice to see him, and he had locked himself in the attic and refused to come out until they left. He didn't say a word to any of them, not even to command he be left alone. Natalie had hovered like a useless idiot and brought Miz Tarbell cup after cup of tea. She couldn't look at the women's pinched, sorrowful expressions. They were too close to the expression she saw in the mirror.

She couldn't even take refuge in calling him out for being childish; the last thing she had was the moral high ground.

He wouldn't speak to anyone, wouldn't interact or so much as smile; he simply buried himself in chores and Natalie wasn't sure why. Because the work was the only thing he had? Unlikely; whatever point his mother had tried to make, she either felt she had made it or had given up. If he flat-out asked her for control of his money back, Natalie bet his mother would have given in. But he wasn't doing that; he wasn't doing anything. Just working.

"Um, Blake, this came for you? The UPS guy brought it?" She could hear her tremulous upward inflection and hated it. *Man up, Nat, you conniving bitch.* She held up the long brown tube. "Do you want it now?"

"It's for you." He didn't look up. "I ordered it for you a week ago."

Oh God. That made it so much worse. "It is? Thank you. Um, I wasn't expecting— What is it?"

Silence. She cleared her throat and tried again. "You know, you're doing a good job. I didn't tell you that enough. Before, I mean."

"Well, you had your work at the bank to occupy you."

Ouch. "So d'you just want me to open it here, or . . ." She swallowed a gasp when he looked up at her from where he was spreading out fresh straw. Those weren't shadows under his eyes, they were trenches. And the swelling! "What's with the bump on your forehead?"

"Margaret of Anjou objected strenuously to the saddle this morning."

"Cheer up." *Oh God, did I really just say that? Buck up, li'l buckeroo!* "She objects to pretty much everything. You know that. It's not personal." A ghost of a smile was all Natalie got, which was a 10,000 percent improvement. She plunged ahead, eager to keep the connection, however tenuous, from breaking. "In fact, I think she hates you the least."

"Ah." He tossed the last of the soiled straw into the wheelbarrow and leaned on the pitchfork. "So she only hates me with the melting intensity of lava engulfing an ice-cream cone."

"You're so odd," she said, not without admiration.

"Is that your professional opinion as a banker, or as a faux farmhand?"

"Okay, that's fair. It's my opinion as . . . as a human being."

Blake said nothing, just rested and looked at her. Now that he was finished laying down clean straw, he'd check the raised beds for weeds, and check on the kitchen garden on the south side of the house (before long they'd be ass deep in basil and mint, but the B and B would buy lots of it for juleps and pesto). He'd make sure the White Rose of York had freshwater and slop to her liking (thank God Roger had weaned her before they'd stolen her—liberated, according to Blake). Natalie wondered why Roger didn't call, or come in person to collect his piglet. Their getaway had not been subtle or quiet. Shannah had probably told him what was going on. Who knew, maybe he was off on one of his sinister vacations again, enjoying his freedom.

Gary or Larry or Harry would be working beside Blake as he did those things. They never worked *with* him; they always stayed parallel: never meeting. She knew he was growing on Larry and Harry. And he could never grow on Gary, nothing to be done about it. Blake could invent a vaccine for male-pattern baldness and never grow on Gary.

"You're working too hard. Seriously, you're barely cute anymore." *Lie.* Rugged exhaustion was an excellent look on him. It made her want to plop him in a hot bath, wash his hair and scrub his back, then refuse to let him have any clothes, so he would be forced to prowl the attic in a (small) towel.

She tried again. "Margaret of Anjou doesn't throw you *every* time."

"No, she's not like Lucy at all."

"Lucy?"

He blinked at her slowly, like an owl. Cripes, he looked done-in and it wasn't even lunchtime. "Charles Schulz. *Peanuts.* She snatches the football away every time, which proves Charlie Brown is something of an idiot. Margaret of Anjou doesn't do that; she cooperates once in a while. She prefers to lull me into thinking she's finally decided to go along. Her method is much more psychologically devastating."

A perfect description of the pony from Hell. Time to switch tactics. "Listen, I'm so sorry I misled you about—"

"Talk about something else, please."

Natalie switched gears as smoothly as she could. "Not even Larry puts in the hours you do."

"Larry hates me."

"Not as much as when you first got here." *God, I suck at this cheering-up stuff.* At his skeptical expression, she added, "Well, yeah, a little."

"As do Gary and Harry."

"It's not personal," she said again, like that made any of this easier, or better.

"No? I assume they knew you were an impostor, and said nothing. They probably laughed almost as much as you did."

"I never laughed." *Bitched, yes. Raved, insulted, cursed his name and all Banaans, uh-huh.* He'd scored a bull's-eye with impostor, though. This farm was the one place in the world she had never felt like an impostor. Whites thought she was playing for their team when she didn't whip out her Native American Decoder

Ring. Dakotas thought she was passing when she celebrated St. Patrick's Day. "That's not hate. It's indifference. They're just marking time and they know it. Please, I don't blame you for thinking like this, but you don't have to look for conspiracies everywhere. . . ." She trailed off and pondered the stupid thing she had just said. *Yeah, I just lied, half the town abetted my lie and never bothered to clue you in, which led to your humiliation in front of your mom and grandma, and maybe all your work out here was for absolutely nothing, but don't be paranoid, it's not personal.* Why, he was bound to feel better soon!

She tried again. "They'd hate anyone doing what you're doing. But they hate you less now."

"And what am I doing?"

He sounded wiped and looked like he'd been in a fight with straw and shit and shit won. "Making it right. Fixing things. They know you didn't have to stick it out. You did, though. That's worth a lot here."

He stripped off his gloves and looked down at his hands. Large and tan, broken fingernails and freckles on the backs. Some blood from a burst blister that hadn't become a callus yet. Raw, and trembling a bit.

"Okay, you need to take the afternoon off." Natalie tucked the tube beneath her armpit, caught both hands in hers and gave him a gentle squeeze, then remembered she was wearing gloves, too, and grinding dirt into his wounded palms, and took them off, and then blew on his palms, getting rid of the dust. Blake sucked in his breath; it probably stung like crazy. "You're wiped; you're done for the day. I get that you're upset, you've got every right to it, but driving yourself to a total physical collapse won't solve a damned thing. I want you to take the rest of the day."

"Pardon me, but a banker who doesn't own this farm cannot dictate when I rest and when I don't."

"Please!" she burst out, and he looked up, startled. "Please, I'm sorry. Please don't punish yourself for my bullshit. Be good to yourself; you deserve the day off, you deserve a month off. I'm so sorry; please, *please* rest for a while."

He sighed. "I dislike seeing you upset. I especially dislike being the cause."

Yes, okay, she could work with this. She had no idea why he wouldn't glory in her being upset but wouldn't question it. "Gary brought a buttload of lemons from the grocery store this morning for God only knows what sinister purpose—"

"He prefers fresh-squeezed lemonade made with a pitcher of well water, a dozen lemons, and a cup and a half of sugar. He makes it at night and lets it chill, then sips it all the next day." He managed a small, a very small, smile. "No vodka."

"Well, let's make some and guzzle it all down. He'll be superpissed. Vengeance will be yours."

He gave her a look. "I'm not interested in further antagonizing a man who could run me over with a tractor."

"He wouldn't dare." *Probably.* "Look, I didn't explain myself very well."

"Sometimes you don't explain yourself at all." At her wince, he looked away. "I apologize. I'm tired."

She put out a hand, then let it drop. "It's okay; listen, like I was saying before, it's not personal. You being here really screws him."

"A familiar refrain."

"No." She felt a bit desperate, he sounded so tired and . . . and *dull;* that was the only word for it. Like he not only didn't care about anything but also didn't care he didn't care. The marked change was startling; she kept running across it and being surprised all over again. From the very first day he'd been vital and interesting. Now he was a shadow. "Not for the reason you think. He was counting on Heartbreak's foreclosure."

Blake politely raised his eyebrows. "Oh?"

"C'mere and sit down. Give me that." She made him sit down. Well, she couldn't *make* him do anything, but he allowed her to do it. She hurried over to the small boxed-in area he'd made for the White Rose of York, scooped up the piglet, then practically thrust her into Blake's arms. She had seen him last night, sitting by himself in the barn and holding the White Rose of York and not looking at anything and not saying anything and oh, *fuck,* what a balls-up this all was.

She fetched his battered water bottle from one of the posts, gave it to him, watched him drink. "Gary *wants* to quit; he wants to leave. But he's tied to this place same as a lot of us. Unlike us, he doesn't want to be, but his wife does. He's too whipped to put his foot down, he's not driven enough to make a fresh start somewhere else, so he just goes along. All the farms going belly-up is his chance to get out without his wife getting pissed. If Heartbreak shuts down, he's off the hook. Can't feel guilty for abandoning a place if it's sold out from under you, right? Easier to tell your wife, 'Hey, there's no jobs around here; it's not my fault; let's go where the work is.'"

There was a long silence while Blake sipped water, scratched the piglet behind her ears, and pondered. Then: "So much of the town loathes me for selling off treasured family farms. But the employees of the farm I'm trying to save are also pissed at me because they're trapped in some sort of hellish agricultural limbo?"

"Pretty much."

"That would explain their increasingly alarming antics."

He said it so dryly Natalie had to laugh. *Okay. Progress. At least he's talking to me. He's not even being as mean as he could, and we both know I deserve it.* "Well. Yeah. Mostly it's Gary; Larry and Harry are ramblers by nature. They're not from here; they go where the work is. They don't mind moving on; they just hate moving on because the bank tells them to. My bank."

"Which is why they didn't let on to your real job. If you're out here working, everything else—including foreclosure paperwork—slows down. It was in their best interest to have you out here as long as they could."

"Yeah. Gary, though. Gary wants out."

Gary had accidentally driven the tractor through the back wall of the garage, then forgotten to mention it to Blake for fourteen hours. (It was a measure of Blake's exhaustion that he hadn't noticed in the first place.) Then Gary had fertilized the tomato plants with weed killer, turned the sprinkler system on to water the driveway (as opposed to the kitchen garden), and added fabric softener to Blake's laundry, if "softener" was another word for "bleach." Again, it had taken Blake a bit of time to notice his gray clothes were now whitish gray. Gary had suggested on more than one occasion that Blake should just fire him already.

"You talked about *Peanuts,* remember? Okay, remember Pig-Pen? The dust that kid kicks up?" That earned her another smile; Blake knew what she was thinking. Gary had decided to host, and be the only guest for, his one-man kegger party last week. He'd walked around all day with a cloud of beer fumes preceding him. Annoying enough, but Gary had decided the next day that the paralyzing hangover wasn't worth it. Instead he unplugged the fridge to defrost it and never got around to actually cleaning the thing out.

"I could summon no pity for the man, though he suffered what appeared to be a devastating hangover."

"And you made him teach you to drive the tractor that morning!" The memory made her positively gleeful. The tractor sounded like a dozen chain saws thrown into a pile of railroad ties. "Diabolical!" In fact, it had earned him some grudging respect from Harry and Larry, who were stuck picking up the slack for the third of their trio.

"It's unfortunate Gary doesn't know I don't have the authority to fire him. Nothing short of arson would result in termination, and perhaps not even that."

"Yeah." Natalie snickered. "Too bad for him."

"Me as well," was the cold reply. Then: "I disapprove of him endangering lives to collect unemployment." Blake paused. "Is that something Heartbreak even offers? Or are you all independent contractors?"

"Depends on the individual. . . . Listen, my point is, you're working hard and almost all of us appreciate it."

"It's kind of you to want to cheer me."

She shook her head so hard, her ponytail almost put out her

eye. "No. I'm not kind. You know that now, don't you? I—I tried to tell you. Before."

"You're referring to your deception."

"Well, yeah."

"And the fact that you only took me under your wing, so to speak, but showed me the ropes, also so to speak, because you wanted my money."

She was startled. She'd been so busy kicking herself about not telling him who she really was, she'd forgotten the reason at the middle of everything: Sweetheart was in trouble because of money: there wasn't enough. Money could save Heartbreak. No one in Sweetheart had money. If Heartbreak could be profitable, they wouldn't have to sell it to Putt N'Go. If Putt N'Go didn't have Heartbreak, they wouldn't want the other farms. Blake had money. Blake was in town for mysterious Banaan-related reasons. Ergo . . .

"I didn't— I—" She could almost feel her voice, low and strangled. What was she even trying to say? Was she denying it? Apologizing for it? *It wasn't so much the money; I just hated you not knowing the real me. But it's okay now, it's okay to trust me* this time, *because* this time *I'm telling the truth.* Oh God, she didn't blame him and she couldn't fix this. "Blake . . . that's not what I—"

"You were only interested in my money." He let that hang there for a moment, then sighed. "I am surprised I am surprised."

"For Heartbreak," she managed, "not myself. And I wanted you to understand us, how it is here, more than I wanted your money. It was never just the money, bad enough as that is; it was everything else, too. I was greedy; I wanted it all."

He just *looked* at her.

Yell, scream, stomp around, throw stuff, break something. Jesus! The look was worse than any of those things; it was worse than all of those things.

"Natalie, do you think it matters to me, the name I write on the check, if it's the reason you tolerated me at all?"

"No, Blake. Now that I know you better, I don't think that. I'm sorry." *Sorry sorry cripes they're just words they don't help anything they don't solve anything shut up shut up shut up.*

"Open your present."

She had no idea what he was talking about, then remembered the long brown tube from Amazon. She went to fetch it (she'd left it on the counter in the tack room), grabbed a twine cutter, and started slitting it open. She realized almost right away that it was a poster and, puzzled, she unrolled it.

She looked at it for a long time.

"I hear you talking about Degas all the time, you and Gary, Harry, and Larry. Garrett and a couple of other people in town, too. You must like his work. I thought— I wanted to show my gratitude. For being so patient with me. And as you know, I didn't have a lot of money; I couldn't show gratitude the way I usually do. So . . ." He gestured at the poster. "This."

Horror and a species of dull shame was creeping through her. She couldn't look at him. Blake must have mistaken that for confusion, or surprised pleasure, because he leaned forward and seemed really engaged for the first time in over twenty-four hours.

"It's called *Two Laundresses and a Horse.* As you know, Edgar Degas is known primarily for his paintings of dancers, but he did several outdoor scenes with horses as well. And I saw that one and thought of us and Margaret of Anjou and I thought— I thought you might like it."

"Blake. You didn't have to—it's too much."

He frowned. "It's not the actual painting. It's only a print. Are you all right? Forgive me for being blunt, but you look awful. All the color's fallen out of your face."

Her mouth worked. Nothing came out. *Don't lie. You can't lie to him. Not this time, not even if it's the last time he speaks to you, which it probably is.* "Not Edgar Degas. That's not what you heard. That's not what they've

(chickenshit!)—

I mean, that's not what *we've* been saying. You overheard people saying 'Vegas Douche.' " Miserable, she finished her sad-ass explanation with, "It's, uh, it's just a dumb nickname. I don't call you that anymore."

"Ah."

Dear God, could you maybe strike me down with a heart attack or an aneurysm or just jab me with a lightning bolt, anything to get me the hell out of here, thanks, your friend, Natalie Lane.

"You're right," he said after a long long long while.

"I am?"

"You're not kind."

She nodded. Then she burst into tears, and for a minute she didn't know who was more shocked, her or Blake.

"Er. Natalie. Please don't. Natalie?" He put down the piglet, who'd almost been dozing on his lap, and then raised his hands until they sort of hovered over Natalie, like he had no idea 1) if he was allowed to touch and 2) if so, where he was allowed to touch. "I take it back."

"Don't you dare take it back!" she nearly screamed, sobs

tearing from her throat like they were trying to escape. "You're right: I'm not kind; it was shitty; I'm shitty—"

"That is *enough.*" She was shocked out of crying and rubbed her eyes with her knuckles, smearing dirt and sweat around like a kid after a fight on the playground. She hadn't known his voice could go so deep and dark. "There are many words I would use to describe you, Natalie Lane, and 'shitty' is nowhere on the list."

"Then you're an idiot."

"I haven't discounted that," he replied, so mildly she almost laughed. He reached out and patted her shoulder, almost as if he was afraid she'd slap his hand away. She couldn't help it; she leaned into his touch, and, bolder, he rubbed circles on her back. "A few instances of bad judgment does not translate to shitty. I know you."

This was all very nice, but she couldn't let it stand. Bad enough to cry like a sorry-ass fraud; she wouldn't take advantage of him being flummoxed to let herself off the hook.

"Blake, you're great and you've certainly proved yourself the bigger person, but give me a break. We've known each other a month. You don't know me. At best, I'm just the thing you wanted to do while you were stuck on Heartbreak."

"My God, Natalie!" The rubbing had stopped and he sounded as appalled as he looked, so pretty appalled. "First, you are emphatically not a thing. Second, I won't deny my attraction to you, but it was to all of you, not just your delightful petite—"

"Stubby."

"—body and striking—"

"Fat."

"—features and stop that! Every day here I couldn't wait to

see you. Why do you think I bought the toaster and the bread? There were days I'd skip breakfast in the kitchen in order to get out to Main One faster, and it's not because I wanted to 'jump' you and it sure as hell wasn't because I was eager to let that demon pony have another crack at me. Though I did think about it," he admitted. "About you. And me. Um. Quite a lot. But sexual fantasies about someone you just met are quite normal for a sexually active male—which might be a misnomer, as I haven't achieved intercourse for several weeks, so really it could have been anyone in my fantasies, it's a physiological reaction that doesn't necessarily translate to emotion—"

"Stop now."

"Yes. Excellent idea."

She paused, flattered and irked. It took her brain a second to untangle. Classic Blake, saying something wonderful and then wrecking it with science. "But if you didn't do that, you wouldn't be *you*, would you, Blake?"

"Do what?"

She shook her head. "Never mind."

"There is nothing wrong with sharing knowledge," he huffed, piqued.

"I agree. I wasn't making fun of you; I guess I was—how can I describe this—enjoying that aspect of you."

"Oh." Mollified, he went on. "I've spent more time with you than anyone else since I turned eighteen. Rake turned eighteen the same day—"

"Because Rake is terrible?" she guessed.

"Yes! See, you know me, too."

"No, you just say that a lot. Half the town knows Rake is terrible."

"The entire town should know." She couldn't tell if Blake was serious or not. "They need to be warned that Venice Douche is at loose in the world."

"Trust me, it's common knowledge all over Sweetheart that Rake is terrible."

Blake clutched her hands in his and she giggled to see her paws swallowed up in his big hammy mitts. "That is the sexiest thing anyone has ever said in the history of spoken language. And I *do* know you, Natalie Lane. I know you love chocolate but hate fudge. I know you left all of Gary's shoes outside in the rain when you found out he'd hidden all the bread from me. I know you're fiercely and equally proud of your Native American and Irish heritage, and that you tell people the reason you're not an alcoholic is because they cancel each other out."

"It's simple math."

"I also know you don't actually think that, not really. I know you admire your mother's ancestors and your father's forebears."

"Don't those mean the same—"

"I know you have a reservoir of deep kindness and you don't like it when people notice. I know you're endlessly patient, and loyal, and fierce, and proud. I know your hair smells like cherry blossoms and I have pondered that mystery for a month."

"It's my cherry blossom shampoo."

"Mystery solved. Most of all, Natalie, I know I will miss you when I've gone. I'll think of you every day for a long, long time. Perhaps until the end of my life."

When I've gone. Of course. And that made sense. She'd always known he was leaving. And certainly nothing had happened in the last forty-eight hours that would have caused Blake to consider changing those plans, for which she did not blame him at all. Still, the news—not that she should have been thinking of it as news—hit her like a jab to the gut.

"Yes. Okay. I— Yes." She began to extricate herself from his warm, comforting grip. "Thank you. For those nice things you said. I'm glad— I'm glad you don't hate me."

"Impossible," he murmured, releasing her.

Yeah? Give me another month, pal.

"I'll just take that—"

"No!" He had reached for the poster and she whipped it behind her back. "No, you can't. It's mine; you said you bought it for me. You said it was my present."

"As you wish." He seemed taken aback by her ferocious defense—if she'd been a crow she would have been flying at him and cawing in his face until he ran away. "I only meant—"

"It's mine," she said again, calming herself. "Whatever the reason, it was a thoughtful gift, and I want to keep it. I didn't know he did horses. I only saw the ballet dancers." She could hear herself and was amazed; she hadn't felt—or sounded—so shy in ten years. "Thank you again." *Enough mush. Back to business—it's what he wants; he wouldn't have touched you at all if you hadn't sobbed like a teething toddler.* "I still say you need to take a break."

"It's my prerogative to disagree," he replied gently. "And your concern is appreciated, but I am fine. And I need to get back to work. Margaret of Anjou will not feed herself. Though I imagine she wishes she could." That last in a dark mutter.

"You're not fine," Natalie replied sharply, and was that still more guilt? Yep. She'd thrown everything at him and he wasn't leaving. He knew the truth about everything—Vegas Douche, the reasons behind Gary's treachery, her job at the bank, Margaret of Anjou's sociopathy, that the nuclear option hadn't worked—and he still wasn't leaving. Natalie knew he would—he'd told her he would, and unlike her, Blake didn't lie—but it would be on his terms.

And he'd been that kind of man long before setting foot in Sweetheart. Shoveling shit didn't change a man in a month. She'd been so stupid, so smug and certain she knew better than a city guy, that she hadn't let herself see his strength. She'd pay for that, because she, too, would think of him every day after he went back to his life.

"Dammit, Blake, don't argue! Your hands are shaking, for God's sake. Come on with me now." She stood and tried to pull him up with her, and after a few seconds he let her. Good thing, too, because it had been like trying to yank a redwood out of the ground.

Blake sighed, so long and loud it sounded like it came from the very bottom of his lungs, and emptied them. Their moment of whatever-it-was was over. "There's nothing to be concerned about."

Biggest lie ever. It was too dusty in here; it was making her eyes water. *Oh. No.* Wasn't the dust. *Do not start crying again, idiot!*

"And you're laboring under a misapprehension," he continued. "My hands aren't shaking because I'm tired. They always do that when you touch me. I— I've been hoping you wouldn't notice. Too late now. Isn't that right?"

He looked around, saw the White Rose of York had settled down in clean straw to finish her nap, and stood. Natalie had the sense he wouldn't be talking like this—that they would never have spoken about *any* of this—if he was in his right mind, or at least well rested. He'd said some nice things when he was drunk, and then out of pity when she blubbered all over him, but she wasn't dumb enough to assume he meant them. Her concern was sharpening into major unease. Cripes, Heartbreak broke Blake! Which she had wanted to happen until it did! "Listen—"

Slowly, so slowly it was almost like watching the minute hand on a clock, his hand came up and, eventually, he had a finger under her chin and was coaxing her head up so she could look at him. Slowly, giving her every chance to punch or kick or spit or just step back, he leaned in and his mouth brushed over her lips once, twice. And once again. He'd been filching toast again. She should be grossed out, being able to taste his breakfast.

(I am not grossed out.)

She blinked at him, realized she'd grabbed two fistfuls of his shirt and things at once seemed quite bright and loud. She could hear everything—Margaret of Anjou's soft snorts from her stall, the White Rose of York's contented grunting, the chorus from the meadowlarks outside and the barn swallows inside. The wind humming through the grass and tree line. Her breathing. His. And she could smell everything, too, which could have been horrifying but wasn't. Clean hay. Dust. Manure. Newly cut grass. Even the sunshine slanting through the barn seemed to have a smell, yellow and bright and lemony.

Then she was clutching air because he'd stepped back out of her grip, and his face was red for reasons that had nothing to do with the heat. "I apologize. It won't happen again." He paused like he was going to say something more, then seemed to change his mind. "Forgive me."

She reached out, not slowly, and grabbed his shirt, not gently, and hauled him back again, not carefully, and then she was discovering that in addition to toast, he'd had orange juice. She was discovering that if she did *that* with her tongue right *there* she could get his breathing to hitch. The power in that moment was heady, almost as staggering as the relief.

(oh God he's letting me he's letting me do this and you said your hands shake when I'm near and you taste like sunshine and toast and your breathing goes funny when we do this, which is good because maybe you won't notice my breathing goes funny, too)

Margaret of Anjou's hiss (before that pony came to Heartbreak, Natalie hadn't known ponies could hiss like pissed-off rattlers) broke the spell. She relaxed her grip, then tried (in vain) to straighten the dust-smeared wrinkles in his shirt. He looked down and watched for a second, then took her hands in his.

"You're lovely." He said it with utter seriousness, the way people said, "It's snowing," or, "Splinters are painful." "And your mouth is glorious."

"I don't—" Ten minutes ago he'd been swaying with fatigue and she'd felt guilt and sorrow in equal measure. Yesterday she was sick over what could only be called her betrayal. Now she knew how his mouth felt against hers, knew she made his hands shake, knew he fantasized about her, and her brain couldn't reconcile the new information with the old. "Thank you. I don't do this stuff normally. Make a habit of it, I mean." God, when *had* she last gone on a date? Between trying to save the bank and, thus, the town (or vice versa), her social life had gone right down the shitter.

"How fortunate for me." This in a low voice, almost a rumble, and she had to actively resist the urge to haul him back in and mack on him some more.

"I'm sorry," she whispered.

"It doesn't matter now," he replied, and kissed her again.

Twenty-nine

Blake Tarbell (Secret Service code name: Vegas Douche) sulked in his mighty Supertruck. He had promised Natalie he would rest, had let her bully him into two glasses of lemonade to assuage her guilt, but the attic was too hot and the lemonade sloshed in his belly, leaving him feeling vaguely ill.

After an hour of rising heat and ever-louder stomach sloshing he couldn't bear it any longer, found his keys, checked on Margaret of Anjou and the White Rose of York, and drove toward town. It was, as always, a peaceful drive. He drove past field after abandoned field, picturing them lush with golden summer wheat, the drone of insects getting drowsy in the sun, the snap of plastic streamers in the field scaring off the birds (easier and more effective, Natalie-the-banker had explained, than scarecrows).

The fields weren't entirely abandoned; it wasn't all desolate, empty landscape. The Darrel twins (each widowed twelve years ago, he had learned, and just two days apart) had their stand up and running, and they waved as he got closer. He returned the wave and pulled over, spotting carton after carton of fresh-picked spring strawberries. He considered purchasing some for Natalie, who would consume strawberry shortcake three times a day if it were socially acceptable. Then he remembered he was sick with hurt at her betrayal(s)

(as she was by yours, you self-righteous ass, and have you forgotten all those sad abandoned fields were partially your doing?)

and decided to punish her by only getting half a pound. *When I could have easily purchased two pounds! That will teach her!* He answered Alice Darrel's questions about Margaret of Anjou

("Are you any closer to killing her? Or her you? There's a pool! So any hints you could give me . . . it's up to four hundred bucks. Seventy/thirty, whaddya think?"),

politely returned Andy Darrel's mild flirtation

("A man like you stuck in Heartbreak with just Harry, Gary, and Larry for company, a damned shame, and a crime against nature"),

and was pleased to accept the small jar of clover honey they saved for him. His second week he discovered Natalie had mentioned his stash of bread and his toaster to the twins, so when they could they pulled a jar and held it for him. Fresh clover honey, he had discovered with deep delight, tasted like springtime. He may have fantasized about using Natalie as a canvas on which he would paint and devour said honey.

He got his bag of berries, wished the twins a pleasant afternoon, and climbed back in the Supertruck. *The Darrel twins are so nice,* he thought, *I wonder if they want Sweetheart to die so they can leave? Or are they like Natalie, they don't ever want to leave? And did Andy's wife really dance herself to death, or is that just a local urban legend? Maybe* dance herself to death *is a eu-phemism. But for what? And why do I want to know? This question will consume me.*

He passed a school bus, obediently stopping when it flipped out its stop sign. The Opitz kids piled out, saw him, and one of them mimed yanking a pull cord. Children loved the Super-truck's droning horn, which was not unlike the sound of a runaway train bearing down on you. Blake obligingly honked. A grin, waves, and off they went.

Once in Sweetheart proper, he had no idea where he wanted to go, just that he was restless and thirsty and his head ached. He parked and considered. *The library?* Closed on Sundays. *The diner?* Not hungry—he hadn't been hungry for over a day. Perhaps his body was finally adjusting to the Heartbreak schedule? *Incorrect,* as he had not been so tired since his first week on the farm.

The gas station? The Supertruck had three-quarters of a tank. *The B and B? No thank you. Las Vegas? No thank you.*

This place, he thought, knuckles white on the steering wheel as he glared through the windshield. *It grows on you like lichen on a tree. The tree doesn't notice and, by the time it does notice, the lichen is part of it, and getting rid of it would be unthinkable.*

That is a terrible analogy. Get a grip on yourself!

The appeal of Sweetheart, he decided, was more about what it *wasn't* than what it *was.* It was not an impersonal city where you locked everything at night—and during the day, too, just to be safe. It was not a luxury hotel; no one was waiting by the phone to rush midnight hot-fudge sundaes to his suite. (They'd done that a few times, he'd come down at midnight for a snack and find Natalie there, and they'd have sundaes or fudge or that potato flatbread she liked, *lefsa*—which had a fascinating history!—and once they got to speculating about Margaret of Anjou's sinister past until two o'clock in the morning.) There was none of Vegas' "make wild revelry, for who cares about tomorrow" vibe.

Things mattered in Sweetheart; the locals had bigger problems than how to hit three breakfast buffets by 9:00 A.M. with time left to gamble away the mortgage payment. The locals weren't afraid to get dirty (except Garrett, but given Blake's family's business, he could not cast blame). Aside from losing their homes, they didn't appear to be afraid of anything. They looked after the land, they looked after one another (the Darrel twins house-sat for Roger when he was off on his mysterious sinister vacations, and Roger watered their dogs when they left town for something called a Romantic Times convention).

Everyone knew everyone else, and at first Blake had found that claustrophobic. He could feel the gazes on him when he went into town for errands, could feel their silent judgment. Everyone knowing everyone was kind of awful if you were Blake Tarbell and people knew you did your best to gut their town until Mommy grounded you. But it was something splendid when you needed a cup of sugar and any one of a dozen people would not only lend it to you; they'd also leave their front door unlocked so you could swing by and pick up the sugar whenever you like.

It wasn't that the people of Las Vegas were terrible. But they were all strangers to one another. That had suited him well until a month ago. And now when he thought of Rake in Venice, up to God knew what Rake-related shenanigans, instead of envy Blake felt worry. His twin was surrounded by strangers in a land where he was not known; Blake would fret until Rake returned. Whatever, and wherever, that meant.

A rap on the window; Blake had been so deep in thought he hadn't noticed the older man who bore a striking resemblance to Sir Ben Kingsley, CBE, if Sir Ben had close-cropped red hair and favored jeans and flannel shirts.

He rolled down the window. "Hello."

"Hiya. Sandy Cort." They shook, and Blake was so used to the burning pain in his palms he didn't flinch. For a man in his early sixties, Cort had an admirable grip. "You're that outtatowner feller, arencha?"

It took Blake a few seconds to translate the midwestern *patois*. He considered, then rejected, telling him "fellow" was pronounced "fell-oh" and "out-of-towner" was technically three words, despite the hyphens, and "are you not" worked just as well as "arencha." "I am. May I help you, Mr. Cort?"

"Naw, Mr. Cort's my dad and he's long dead, that stubborn bugger; I'm Sandy. Just wanted to say h'lo. Me and Roger—you know Rog, he's shacking over at the B and B?"

"Yes, I have stolen his livestock."

Cort didn't even blink. "That's the one, yep; we tickle trout together."

Blake managed, just, to swallow the inappropriate giggle that wanted to leak out of his lungs.

"Said you were a nice feller and I should say h'lo. So: h'lo."

"It's nice to meet you."

"He said you talk like books."

"I suppose I do." He was a bit taken aback, then decided there were worse ways to talk and warmed to the comment. "I read a great deal."

"Yeah, sure, t'be expected. Shannah's boy, arencha?"

"You know my mother?"

"Oh, sure, her an' all them Banaans." Blake was surprised to hear Sandy pronounce it "ban-anns" instead of the more typical "buh-nons." "She was always like that, even as a little 'un; the other kids'd be playin' outside and she always wanted to hole up with four or five books. Not comic books, either!" he added, as if Blake were making ready to scorn his mother's reading efforts. "*Big* books, for grown-ups. My dad got kicked out of the nursing home because of all the candy he kept sneaking to the diabetics, came home to die."

"I'm sorry?" And here he thought he had been following the conversation so well.

"Howwcum?" Sandy fished around in his jeans pocket and extracted a pack of Hubba Bubba bubble gum, which he offered to Blake (who declined, as a stint with braces as a teenager had left him disinclined to anything sticky except honey). Between chomps, Sandy continued. "He wanted to be home; we wanted him home; he was on the porch or in bed most times, wasn't any trouble. Knew he didn't have long—if you don't fight cancer with chemo, it's not s'bad, he was just mostly tired, and the docs helped with the pain at the end. Your mama, she'd come over and read to him."

So difficult to picture the competent, uncompromising Shannah Banaan Tarbell as a little girl; when Blake tried he could only physically shrink his mom, not reduce the woman he knew to the innocent nature of a child.

"Ah, Gawd, she read him all those Little House books; Dad loved those; he had a big crush on Karen Grassle, the actress who played Caroline Ingalls on the TV show—no?

Never mind, doesn't matter now. God, he wanted to get in her petticoats so bad."

"That's adorable, Cort."

"Anyhoo. Your mama was sweet as sugar, and after my dad passed we found out he left her a thousand bucks! And he said she could do whatever she wanted with it, but he hoped she saved it for college or bought books with it." Sandy grinned, leaning on the truck door and blowing a bubble almost as large as his head. "She didn't save it for college, tell you that."

"The nook!" Blake cried, shifting so suddenly he blared the horn. Sandy, in mid-bubble, almost choked. "When we were little we had this tiny apartment in Vegas—this was before our father passed away, so she was supporting us on tips, more or less. It was a dreary two-bedroom apartment, one for my brother and me and the book nook, we called it. That room was floor-to-ceiling books, with shelves everywhere, books everywhere, even piled on the floor in stacks as high as her hip. There wasn't room for a bed. Our mother slept on a hide-a-bed in the living room until my father died, because that was preferable to getting rid of the books."

Sandy chuckled, delighted. "Yep. Sounds about right." Sandy leaned closer, as if confiding a great secret. "Y'know, it wasn't her fault, what they did. It was her family, not her. Lotta people, they won't get that. They think once a Banaan, always a Banaan. And maybe if your mama hadn't ever left Sweetheart, that'd be true. But she *did* leave. So it's *not* true. I know, because Sweetheart's in trouble and she came on the run. She's here, ain't she?" A pause while he blew another bubble, snapped it, chomped, finished: "So are you."

Blake leaned forward, intrigued and almost dizzy with the

influx of information. "What do you mean by what her family did?" No response. "Sandy?" The older man straightened suddenly, smile lines replaced by frown lines. Blake glanced to his left and saw Garrett Hobbes walking toward the truck in the company of a tall, thin elderly man he didn't recognize.

Oh, look. It's Satan's intern.

"Hey, cripes, we were just talking about you!" Garrett jogged over to Blake, the twenty seconds of exertion bringing sweat to his brow, armpits, nose, chin, chest, and scalp, Blake noticed. The elderly man followed in Garrett's wake, not rushing. He stared at Blake, which was nothing new in this town.

"Sorry I'm all out," Garrett wheezed, stopping before he ran headlong into the Supertruck's cab. "Of breath. Just got done. You know. At the gym."

That explains the dreadful shiny suit and the wet shiny hair. "They were out of towels?"

"Not a lot on hand *this time of day*. They're not used to people being there *this time of day*," he said with misplaced emphasis and an odd note of pride Blake found puzzling for four seconds.

"How fascinating. I don't—" And then he did. He saw it at once and shook his head, unsure if he was amused or annoyed. "You think scheduling an exercise regime during business hours will arouse envy in your fellow townspeople. That they will marvel at how you can break away from work for organized sweating on a treadmill. I regret being the bearer of bad tidings, Garrett, but it doesn't arouse their envy. Just their annoyance, often laced with contempt."

"What the fuck do you know?"

Blake almost missed the rebuttal over Sandy's guffaw. The

man actually slapped his knee, something Blake had assumed no one did outside of Westerns. Though Blake knew the futility of introducing people who knew each other, he was a slave to the lifelong habit of stiff manners. "Sandy, this is Garrett Hobbes. Garrett, this is—"

"I know who he is, cripessakes. Look, when do you jog or lift or whatever? Big guy like you," Garrett added almost resentfully, "you must be in there a lot. Prob'ly got big fancy gyms in Vegas, right? I might move there, if I don't find anything good in L.A."

Mental note: Burn Las Vegas to the ground and never return. Possibly the entire state of Nevada. Cannot be too careful.

"Really, Garrett? We're still discussing your sweaty regimen? Since you're so keen to know, I was a one-percenter, now cast into the other part of that equation, and I used the hotel treadmill—"

"Don't like jogging in the desert?" Sandy cracked, and slapped his knee again.

"Good Lord, no. I'd be on the treadmill around two thirty A.M. And that's because I was a) an insomniac and b) not an incurable ass." *Probably not an incurable ass. Well, not as big an incurable ass.*

"Fine, enough, don't even know how we got on that topic—"

"You brought it up. Don't you remember? It was fifteen seconds ago."

"—but I've been thinking about you, stuck there with a bunch of jerks who want you to fail—"

"Are we still talking about Las Vegas?"

Garrett would not be deterred. "And I thought of someone

who might be able to get you to see sense, and as it happened he was swinging by town today anyway, so I reached out and, you know."

"What?" Blake had no idea where this was going. The elderly man had by now joined them. He was slender going on emaciated, the weathered skin of his face stretched so tightly you could easily make out the shape of his skull. His neck was too long for his body, his shoulders too narrow. He was neatly, dully dressed in gray slacks with a black leather belt, a tan dress shirt, and black dress shoes. Clean shaven, with a head full of scrupulously trimmed white hair and pale brown eyes, almost sand colored. He held himself with stiff pride, and stared and stared at Blake and said nothing. His mouth was small and tight with . . . disapproval, perhaps? Disappointment? A recent lemon dessert? "I know what?"

"This is your grandpa, Mitchell Banaan."

Over the sudden roaring in his years, Blake replied, "No, it isn't."

"It is, though."

"Isn't. My grandfather is dead, as are his wife and three of their four children, my mom being the fourth. It's the reason my mom and I came to Sweetheart; it's why she inherited the unholy mess of bankrupt farms. Ergo, this man is not my maternal grandfather."

"They gave up the farms," Sandy explained, effortlessly inserting himself into private family business, or Garrett's delusion, or both, "but not because they died. You thought they were dead? Who'd tell you something like that?"

No one, he realized with startled dismay. Questions shoved aside, evaded, or not even asked were at once much clearer.

Who died? he had asked, and Shannah had not answered directly, merely going on to discuss the farms she inherited.

If they hadn't died and left her the property headache, he had pointed out, *we wouldn't be out here.* He had seen her puzzled expression and wondered at it.

Died? I'm not getting you. They didn't— He had wondered, but then Mom had cut Natalie off and it never occurred to him to revisit the question.

Blake then did something he had never done before and hoped would never do again: he did what Rake would have called a "headdesk" on the steering wheel, hard enough to make the horn blare, and roared, "You colossal jackasses are *alive?* Because if that's so, I am going to kill *all* of you!"

Thirty

"So. One of Shannah's boys." The old man
(his grandfather the old man was his grandfather who is not
dead *for the love of all that is unholy and when did my life become
a soap opera)*
sized him up with the warmth of a snake glaring at a robin's
egg.
*(what? stop thinking like a laid-back NoDak and reclaim your
identity, your big-city cold, intense, soulless identity)*
sized him up with all the warmth Margaret of Anjou (the
queen, not the hell-pony) had for Richard, the Duke of York.
Whew! Better.

"Which one are you, then?" This in a tone often used for
questions like "paper or plastic?": chilly indifference. Five seconds into their first meeting, Blake understood why his mother
had fled Sweetheart.

"Blake." *I suppose we're to have a conversation now? Or*

something? "The oldest." *Because Rake is . . . not going to believe this when I tell him.*

"You don't look like a Banaan." The relentless frigid regard was getting difficult to bear. Blake imagined he would drop his gaze, soon, and direct his responses to his feet. "Not at all like Shannah, or me."

Then Blake pictured his mom, the generous kindhearted child who read twentieth-century literature to a dying man because that was a respite from her life, that was a wonderful warm experience compared to any interaction with her father, and just like that, the ancient troll's evil spell was broken. Blake's head came up and he took a step forward. His grandfather did not step back. *Good.*

Keep not backing up, old man, let me get in there chest to chest. See what I did *inherit from my mom.*

"We favor our father's side." *Thank* God. The nuclear option, while devastating, respected, if not loved, Shannah and adored the twins without condition. The moment she found she was a grandmother, Nonna bent her will to securing every advantage she could for Shannah and her sons. This man, now. This man was something else. "In almost all things."

"What are you doing here, boy?"

Excellent question. And if there had been no easy answer half an hour ago, there certainly wasn't one now. He stared at the man in mingled frustration and annoyance and finally came out with, "I don't know."

A snort. "Typical. Your mother's the same. She didn't know what the hell she was doing; she just left. And then look! Got caught with you and your brother. Tell you what, she was a sorry girl after that. Told her. We said, 'This is what happens when you turn your back on family.' We said, 'Being smart got you into this, better hope being smart can get you out of it.'"

I cannot imagine the courage Mom used when she found she was pregnant and realized she needed her family. Asking this man for help must have been like asking for . . . for . . .

His historical knowledge failed him. For the first time in his life (when he was sober, anyway), he could not complete the metaphor. Instead he reached out, found his grandfather's shirt collar, twisted, pulled. They were close to eye to eye; his grandfather was two inches taller.

"Old man, I have had a shit week and am giving serious contemplation to beating you to death."

"They teach you to push around old men in Las Vegas?"

"No, they taught me to never bet against the house in Las Vegas. Your *daughter* taught me! 'No one is an unjust villain in his own mind. . . . Some of the cruelest tyrants in history were motivated by noble ideals.'* She taught me 'those who are capable of tyranny are capable of perjury to sustain it.'† She taught me 'under tyranny it is right to be a rebel.'"‡

"What—"

"The daughter you turned your back on helped me learn my letters, got me my first library card, showed me the universe as best she could, and never quit. You, though. You quit. That's all you do, isn't it? That's why people pronounce 'Banaan' like it's a curse around here. Your daughter wanted to be better

---

*Jim Butcher, *Turn Coat*.
† Lysander Spooner.
‡ Robert Fanney.

than that. And she is. She's worth fifty of you, old man, and you have no idea how badly I want to break your nose."

There was a *snap!* and they both looked to their left; Sandy Cort was popping his gum and watching with an avid gaze. "To think I almost didn't head to town today," he said, as if amazed there could be a universe where he missed the confrontation.

"Piss off, Cort. This is family business *kakk!*"

Kakk because Blake had tightened his grip. "*You are not family.* You turned on my mother when she needed you. You sulked when she left and punished her when she tried to return. Do you know what all of this means?" He took a deep breath and bellowed, "You're the reason I'm in Heartbreak, you judgmental sack of shit! And coming to Heartbreak is both the worst and greatest thing to ever happen to me! Do you think I want to be beholden to you for anything? I would rather be Rake's personal assistant for a calendar year!"

"You're busy," Garrett said. "We can talk later."

Blake had forgotten him, too. "Busy, yes, and also, 'Power-lust is a weed that grows only in the vacant lots of an abandoned mind.'"

"What the fuck are you talking about?"

"Not me. Ayn Rand. Do you even have a library card?"

"I only read *Men's Health* and *Maxim*," Garrett replied, puzzled.

"*Maxim?*" Sandy said, rolling his eyes. "For God's sake, Garrett. That's porn for kids not old enough to legally buy porn who don't have Internet access."

"It is not! They have sex tips and sports articles."

"'The Hottest NFL Cheerleaders' is not a sports article."

"You seem to know a lot about it," Garrett shot back.

"That's true, Sandy," Cort added, amused. "You do."

Another *snap!* of bubble gum from Cort's jaws of life. "Yeah, my grandson reads it and leaves it lying around. Kid just got his driver's license last week."

"Rebuttal, Garrett? No?" Without loosening his grip on his hateful grandfather, Blake shifted his attention to the sweaty, greedy, pathetic man who somehow thought that arranging a meeting between grandfather and grandson would fix everything. "I had to work and live here for weeks to understand why places like Sweetheart are necessary. Because one piece of earth is *not* just like another."

"Oh, for God's sake," he huffed, already looking around the quiet street for an escape route.

"In Las Vegas, the lights are always on, but not because anyone who cares about you is waiting. No clocks, so you aren't reminded how much of your life you're pissing away betting against a house that never loses. Vegas can suck you dry and then turn her back on you; Sweetheart is the pitcher of lemonade on the lit porch." *Not my best.*

"What the fuck does this have to—"

"I don't know; I am tired and confused and angry!" And hot. No one had warned him that North Dakota springs could be downright tropical.

"Atta boy." From Sandy Cort, who blew a bubble of approval.

"And you want to make this place a miniature Vegas, with casinos and miniature golf and bright lights at ten o'clock at night, you soulless shithead! Which you never would have thought to do without wretches like *this* enabling such a toxic mind-set." He gave his grandfather a light shake for emphasis, then released him. *"And I helped you.* You could never have taken it this far if I hadn't also been a soulless shithead. Thank Christ I came to my senses in time." He was so staggered by the epiphany he was dizzy with it. And for some reason his hands no longer hurt. "Forget your ill-conceived plan, Garrett. I'll do whatever it takes to save Heartbreak, whatever I have to in order to get the funds. If I have to crawl, naked, the length of downtown to my mother on broken acid-drenched glass while listening to an audio of *Angela's Ashes* as narrated by my brother and follow my undignified pleading with an hour of interpretive dance, I will."

"Jesus," Garrett said with a flinch, doubtless picturing the tawdry scene.

"Yes! That's how determined I am. The place doesn't have to be profitable, either, so don't hang on to that hope. Heartbreak could *burn down* and I wouldn't let it go, do you understand?"

"What the fuck did they do to you out there?"

"Worked me half to death, starved me, put me in danger, let me operate heavy machinery while fatigued, made me eat *lefsa* and haricots verts, and put me in charge of an animal who yearns for my death," he replied happily. "This might be Stockholm syndrome. Don't care. Go away."

Here comes "this isn't over." That was unoriginal but vaguely badass, just the sort of thing Garrett—

"This isn't over!"

—couldn't resist.

"And you!" he continued as Garrett stomped off. Cort nodded to show he was still listening and Garrett almost giggled. No, that noise Blake heard *was* him giggling. The man was so unabashedly eavesdropping, and it was clear he would be gossiping about this for weeks, and refused to exhibit shame. It was glorious. "You tell Roger he will *never* get the White Rose of York back. She is going to live to the ripe old age of . . . of . . ." His research failed him. ". . . to whatever a ripe old age is for swine."

"I'm tellin' him a lot more than that." With Garrett's absence, Sandy seemed to realize the confrontation was winding down, and failed to hide his disappointment. "Welp, better get goin'. Nice to meet you, Blake. You say hi to your mama for me."

"I will, Sandy, nice to meet you, too."

An indifferent nod to the man so recently in Blake's clutches. "Mitchell."

His grandfather's head moved a half inch in acknowledgment. "Cort."

"And you! Awful, horrible old man." Blake could not recall ever feeling so manically cheerful. He had no idea where he was going from here and did not care. His life had crashed and burned and he did not care. He kept having to stifle the urge to giggle and he did not care. It wasn't that a weight had been lifted. It was more like he had lived his entire life on a high-grav planet and moved to the moon: an entirely new world to explore while weightless and free.

"I'm done with this," his grandfather replied with chilly mien, but didn't get far once Blake's hand closed around his elbow.

"Of course! Things are out of your control, thus it's past time to run along, isn't that right? Our meeting didn't go the way you planned? You thought I'd be small and stupid and timid? Hoped I'd be? Thought I'd be bullied by my mother like you bullied her? Okay, that part's a little accurate. . . . Garrett told you I was having trouble and you came right over, didn't you? But not to help. You wanted to see Shannah's mistake up close." The man's disgruntlement was so plain, Blake could not stifle a smirk.

"Let me go."

"Not yet; my brother would tell you I love the sound of my own voice, and he would not be wrong, though Rake is . . ." Now that Blake had met a blood relative who was genuinely terrible, he would have to think of something else. ". . . perhaps a bit less terrible than I previously thought. So I'll leave you with what I think happened, why you're a pathetic shit, and what will happen next.

"She left to get away, to see more of the world than Sweetheart, as teenagers have been doing since there were teenagers. But that's not what you told yourself. You decided she left to find a husband, to—what's the phrase? put on airs?—because for some reason you also thought it was 1950." He watched the old man's mouth get smaller and smaller, the only indication of his anger, and had a flash of inspiration. "You didn't know my father was wealthy! She came to you for help and you turned her away. You didn't reach out until after my father died, after she controlled the trust fund. And she told you where you could put it!" Blake could not recall the last time he was so delighted. "You assumed she was still the small scared girl who left. Don't you see, you ancient ghoul? She couldn't be that girl anymore; she had to be strong for her children. When you finally unclenched and called, she was the person *you* inadvertently made, strong, like obsidian, but brittle, also like obsidian."

"She owed loyalty to her family."

"*So did you.*" Hard to talk through clenched teeth. "Run along back to whichever hole you crept from, old man, and don't dare to seek out my mom without a written apology of a minimum of five pages."

"Boy, you don't dictate my behavior."

"Do not call me that! My name is Vegas Douche!" *Dear God. What have they turned me into?*

Without a word, his grandfather turned and walked away, stride brisk, shoulders back. You could not tell by looking at him that anything was wrong. Blake had seen that quality before, but in his mom it was something to admire. In his grandfather it was simply the old man's place to hide.

"Five pages, single spaced!" Blake shouted, and noticed Bev and Cameron Harmon stopped short across the street, then waved at him.

He smiled and waved back.

Then he passed out.

Thirty-one

It's okay he's fine everything is fine his hands don't even hurt
so how could everything not be fine and yes a bit dizzy but it
had been an interesting week so no wonder and he told the
Harmons he tripped they rushed over when he didn't trip
when he went down and his grandfather never slowed never
stopped and good riddance you wretch you monster you are a
dead thing and rumors of your not-death were exaggerated
because you have always been dead for her and now she can be
dead for you and we will be too the nuclear option has love
enough for all of us and it was so hot but it was fine everything
is fine and why is the road moving while the Supertruck stays
still oh well home again home again and hurrah here is Heartbreak and Gary is pretending he doesn't know the difference
between *Lactuca serriola* and *Lactuca sativa* and surprise Gary
the Supertruck and I are in the garden with you and oooh look
at him dive out of the way and shall I park beside the basil row
or the tomato row oh I seem to be on the muskmelon row and

this garden will not weed itself so Blake to the rescue and don't forget Natalie's strawberries ooops forgot to put down the ladder and now my head is in the muskmelon row which is all right no time to waste it's quicker this way much quicker and what is that terrible crash-bang noise and who is breathing on me who is snorting and breathing gusty hot breath on me and it's nap time now.

Thirty-two

It wasn't a nightmare, but Natalie forgave herself for thinking so at first.

First Blake managed to take the Supertruck to town without her noticing (that whole "give him space" thing really backfired). Then he came back, *roared* back, almost took out Gary, *did* take out half the kitchen garden, then conked out (on top of the muskmelons, no less).

All that was alarming enough, but the final surreal touch was Margaret of Anjou kicking free of the corral and galloping full tilt across the drive and around the house, running straight to the kitchen garden, Natalie had assumed, to seize her chance to stomp him to death. Instead she screeched to a halt beside Blake, who was facedown in muskmelon plants, then stood over him, nickering and gently pawing at him and giving every sign of a horse in emotional distress over an owner she cared about. Which wasn't possible.

Natalie ran. She felt a dull pain over her eye and realized she had run into a closed door. Opened the door, ran more, kept running, ignored Gary

"Cripes, all he hadda say was, 'I already weeded the patch,' didn't have to, y'know, try to kill me!"

shoved Margaret of Anjou, gave up trying to move her, and in the end nearly ended up facedown herself. In the end she crawled the last few feet to reach Blake. She put a hand on his shoulder and started to gently turn him over. Tried, anyway; he was a big man. She put both hands on his shoulder and grunted and heaved and after what felt like half an hour he flopped over on his back.

"Blake?" She gasped in horror; his entire front was soaked in blood! *No, wait.* Squashed strawberries. The smell should have tipped her off.

She carefully brushed dirt from his face and hissed when she touched him. *Oh, Jesus. Hot.* A fever, then, and . . . yep, she checked his hands and they were so raw, she could almost feel them throb against her skin. Infected, then, which had brought on the fever, all of it exacerbated by exhaustion and dehydration. He would be deathly ill for days in a place he felt unwanted, surrounded by people he was sure despised him, watched over by someone he knew had lied to him.

She could hardly believe there was a time she'd gleefully anticipated Heartbreak breaking him.

Something kept nudging her and she pushed back without looking. "Blake?" She shook him, brushed away more dirt. "Blake, can you— Dammit!" She turned and realized the source of the shoves. "Margaret of Anjou, I am *working on it.*" The pony let out a plaintive nicker, then promptly nudged her again. Cripes, what a nag.*

But the yelling did what her gentle concern had not. He stirred a little and mumbled, "Go away, Natalie. I don't care if Margaret of Anjou has a fever; *you* take her temperature. I don't have the courage."

"She's not the one with the fever, Blake. Can you see me okay?"

He blinked up at her, eyes watering. "No, you're all blurry and dark." She brushed away more dirt and he smiled. "Now you're brighter. Why is it so dark in here?"

"You're in the kitchen garden. If I help you up, do you think you could walk with me to the house?"

"Impossible." *Shit. Well then, get the guys to help or call an ambulance. Maybe both.* "I already weeded today."

"You're not in the kitchen garden because— Easy, easy!" He sat up, blinking around at her and the pony looming over them. "Okay, we're just gonna rest a minute, okay? And then we'll go into the house and figure out what to do next, okay?"

"Why are you saying 'okay' so often?"

"Because I am freaking out, Blake!" She forced herself to lower her voice and continued. "I told you to take care of your hands! I told you that you were working too hard." Then she was crying. She wasn't sure when she had started—when she heard Gary's screech? When she realized Blake had gone, and wondered if he'd ever come back? "It's my fault. You didn't know. I should have looked after you better. I should have done everything better."

"That's a lie. You are unimprovable." Then he passed out.

---

*Heh. See what I did there?

Thirty-three

Blake burned for three days.

Thirty-four

It took her twenty minutes to help him into the house. She covered her terror by scolding, and he laughed at her.

"I can't believe I let this get so far."

"So say all who embrace the dark side."

"You're brilliant, Blake—"

"And I've never had a cavity!"

"—how could you not know this was a pretty inevitable conclusion?"

"Victim blaming, for shame, Natalie."

"Argh, you're right, careful, porch steps coming up."

"Victim *shaming*. That's what happened to my mom, you know. Do not, if you have any tender feelings for me, do not ever tell her I said that."

"No prob. She'll be plenty pissed at what I let happen to you, no need to stoke that fire."

"Yes! Correct! That fire needs no stoking whatsoever. That

fire should be left to burn out. We should do the opposite of fanning the flames."

"Oof, heavy!"

"That's not nice, Natalie," he whined. "I'm at my winter weight. Victim blaming, then fat shaming, and you call yourself a feminist. Actually, I've never heard you identify as a feminist—"

"Shouldn't have to," she grunted, staggering forward in step with him, "should just be assumed."

"Regardless, I am forced to report you to the good people at Jezebel dot-com."

"How do you even know about Jez— Never mind. Here we are. Just several dozen more steps to get to the attic."

"Rake is not terrible."

She groaned, and not just with Blake's weight. He had an arm slung over her shoulders, she had an arm around his waist, and they were averaging about two feet a minute. Even if his heat hadn't been searing her wherever they touched, that statement would have told her everything. "Oh, man, now I know you're delirious."

"I've never been more clearheaded in my life. Sweetheart is great! Down with Vegas! Rake is much less terrible than I ever suspected! I bought you strawberries!"

"Blake, honey, you're shouting."

"Call me honey again!"

"I should be calling an ambulance, honey. And yeah, I saw the strawberries."

"I am so sorry."

"Why?"

"I could have bought you many more. I only bought you one bag. For spite! They were the strawberries of spite and I am ashamed." His head drooped and his skull *clonk*ed against hers. Sparks flashed before her eyes

(that's what they call seeing stars maybe?)

and she staggered, then straightened. "Okay, please don't do that again. The thing with your head. And don't worry about the strawberries of spite; I didn't deserve any. Besides, they got all over your shirt when you pitched out of your truck, so it's just as well you didn't buy a ton."

"When I pitched out of my *Supertruck*," he corrected. He began scraping at the berries all over him. "I'm not sure I'll be able to get these stains out."

"Who the hell cares? I'll buy you a new shirt."

"You'll have to," he said with strange cheer. "I am poor now."

"Done. Okay, we're almost a fifth of the way there."

"Smooth sailing!"

"Sure, sure. Don't worry about your shirt; I'll help you get undressed."

"You insatiable slattern! I might have known you'd leap at the opportunity to molest me. That's why you got rid of everyone else, isn't that right?"

"Gary went to town to get the doctor. Harry and Larry took the day off to go trout fishing. It's just us right now."

"Outstanding! I stand ready to be molested, Natalie, my darling, my dove."

"Blake . . ."

"Oh please, please molest me."

"If you still want me when you're better—"

"Oh, I will! I want you more than Henry the Eighth wanted a son."

"Wow." She wouldn't deny it; she was touched. She might have done a little research about the people Blake talked about like they were still alive. So she might have read that Henry VIII basically split his country down the middle out of lust for Anne Boleyn's loins. (The end of that great love story was somewhat less romantic.) "Then I guess it's a date. Don't worry; I won't hold you to it when you come to your senses."

"I will never come to my senses!" He flourished his free hand and they nearly fell back down the steps. "Why are there an extra five hundred steps here?"

"Wondering that myself," she grunted, helping him farther up the stairs. "No more flailing, please."

"Why are you so beautiful?"

She snorted. "I'm not."

"Only beautiful people deny being beautiful."

"Unattractive people deny being beautiful, too."

"Ha! That tickles!"

"Is it your phone?" It was in his back pocket, so every few minutes his butt vibrated, which prompted a burst of giggles from him. "Tell your butt to take a message."

"Ba-dum-tsshhh!"

"Cripes' sake."

"This was all worth it to have you touch me. Infections, fever, the possible onset of delirium—"

"Possible?"

"Worth it. All of it."

"You've lost your damned mind," she said, not without admiration.

"It's probably Venice-Rake. Messaging my butt. Venice-Rake is different from Terrible-Rake."

"Okay."

"Rake is not terrible. Mitchell Banaan is terrible."

This time she was the one who nearly pulled them back downstairs. "Oh, man. Got to have a face-to-face with the prince of darkness, huh? What was he even doing in town?"

"Satan's intern."

"Okay, that didn't clarify anything."

"Well, Satan needed an intern; what's so difficult to understand?" Blake shuddered against her. "He was terrible, Natalie. My grandfather. Not Satan. If Mom gives me my money back I will buy every company he ever works at and fire him, except he's probably retired, so I can't actually do that. I'll just dislocate his arms."

"Blake . . ."

"I know; it's not a perfect solution."

"Almost there, Blake."

"Not almost." He leaned down and nuzzled the top of her head. "Cherries. Odd."

"It's just shampoo."

"You're not 'just' anything. Not almost. Home. We're already there, didn't you know? Not almost home. Home. Even if Sweetheart is dying."

"It's not." *Step, step, heave. Step, step, heave arrgghh so heavy!* "Town's like you; it's going to recover."

"What a tender metaphor. I may be in love with you."

She closed her eyes. This was worse than finding him unconscious in the kitchen garden. He was saying things she never knew she wanted to hear, wonderful things she could see herself getting greedy for. She wanted him to never stop. And of course he was going to stop. He loved her in his delirium; in his right mind he would remember she had lied because of money.

"It's fine," he said when she hadn't responded. "I know you aren't. I would never have expected it. I don't look for it now."

"Blake." It came out a croak; she had wept more this week than she had in the last five years and dammit now she was crying *again*. "Blake, you're right; I don't feel the way you do."

He sighed into the top of her head. "Ah."

"I *know* I'm in love with you."

I'm in love with you. Cripes, was it really that simple and stunning? From the beginning she had wanted him to think well of her, wanted to impress him, had taken pride in how hard he worked, and hated him because she knew he would leave. Told herself she hated that he was leaving *the town*. The deeper she got with her lies and manipulation, the worse for both of them—him because he deserved the truth. Her because she knew it would all end soon enough and she'd have no one to blame but herself. Her mother had called her Irish/Native American . . . Irarican! "The pride and stubbornness of both cultures, Nat, poor kiddo." In that moment, she wanted her mother more than she had since the dizzying numb weeks after the funeral.

"I should have told you. I was too chickenshit. I love you and I love all your weird ways, because our weird ways complement each other."

"This is a wonderful day."

She smiled. Only four hundred steps to go, subjectively speaking. "Is it?"

He squeezed her waist, radically reducing her air supply. "Are you in love with my fever?"

"Definitely not. What's funny is, even though you're delirious, this isn't even the weirdest conversation we've had."

"Is this Florence Nightingale syndrome? No, that would apply if it was me falling for you." He gasped. "Do *I* have Florence Nightingale syndrome?"

"There's a lot going on with you right now, Blake, but Florence Nightingale syndrome isn't part of it." At last they were in the attic. "Going to put you on the bed now."

"Finally! Ravage me, Natalie Lane!"

She eased him down as carefully as she could, relieving him of his phone on the way. "Okay, first things first, time to make some calls."

"No, you have to undress me first; I don't think we should explore the kinky end of the spectrum just yet. It's not that I won't make love with you while you dial random strangers; I would just prefer something more straightforward for our first coitus."

"For God's sake."

"Rake said using 'intercourse' to describe coitus was preventing me from having intercourse."

"Yeah, but that's . . . that's not better."

"Call it what you will." He flung out his arms dramatically, tried to roll over, failed. "Ah, you don't mind the woman-superior position, do you? I'm feeling a bit light-headed."

"Here's what I like: missionary for intimacy, on all fours for intensity, and me on top for fun."

He *stared* at her. "I can work with that."

She felt bad for teasing him. "Never mind. When you're

feeling better, okay? I mean . . . if you still want to. I meant what I said earlier. I won't hold you to any of this."

"How unfortunate for you, because I intend to hold you to all of it. Also, did you take my phone so you can strip me, pose me in humiliating positions, and then take pictures and send them to everyone on my contact list?"

"I took it to call your family, ya idjit."

"I love your adorable pet names for me. Idjit, moron, Vegas Douche—"

"I don't call you that anymore," she was quick to assure him. "And I'll beat the shit out of anyone who does."

"Excellent! You'll solve my Mitchell Banaan problem; how clever you are. This is odd."

"Got *that* right." His iPhone was passworded, which wasn't acceptable. She needed family contact info.

"This is odd."

"You said that, baby."

"Baby. Yes. I want to have your baby."

She giggled. "It *has* been a long time since you've had intercourse if that's what you think will happen."

"Odd."

"Yes, okay, what's your password?"

"When I've pictured you standing over me while I'm in bed, I'm always erect."

"It's just the fever, baby; you'll be getting it up again in no time."

"I like that you aren't afraid to show confidence in my penis."

"Password, moron." She tried for stern, but exasperated fondness came out instead.

"WWND."

"Okay. Something to do with the House of Lancaster or Richard the Third?"

"What Would Natalie Do."

"Dammit, Blake!" She bent and kissed him swiftly on the mouth. "You're wonderful, even when you're out of your head.

"Did you hear that?" He was relaxing into the bed after trying to grab her and missing by two feet. "You said I was wonderful."

"Rest, Blake."

"You always have good advice."

"Close your eyes, baby."

He did.

Thirty-five

When Blake next opened his eyes, his mom and grandmother were bending over him. "Aaagghh! My heart. Christ."

"How are you, boy?" Shannah asked, anxiety making her normally firm contralto thready and unsure.

"My brain is on fire."

"That's not far from the truth." Blake noticed another woman preparing to leave. She had gorgeous deep brown skin with reddish undertones, high cheekbones, and small, wide-set dark eyes. Her hair was cut in a neatly trimmed Afro streaked with silver, and she was holding a bag, preparing to depart, but turned when he'd shouted. In his fright upon waking with Shannah and the nuclear option looming over him, he hadn't noticed anyone else at first. "You've got an infection, Mr. Tarbell, and a temp of one-oh-two, an improvement over one-oh-four, which we're bringing down."

"It's okay, Blake," his mother said, as if worried he was

going to leap to his feet and charge the woman with malpractice. "I told Dr. Wen about allergies and things."

"I'm not allergic to anything."

"I told her that."

The nuclear option spoke for the first time. "You'll be eating antibiotics for a few days, Blake."

"The breakfast of champions," he muttered. He took a closer look at the doctor. "What is this? Is this a house call? Really?"

"Really," Dr. Wen assured him. "The clinic closed down and the nearest hospital is over two hours away. For something like this, unless your fever won't break or the infection worsens, it's fine to treat you at home. If it does worsen, there's always the air ambulance."

"A house call," he mused. "Then . . . how long have I been asleep? How did I go back in time? It's 1920, right?"

"If it was 1920," was the dry response, "would I be a doctor?"

"Excellent point. All right, run along to the next century, then."

"Good advice." She glanced at Natalie, who was sitting on the foot of the bed, gnawing on a knuckle. "You're right. He's engaging."

"Yes, I'm engaging to Natalie! And she's engaging to me. After I propose. Mom, may I have some money for a ring?" There was no response, and her eyes seemed overly bright. He peered at her and realized, "Are you in your pajamas?"

Shannah glanced down at herself. "Yes."

"Pity, I was hoping it was a fever dream." His mother was inordinately fond of ankle-length velour nightgowns and matching velour robes and slippers in various pastel shades. In winter, she was a walking electric chair, at times generating so much static she fried the thermostat.

"We came as soon as Natalie called us," the nuclear option explained. "Your mother had more important things on her mind than outfit coordination."

"S'fine, Nonna," he said, drowsy again. "Natalie will fix it."

"Whatever you say, Blake." A soothing pat, and Blake noticed his hands had been cleaned and bandaged. He was also wearing his last pair of clean black boxers, and a clean T-shirt.

"No!"

"What?" Every woman in the room turned her full attention on him, including Dr. Wen, who hurried back to his bedside.

"What is it? Pain? Are you having trouble breathing?"

"I missed our sex!" he cried to Natalie, gesturing to his clean clothes. "It must have been incredible!"

"You . . . um—" She was so pretty when she blushed. "We didn't. Do that, I mean."

Oh. He hadn't realized he'd been speaking out loud. No problem, it wasn't at all embarrassing, like it would have been if he had said he dreamed of pressing his lips to every inch of her, repeatedly, for the next fifty years.

"Blake."

He knew she would taste even better than she looked and he couldn't wait to catalog all her flavors.

"Blake! Maybe we can talk about this later?"

My God, Natalie is telepathic! She's reading my mind! This is incredible!

"I'm not telepathic, ya idjit. You're still saying these things out loud."

"The last ones," his grandmother said helpfully, "you shouted."

"So wise, Natalie." He sighed. "Come here and sex me again. I promise to pay attention this time."

"I didn't sex you the first— No. I'm not going to try and have a logical discussion while you're sick."

"So wise. If I die, clear my browser history."

"Now that," she said with a grin, "is the first sensible thing you've said in a while."

Blake slept.

Thirty-six

Natalie woke with a start; she'd nodded off in the chair beside Blake's bed, which was a miracle. It was a rickety wooden chair she'd dragged up from the kitchen, and not even a little comfortable. It was late morning by the looks of it; the attic was splashed with sunshine and she realized for the first time in forever that she was ravenous. And that she needed to brush her teeth.

As if picking up on her hunger

(heh, maybe Shannah's the telepath),

the door to the attic opened and Natalie heard Shannah and Ruth coming up the stairs. She could smell the muffins and met them at the top.

"Mind readers," she said, then promptly snatched a blueberry muffin and wolfed it in four bites.

"Chew, dear; you're no good to Blake if someone has to give you a tracheotomy. Here." Ruth handed her a large glass of orange juice, which Natalie decimated in three swallows.

"Oh God, thank you. I had no idea how much I needed that until I smelled you." She was already settling back in the chair beside him. "Uh, smelled the food, I meant. Not that you guys smell." *I probably smell*, she realized. *I think I showered the morning Blake got sick . . . or was it the night before? Cripes, what day is it?*

"Natalie, I want you to take a nap," Shannah told her. "I haven't seen you sleep since we got here."

"No, I'm fine. He might want me. I'm fine."

"He absolutely does want you," Ruth said dryly, "and don't you think you should get your rest so you'll be ready when he is?"

Is Blake's grandma telling me to rest up for sex?

"I'm fine."

Blake rolled over on his side and slept on. Every woman tensed when he moved and relaxed when he kept sleeping. Natalie didn't know she was going to brush his hair away from his eyes until she did it.

"It's my fault he's sick."

"Do not start, young lady," Shannah warned her. "My son is a grown man and has been taking care of himself since before he was voting age. I warned him about his hands myself."

Natalie couldn't accept it. Shannah was just being nice. Granted, she didn't exactly have a strong rep for that behavior, but it was the only explanation that worked. "Dammit! I knew he felt too warm when we were hugging in the barn."

Ruth cleared her throat. "Oh? Is 'hugging' a euphemism for—"

"Hugging is *hugging*, ma'am. Cripes."

Shannah was staring down at him with an expression Natalie had never seen, thought no one could ever see, on her face:

helpless and hopeless. "If you're to blame, Natalie, then I am, too. I put him out here and I knew he'd be in over his head. You at least showed him what to do. I just abandoned him there."

"Not true. I know you kept calling him, offering to come to the farm, or asking him to come have supper with you at the B and B. He's the one who didn't want to—" *Spend time with you,* but that wasn't at all tactful, so she swallowed the rest.

"But when it all came out—when you were having lunch at the bed-and-breakfast the day Ruth came—"

"I remember." She did. A day of infamy, to be sure, and one she never wanted to relive.

"Why didn't he just ask me for his money back?"

Natalie stared at Shannah for a long moment, and Ruth leveled her with a look. "What an insanely stupid question."

"Oh." She seemed to hear herself, and her mouth twisted into a wry smile. "Well, yes. I suppose it is."

"He gets a double dose of pride," Ruth added. "Tarbell-Banaan pride."

"Banaan-Tarbell pride." Flustered, she started to pace, and Natalie realized with utter amazement that Shannah Banaan was *wringing her hands* like a helpless heroine out of a fairy tale waiting for the men to swoop in and save her. "D'you know what Roger told me?"

"Roger's a soon-to-be-retired pig farmer," Natalie explained. "Blake stole his last pig. Um, liberated the White Rose of York is what I meant."

Ruth remained unruffled. "All right. I want to hear the rest of Shannah's story, but then we're going to come back to the pig thing, dear."

"Yeah, I don't blame you. Half the town thinks he's crushing on your daughter-in-law."

"Really? Any truth to that rumor?"

"I think so. And I'm pretty sure she likes him back. She tolerates him way more than she tolerates anyone else. I think if she wasn't hanging with him, she'd be a lot less pleasant. I mean, coming back here to try to fix her family's mess before the judgment of the whole town is her worst nightmare. Roger makes it bearable, I think."

"Why, he sounds lovely."

"*Ladies.*" Shannah saw she had their attention and continued but didn't look as irked as Natalie would have anticipated. "Roger told me my father came to town and he and Blake almost got into a fight! That was how he met his grandfather."

"That pompous ass," Ruth said dismissively. Natalie felt her eyebrows arch, and Shannah swung around to stare at her mother-in-law. "What? He is."

"Yes. But how did you know? You haven't been in town long enough to hear much gossip about him."

Ruth said nothing, just stepped to the dresser and began arranging Blake's medication bottles.

"Mrs. Tarbell?"

No response. Natalie started to get nervous. What was she missing? And would the women come to blows? Was she expected to referee? *Maybe I'll take that nap. Is there a way to retroactively nap so I miss the entire conversation leading to the brawl?*

Shannah tried again. "Ruth?"

The nuclear option turned back around and beheld her

daughter-in-law with an expression of fond annoyance. "I called him, of course."

"You— *What?* When? Before you came to town?"

"Years ago. When the boys were teenagers. When I got to meet you for the first time. And you were very polite, though you didn't want me there, and the boys were lovely, and so protective of you. Even when I explained who I was they wouldn't take that at face value. They watched how I behaved for a long time before relaxing their guard. Before letting themselves think of me as family. I thought— I thought if your family knew how hard you had worked and what a good mother you were, and how wonderful the boys were, they would regret cutting ties. They would want to be in all your lives. I thought they would help you."

Shannah smiled, a bitter grimace that made her look like she'd been chewing lemon rind. "They weren't interested, though, were they? Not until you told them your son had left their grandsons millions of dollars. I always wondered how they found out. I knew I didn't tell them."

"I told them a few other things, too," Ruth muttered. "At length. And I might have called back twice, because he kept interrupting my train of thought by hanging up on me."

A strangled sound from Shannah, which Natalie suspected might be a gulped laugh.

"I've always admired you, Shannah. You're hard, but only because you had to be. And you love your boys. That would have been enough for me, but the twins are a part of you, my dear; you and my son made them; they are the *best* part of the two of you. Did you really think I didn't love you, too?"

Shannah shook her head. A lone tear tracked down her cheek and she rubbed it away with a savage gesture.

Ruth just *tsk*ed. "Like I said: hard. Oh, Shannah. There's not much I wouldn't do for you, silly girl."

Oh my God someone called Shannah Tarbell a silly girl and wasn't knifed! What is happening in this weird wonderful town?

Somehow the women were hugging, and Natalie brushed her hands over her eyes to make sure she wasn't leaking, because they felt suspiciously moist. There was movement on the bed and she looked down to see Blake blinking up at them.

"My fever's back," he said, observing the embracing women, then caught her hand and kissed the knuckles. "I don't mind."

"Shut up," she said with all the warmth she would have put into *God, I adore you and would love for you to have my children.* "Rest."

"Captain, my captain," he mumbled, then dozed off. He didn't let go of her hand. Natalie didn't mind.

Thirty-seven

She woke with a start to find Shannah easing her out of the chair and into bed beside Blake. "Hmm? Is he okay? What? Are there muffins? What?"

"Hush, you'll sleep easier on the bed. We've given up trying to make you go to your room. Or to take a shower," Shannah added in a mutter.

"You caught on quicker than my parents did." Natalie yawned. Then stiffened. "Margaret of Anjou and the White Rose of York! I've got to—"

"Shush." A less-than-gentle shove and Natalie sprawled beside Blake, who slumbered on, oblivious. "I know about the piglet . . . are you talking about that strange grumpy pony? She refuses to be moved. Sit up a little, hon, and look out the window."

Natalie did as she was bid and wondered if Blake's delirium was catching. It was light again, but not for long, and she could see the pony was alternately cropping grass and staring up at the attic window. *Stalker. Stalker pony!*

"What the hell has gotten into that thing?" Natalie wondered aloud. "If it was any other animal, any other animal including a black mamba or a wolverine or a scorpion, I would assume she'd gotten fond of Blake. But she's not any other animal."

"I'm afraid that's the only explanation, unless your pony is in it for some elaborate long con and this is how she's going to lull Blake so as to eventually kick him to death."

"See, *that* makes sense. But I need to make sure they're—"

"You need to stay with my grandson." Ruth spoke for the first time and Natalie started. More proof of exhaustion; the attic wasn't so big she wouldn't notice the nuclear option. "You've made that plain. But don't worry about the chores. That strange man with all the freckles said he would take care of them, and he has been."

"That's actually weirder than Blake's delirium."

"I think my grandson nearly committing vehicular man-slaughter on the man made an impression. I've never seen such a hard worker."

Natalie started to laugh and, for a moment, was afraid she wouldn't be able to stop.

"So go back to sleep." Shannah's firm hand was on Natalie's shoulder, pushing her back down on the bed. "Heartbreak is in good hands." That couldn't be true, Natalie decided, but was too exhausted to question it. "Blake is better. Dr. Wen said he should get up tomorrow. Time for you to rest, my dear."

My dear? This can't be real life. I think we've all got Blake's fe-ver. I've never seen Shannah smile so much. And I think I heard Roger downstairs last night wooing her—God, I hope he didn't take his piglet back. And the nuclear option is pretty great. I'm not sure Blake had any idea he had such a wonderful family.

"Just for a little while," Natalie temporized, then ruined it by yawning.

The moment the door to the attic closed, Blake muttered, "Alone at last."

She jumped, startled, and tried to sit up, but he threw an arm across her waist and held her beside him with gentle strength.

"No, no. Not when I've at last gotten you in my bed. I had to fake an infection and a fever—"

"And two days of delirious bullshit, and almost running Gary down like a gopher, and inadvertently helping your mom and grandma bond."

"See the lengths I'll go to in order to have you?"

"Idiot. You're not fooling me. You didn't plan shit." She curled into his side and felt herself relax for the first time in two days. "I'm so glad you're better."

"Mmmm."

He's better, yeah, and that's a good thing, a wonderful thing, but it's time to make good on my promise.

"Uh . . . Blake."

"No."

"Listen, I don't think you'll remember, but you said a bunch of crazy stuff—"

"No."

"—and I promised I wouldn't hold you to any of it—"

"No."

"—and I wouldn't want you to think anything has to change between us."

"No."

"I mean, I hope you can forgive me for lying and tricking you, I'd like *that* to change, but as for the rest of it—"

"Nothing has changed."

"Oh." *Don't cry. At least, not lying beside him like you are. Find an excuse and get the hell out of here and then have your break-down. Then find Gary's stash of cookie dough and gobble every bite.* "Okay. Listen, my teeth feel like they've got little tiny sweaters on, so I'll just hit the bathroom and—" *What? Never return to the attic?* Return but accept that she loved him too late and would pay the price by never seeing him again? Pretend they were pals and wave and smile when he went back to his life? "So I'll just, um, go? I guess?"

"Nothing has changed," he said again, sounding so confident and calm she wanted to smack him, then kiss him, then burst into tears. And maybe smack him again. "You're in love with me. I'm quite certain I'm in love with you. I'm going to kiss every inch of you, and have your baby somehow." He turned to her and pressed a kiss to the corner of her mouth. When he spoke, his deep voice vibrated all through her. "I. Remember. Everything."

And just like that, she was crying *again*. But this time, the tears didn't scald. They seemed to sweep away doubt and fear. She hadn't known crying could do that. She thought her mom might have known.

"When did you know?"

It was twenty minutes later. He had insisted on walking to the bathroom under his own power and emerged after a few minutes with a clean, scrubbed face and minty breath. Natalie had done the same. What she really wanted was a shower, but she wasn't willing to leave him that long and wasn't yet prepared to share a shower with him.

Soon, though, she thought, and the certainty filled her like a warm glow. *After we make love for the first time, then we'll take a long, hot shower together.*

"Know what?" she said, stifling a yawn.

"That you . . ."—he paused, then continued almost shyly, "loved me."

"Well." She drummed her fingers on his chest, thinking. She loved resting her ear against his heart, hearing his baritone rumble through her. She hadn't known before Blake that she had a voice kink. "I don't know the exact day. Your mannerisms started changing, if that's the right word. Don't spit out a dictionary definition of 'mannerisms,'" she added in alarm as Blake's lips parted. She kept going so as not to give him a chance to interrupt her with an Oxford definition. "I almost *didn't* notice until it was too late. One day I realized you used to ask, 'Where do you keep the pitchforks?' 'Where do you keep the BENGAY.' Like that. But after a while it was 'we.' 'Where do we keep the BENGAY? What did Gary do with my pitchfork?'"

"We keep it in every medicine cabinet in every bathroom in the farmhouse," was his prompt reply, which earned him a bright smile, "and some in Main One. We're almost out. Again," which earned him a snicker. "So my constant need to smear terrible-smelling ointment all over my aching muscles endeared me to you, eh?"

"Irresistible. Naw, that's a lie; you were pretty cute before that, too. But I was able to tell myself it was strictly physical.

It's okay to find a jerkass physically attractive if you tell your-self it's only about his broad shoulders, his hair the color of late-summer wheat, his piercing blue eyes, blah-blah."

"Why were you at the B and B my first day here?"

She burst out laughing. "God, that's right; you saw me in a suit and everything. You looked so *weird*, high up in that damn truck; you looked so out of place but kind of determined, too. I liked you right away."

"Until you found out I was Banaan spawn."

"Well." She coughed. "We had to close the bank for a couple of days; they found asbestos."

"Studies have shown sometimes it's actually safer to leave the asbestos where it is, assuming it's intact, of course, and—"

"Yes, Blake, I know, it was my bank and my asbestos, and I paid for a couple of expert opinions and did my own research, too, okay?"

"Sorry."

"Show-off," she said without heat. "Anyway, it worked out fine—that one thing worked out fine—but we were working out of the B and B for a couple of days. It's down to me and a couple of part-timers now, so it wasn't a perfect solution, but it was what we had."

"I liked you at first sight, too," he said, pulling her more firmly against him. "God, you feel good. Dammit, I have to insist Dr. Wen issue me a clean bill of health immediately."

"So we can perform coitus on each other?"

"Wow. Rake is right. That is terribly unromantic."

"Coitus me, Blake. Coitus me till I scream. Coitus me all over!"

"Point made, my God, stop it." He poked her in the ribs,

smiling when she giggled. "I'm half-afraid *this* is the fever dream. That I'll wake up and you'll be back to hating me again."

"Nobody hates you. Not even Margaret of Anjou."

He had been leaning in for another kiss and snickered against Natalie's mouth. The snickering turned into kisses, and though they didn't exactly insert Tab A into Slot B, they explored each other's bodies with gentle hands and light touches, and sighed into each other's mouths, and at one point she was trembling so hard she thought she might die from it, and what a sweet death it would be, and Blake whispered over and over, "Natalie Lane, Natalie Lane, I love you. I love you." And maybe Blake was right to worry; maybe this *was* the fever dream. In which case, Natalie hoped they never recovered.

Oh, that's not healthy, was her last drowsy thought. But she couldn't work up enough concern to truly fret and so slept instead.

Thirty-eight

Gary worked tirelessly, which Natalie and Blake giggled over and chastised each other for. "It's awful: He's scared to death; he thinks you really tried to kill him."

"I know; I've tried to approach him to apologize, but he just runs away from me and works on something else."

Dr. Wen came, examined, pronounced Blake much improved, left.

Harry kept sending up the most delicious invalid food Blake had ever tasted. "What, exactly, is my incentive to get better?" he asked, moaning around a mouthful of poached egg. Harry had gently simmered the farm-fresh eggs, with their bright orange yolks, in water. When the yolks were runny, but the whites were firm, he slid them onto two thick slices of perfectly toasted homemade potato bread, then topped them with chopped prosciutto. The day before he had simmered a gorgeous chicken soup all afternoon on the stove, tormenting everyone with working nasal passages, and Blake's bowl was thick with noodles and fresh vegetables and meat so savory and tender it nearly dissolved in his mouth. The Darrel twins had dropped off five pounds of strawberries, so the household enjoyed fresh fruit smoothies for breakfast (blended with yogurt, ice, orange juice) and strawberry milk shakes (berries + homemade frozen custard = *oh my Gawwwd*) for dessert.

"Just when I thought he couldn't top the chilled cucumber soup." He slurped down the rest of the egg. "I'm sorry; I'm aware this is disgusting to watch."

"It's not disgusting to watch. I'm glad to see you feeling better."

"And I repeat, where's the incentive to get well? I have you all to myself; my mother and grandmother are getting along; Gary is doing an insane amount of work; Margaret of Anjou almost doesn't loathe me. . . ." He paused, finished his toast, considered, and then said in all seriousness, "I think these last two days have been the happiest in my life. Isn't that wonderfully insane?"

"No. And the incentive is missionary for intimacy, me on all fours for intensity, me on top for fun."

He had frozen in mid-chew, then gulped and managed, "Fun?"

"I just really like to bounce around up there, y'know? Have a good time. You can hang on to my hips and watch. Jeez!" She dived and barely caught his plate in time.

"Sorry. I lost all sensation in my hands because the blood left my fingers and rushed somewhere else. Now I feel vulnerable and scared. Hold me?"

"I still want to hear how you're going to have my baby."

"Practice," was the solemn reply. "Hold me? Never mind. I'll hold you. It's easier to hold you when you're naked."

"A-*hem*."

They looked over and Blake saw the color rise in Natalie's cheeks. He'd been so busy picturing her charms bouncing around that he hadn't heard his mom and grandmother come up the stairs. "Away, harpies!" he commanded. "I'm not well enough for visitors."

"Shut up, boy; say hello to your guest."

Roger, the last one up the steps, peeked around Blake's mother and waved. "Hiya, Blake. Feelin' better?"

"You can't take the White Rose of York!"

"*Blake Tarbell!*" his mother hissed.

"Hello, Roger, I'm feeling quite a lot better, thank you so much for asking, and if you touch my piglet I will break this plate over your head. Then I will unleash my love, Natalie Lane, upon you and you will feel as if the Furies are plucking at your internal organs. Death will be a welcome respite."

"I don't know if I'd do all that," she confessed, elbowing him. They had been sitting on his bed, knees touching, while they ate breakfast. Now Natalie stacked their plates and beckoned the visitors closer. "We were just—"

"Yes, we heard your plans for the afternoon," Ruth said, eyes gleaming as she smiled. "So sorry to interrupt."

"Liar."

"Well, yes."

"So guess who I ran into?" Roger said, making himself comfortable in one of the several chairs Natalie had brought up when townies starting showing up to pay their respects and wish Blake a speedy recovery.

"Sandy Cort," Blake replied at once.

"Dang, you're good. Said you and your grandpa got into it downtown the other day."

"Apparently I was feverish even then. It's the only explanation for why I didn't wring his wattled rooster neck."

Shannah burst out laughing, checked herself, and tried to reestablish her stern *mind me, boy* expression.

"Before he left he was tellin' everybody that he guessed you were a real man on account of standing up to him, and maybe Shannah hadn't done such a bad job."

"Oh-ho," Natalie said. She had such a mischievous look on her face Blake almost forgot his deep regret at letting Mitchell Banaan live to see the sun come up. "So that's how he's playing it."

"I don't understand." Nor did Blake care, but he did adore that expression on her face, and resolved to do whatever he must to cause it to reappear.

"His little ambush didn't go how he planned, so he's putting the 'you stood up to me; that was the test' spin on it. You know, pretending that he provoked you to *make* you stand up to him, as opposed to what really happened: You were disgusted with him, unafraid of him, and he knew it, and everybody knows it, and he's humiliated while pretending he's not. He won't be back. Uh, sorry, Shannah, I didn't mean—"

"That," Blake's mother replied, "is a dead-on analysis. Why in the world are you apologizing?"

"Social pressure," she confessed, and now it was Blake's

turn to poke his elbow into her side. "Oof! I didn't know you were back, Roger. That was a quick vacation."

"Oh. Yes. The ticket was nonrefundable, so I didn't want— But it wasn't as much fun as— I mean, I didn't know how long your mama was going to visit, and didn't want to miss— I can go back anytime."

My, my. Roger, you balding dog, you've got designs on my mother. That alone would be intriguing enough, but from the way his mom was blushing and looking everywhere but at Roger, it appeared to be mutual.

Blake supposed if he were a better son he would be over-protective and bristling and give off a strong *you hurt her, I'll kill you* impression. But the thought of his lonely mother liking someone, and someone as pleasant as Roger, was a welcome one. Now that Blake had Natalie

(I cannot believe she loves me I should fall prey to infection every week)

he wanted nothing more for his mother (and yes, Rake, too, terrible as the man was) than the happiness he had been fortunate enough to find. Stumble into. Blunder onto. Whatever.

"Yes, but where do you go when you visit these places?"

"Oh, just . . ." Roger made a vague gesture. "You know."

Not at all, actually. Perhaps the townspeople are right; perhaps he is a former spy disguised as a former pig farmer.

"About the White Rose of York." Roger cleared his throat and the rocking chair creaked as he fidgeted. "Didn't come here to snatch her back. It's fine if you want to keep her; I just didn't have the heart to let her starve when her litter rejected her. But what will you do with her? I mean—" He looked around the attic. "What happens next? Where will you go? *Will* you go? I only ask because of the piglet."

"He can go anywhere he wishes," Shannah replied quietly. She went to his dresser, plucked up his checkbook, then walked to the bed and handed it to him. It didn't actually confer any privileges on him—his mother didn't have signatory power on *that* account, thank you very much—but Blake understood the symbolism of the action. "And do anything he likes. He's a grown man with a trust fund of several million. It's not for— It's not for anyone to say what he'll do or not do."

Wrong, Blake thought. As far as he was concerned, Natalie Lane had a say. But no one else. Well. *Maybe* Rake. And his mother. And the nuclear option. At the least, Blake would bend an attentive ear to their advice in the future. He was not unaware that his own arrogance played as much a part in landing him here as his mother's.

"Ah!" he said, not hiding the pleasure in his tone. He waved the checkbook like a flag. "No longer grounded! To celebrate my good fortune, I shall throw a kegger party tonight when you aren't around, Mom."

She didn't smile. "I was wrong."

His own smirk faded. "Mom, I understand why you did it. I'm not holding you up to shame."

"I was wrong," she said again, as if he hadn't spoken. *Guess some things never changed, and thank goodness. And is she really doing this in front of everyone?* "Wrong to judge you and wrong to penalize you for what my family did." *She was! She had an audience and didn't give, as Natalie would put it, a ripe shit.* "My family—you have to understand. It's not that they didn't love me or take care of me. My sibs certainly turned out fine. *I* turned out fine. It's just . . . the minute things get hard—and they almost always do—my family quits on whatever it is. Farms, businesses—"

"Daughters," he suggested quietly.

"Yes," she replied, and sniffed. She looked at the floor for a moment, thinking, then looked up, and they locked gazes again. "And I swore—I swore on my life and yours and your brother's, I swore I'd never, ever pull a Banaan. That's what they actually call it here, did you know? If you give up on something, you're pulling a Banaan. You heard about Heartbreak, how it came to be built and why they call the barn Main One—"

"Yes indeed. One of our relatives."

A wry smile. "The only Banaan to ever stick to anything, and it cost him his happiness. He was our cautionary tale, you know? He was the lesson: see what happens when you don't know when to walk away? And we've been giving up ever since. It's practically on the fucking family crest."

Holy God. Blake could count on one hand how often he'd heard his mother drop the f-bomb.

"I wouldn't let it happen again," she finished. "And you paid for it. I have no excuse."

"With respect, Mom, I must disagree." This, as he realized on the street while confronting his grandfather, put his mother's horrified rage in an entirely new light, why her calls to Blake in Vegas were getting increasingly desperate and strained. She was seeing her family history unfold yet again and would have wanted to do whatever she could to change it and not count the cost until late in the game. "Or perhaps we must agree to disagree, like we did the second time George W. Bush got elected—"

"He did not get elected a second time!" she screeched in response.

Ah! There's the mother I grew up with.

"I understand, and I'm sorry for giving in to what appears to be the Banaan genetic flaw—"

"It was a terribly unfair thing to do to you. I'm so sorry, Blake."

Blake worked to hide his astonishment. Apologies were as rare as the f-bomb. Not that she didn't feel remorse, but Shannah tended to *demonstrate* her apologies: being extra nice, buying him something she knew he wanted, bending a few household rules. She would show, never tell. She had paled a bit when he didn't immediately reply, and he cursed himself for the lapse. "Mom, I—"

"Forgive me," she whispered as a lone tear tracked down her soft, barely wrinkled cheek.

"For heaven's sake." He tossed back the blankets and stood, squashed the dizziness that made the room jump for a second, then pulled her into a hug. "I forgive you, and you'll forgive me, yes? And then we can plot your father's kidnapping and mutilation."

"Agreed," she said, and laughed while the last tear escaped her eye.

"Welp," Roger said, getting out of the chair, "don't want to tire you out. Sandy Cort made me promise to visit you and so I have."

"You two make each other promise things often, don't you?" Blake asked.

"Yep." Roger grimaced. "He's the one got me into my hobby in the first place." Then, to Shannah, he asked diffidently, "Walk me out?"

"Yes. Of course." She kissed Blake's cheek and stepped out of the hug. "Back in a few minutes."

"See you around, Vegas D—"

"Don't!" Natalie shrieked.

"—ude. What?" Roger glanced around, surprised. "That's what we call him. The kids at the bus stop started it; they love that damn truck you're always tooling around in. The loud horn, y'know, you're always honking it for 'em."

"I don't mind," he replied, outwardly flustered and secretly pleased. He loved that horn. He was giving serious thought to buying the Supertruck outright. Or did they make them in hybrids? A hybrid Supertruck with a tremendous loud horn would be spectacular.

"Right, well, they started calling you Vegas Dude and the name stuck after a bit."

"I thought it was Vegas Douche."

"Oh. Well." Shrug. "A few people call you that. No one whose opinion counts, though, so that's all right."

"I guess it is," he replied, amused, and watched Roger escort his mother down the stairs. Then: "Is it too soon to ask for more poached eggs?"

Thirty-nine

Outside, they visited the White Rose of York and then Shannah walked with Roger to his truck. Once there, he seemed to be having difficulty saying whatever was on his mind. He plucked his phone from the front pocket of his bib overalls and looked at her, then at the phone, then back up at her.

"Roger?" She made her voice as gentle as she could. "Is something wrong?"

"Noooo. I don't think. I guess it depends on if you like it."

"All right."

"My last vacation." He did something to his phone, then thrust it at her so quickly she fumbled and nearly dropped it. "Cripes! Sorry. There. Look now."

She did, and it took a few seconds for her to realize what she was seeing.

"Are you . . . Is that Brad Pitt?"

"Not the real one." He looked away for a second, then met her gaze with a sheepish smile. "I, uh, I love museums. All kinds, but especially that kind. That's where I was, the Holly-wood Wax Museum. I sort of play God there."

This was it. She was about to have the stroke her family had long predicted. Though they hadn't predicted a happiness stroke.

"I like to rearrange the exhibits when the staff isn't look-ing," he practically whispered. "In my head canon, Brad Pitt adopted a pack of orphans with his life partner, Jamie Foxx. Plus, I always thought Sandra Bullock and Elvis Presley de-served a chance to be together. And at the museum, they *are*. I, um, I know that's strange."

Her lips were moving. Her voice box was vibrating; she was making noises. Speaking, probably. She had no idea what she was saying until he leaned forward and pressed his mouth to hers in a firm, unapologetic, wonderful kiss.

"Oh, good," she murmured against his mouth, which was now curved into a delighted smile. "I told you to kiss me. I was wondering what I was saying."

"You told me to kiss you," he agreed. "Best order I ever got in my life. You gonna tell me to do that again? I'd sure like that."

"Oh yes. You'll have to come with me to see the boys for their birthday. I'll show you my scrapbooks. Have you been to Madame Tussauds?"

"London? Sure."

"The one in Hong Kong?"

He pulled back and gave her a long, loving look. "Nope. That one got by me."

"You'll come with me," she decided. "You want to, don't you?" His smile was reply enough. His big, rough hands had gone around her waist, but she had seen him handle the White Rose of York and wasn't afraid of his touch. "We'll go to the one in Washington, D.C., and the one in Berlin, too." She paused, considering. "Don't you think Marilyn Monroe and Gwyneth Paltrow would make a lovely couple?"

"I think," he said, after kissing her again, "it's goddamn genius."

Forty

"Your mom's apology was really good," Natalie said when she and Blake were alone again, "but you never answered Roger's question. What are you going to do now?"

Blake pulled back from where they'd been sitting shoulder to shoulder on his bed and gave her a look. "Don't you know?"

"I know what I hope you're going to do," she said after thinking about it for a few seconds. This was tricky ground; she wanted to make sure she said what she meant. "But it's like Shannah said. It's not for anybody to tell you what to do or where to go; it's for you to do that."

"Oh no, that's not at all true, Natalie, with respect to you and my mother. But here is what I want to do, and I hope it resembles what you hope I'm going to do." He reached across her, found his phone, and pulled up his Notes app.

"Oh God. You have a list."

He glanced up. "Of course I have a list, I keep several lists, I'm not a savage. Let's see: 'Rake Is Terrible,' 'Gary Must Die,'

'Mom Is Terrible,' 'Why the Nuclear Option Might Backfire,' 'The True Fate of the Lost Princes'—ah! 'The Rest of My Life.' Here it is."

    a) propose to Natalie

    b) be engaged to Natalie for a period of no less than 30 days and no more than 730 days

    c) pay Residence Inn invoice

    d) remove all personal items from Residence Inn

    e) buy Heartbreak from seller

    f) put Heartbreak in Natalie's name

    g) move into Heartbreak with Natalie (see above, remove all personal items from Residence Inn)

    h) ensure Putt N'Go deal is off the table forever

    i) buy back foreclosed farms from Putt N'Go

    j) figure out a way to have Natalie's children

    k) if unable, discuss the possibility of Natalie bearing her own children

    l) if unable or unwilling, discuss adoption

    m) if children follow, research what is needed for them to be considered full members of the Lakota tribe

    n) also take them to Ireland

    o) and Great Britain, specifically the Tower of London, Bosworth, Stoke, Leicester Cathedral, Coventry

    p) but never Disney World

    q) slowly acclimate Margaret of Anjou to the children of my and/or Natalie's loins

    r) never eat the White Rose of York

    s) live another five decades with Natalie

    t) die

u) preferably within a half hour of Natalie
v) find out if there is an afterlife
w) if so, find Natalie
x) be together forever

Forty-one

He misread her astonishment. "Oh, sorry, too fast? Too vague?" He frowned down at his phone. "I know there is room for improvement on my list, and perhaps some of the items need to be renumbered. And of course, I'm happy to add any codicils you might have."

"Good to know," she managed. "Thanks for clearing that up. I was a little worried. About the renumbering thing." *He wants our babies to have full Lakota citizenship. Wants to find me in the afterlife. All this on a list like you'd use for groceries. God, he's so strange and he's mine.*

"So then, it's settled. Excellent. Henceforth I will take the stance that anything I must decide about my life *we* must decide about *our* life. But Natalie, I don't want to overwhelm you—"

"Too late."

"I'll wait, of course." He didn't smile, just looked at her like there wasn't anything else in the world worth looking at. "I know this is abrupt. Six weeks ago we hadn't so much as a hint the other person existed, and now our lives will be entwined until death, and hopefully afterward—I am an optimistic agnostic. Some of my items might not be at all easy, like how to restore the farms to Sweetheart and, if we can get that done to the satisfaction of all, how to get people to work the land."

"Oh." She had never been so flummoxed, or happy. "You're right; that'll be tricky. We might not get everything on your list. Er, why the time limit?"

"Beg pardon?"

"On our engagement. No less than thirty days—"

"My understanding is that even a 'quickie wedding' takes time to plan. Also, a Las Vegas wedding is not on the agenda. Never while I live. In fact, regarding the venue, I'd like to present a list of places Rake loathes. Aside from the pure joy of making you my wife, knowing Rake had to travel to a place he hates will make our day that much more meaningful."

"There's something wrong with you. What's with no more than seven hundred thirty days?"

"Yes, two years."

"Why?"

"Because." He saved his list and put the phone back on the end table. "I don't want to wait more than two years to be your husband."

"Oh. All right then. Yes. Yes to all of it. Today and forty years from now and after we've died within half an hour of each other: I'm in."

"Thank heavens." He sighed, slumping back against the headboard. "I loathe suspense. Why do you think I study history? I always know how the book will end."

"Time for a new book."

He laughed. "We've been living the new book for thirty-nine days, Natalie! We only just realized it this week."

"This is a great time to shut up and kiss me."

To her delight, Blake obliged.

"This is a terrible idea." Natalie groaned, clinging to him. "We're gonna break our fool necks."

"Worth it," Blake managed.

The reading of Blake's list had led to kissing, which led to groping, which led to showering. The attic bathroom had everything they needed, including a double shower. Natalie made Blake drink a large glass of orange juice before she stripped him, then herself, and then nudged him into the shower. As the water hit them they groaned in unison, stretching beneath the warm spray.

At first it was (mostly) business, washing each other's hair, scrubbing each other's backs. Natalie had brought her OGX cherry blossom shampoo and scrubbed the thick lather through Blake's dark blond hair. He rested his hands on her waist and luxuriated under her touch.

"I have never been sexually aroused by shampoo before."

"You've been missing out." She coaxed him into tipping his head back to rinse out the lather, then wriggled a bit as his hands slid over her ass and he pulled her closer. She was pleasantly un-surprised by the size of his cock, which was flushed deep pink, firm and fleshy and nudging up to hit his stomach. *Well, he's a big guy, tall, big hands and big feet. Oofta.* She still had shampoo on her hands and reached between his legs, gently running the soap over his balls, fondling them in her soapy palm, then stroking his lovely long length while he shivered against her.

He must have thought her breasts and ass were filthy, because suddenly cherry blossom shampoo was everywhere, so much that his grip kept slipping, which made them laugh as often as they moaned. Then his mouth was on hers and this kiss wasn't at all tentative like their others. He crowded her against the back wall of the shower, hands sliding around her slippery, soapy body as he licked into her mouth and all she could see and smell and feel and taste was Blake, Blake, Blake.

"We've got to get out of here," she gasped. "We've got to rinse off and get out and finish before I explode."

"That's my line, darling," he whispered into her mouth. "But you're quite right. The water will wash away much of your natural lubricant, which is why sex in hot tubs is a terrible idea. Those poor souls are just asking for a case of bacterial vaginosis."

She groaned, equal parts revolted and amused. "God, so romantic . . . love when you talk to me about infections. Now talk to me about antibiotics and flu shots."

"Hush." He shut off the water, pulled the curtain aside, braced his weight, then reached around and picked her up, holding her against him by the backs of her thighs. Her feet dangled far from the floor and she held very still. *This might be a terrible idea. But it also might lead to more of the sex. More of the sex is good.* She let out a nervous squeak as he carefully stepped out of the shower, then stood on the rug for a moment, both of them still dripping, then carried her to the bed.

"Ahh, careful, hardwood floors! Don't slip, don't slip!"

"I understand. But don't worry; if I go down, you'll likely squirt out from under me like a giant tiddlywink."

"Oh, definitely not worried now. What a relief." *What the*

hell is a tiddlywink? Maybe it's some kind of Vegas-themed sex toy.
Then, as he eased her down on the bed: "Blake, no, we'll get
your bed all wet, towels, towels!"

"Fuck towels," he growled, and in less than half a second she
lost all concern for the state of his quilt and blankets as his chest
settled against hers, his solid warm weight pressing her into the
mattress. When other men had done this she had felt almost
claustrophobic. With Blake, she couldn't get close enough.

She put a hand on the back of his neck and brought his
mouth down to hers, kissing him with all the frustration and
hurt and anger and remorse she had felt over the past month,
putting every bit of *I love you I'm so sorry I forgive you and you
forgive me* into it, and it must have worked, because he only
broke the kiss to whisper to her in his deep, dark voice, words
she felt as much as heard.

"Beautiful, you're so beautiful, Natalie, lovely Natalie I love
you I love you. . . ."

She took his hand, kissed his fingers, then drew them between her legs, let him feel how slick and wet she was (despite
the shower), and he groaned as she spread her thighs and
wriggled helpfully against him.

"Can I? Please please, I have to be inside you, Natalie,
please. . . ."

"Yes," she managed, and he leaned over and groped in the
end table drawer—she had brought condoms when she'd gone
to fetch her shampoo—and his hands were shaking so badly
she took the small foil-wrapped packet from him. Not that her
hands were steady as stone, but he'd only just gotten his ban-
dages off that morning.

"Okay. I've got it—there."

"Thank Christ," he groaned, "all praise to your miraculous hands." She fumbled a bit and he had to help and, in the end, between the two of them

("Good God, we're both consenting experienced adults and this is taking *too long*," which got her laughing so hard she almost fell off the bed.)

they rolled the condom on.

"Now?" he murmured. "Yes? Okay?"

"Yes! Jesus, yes, get in me already."

"The most beautiful words in the history of language," he moaned, then shifted against her, and suddenly he was filling her slowly and sweetly. "Oh thank God for that prophylactic or this would have just ended."

She giggled, then gasped as he moved, wrapped her legs around him, and pulled him as close as was possible. She could feel the big muscles in his back shifting as they moved together, and was astonished to find she was close, so close, though they'd barely begun. Usually it took several minutes and specific stimulation for her to reach orgasm. Then she remembered what he'd said about how they were living a new book, realized she'd wanted him, wanted this, for a month, thought of this and hoped for it, touched herself in her lonely bed and thought about him, and despaired of ever having it, and then she was crying out and clutching him to her and then his eyes rolled back and he leaned forward and groaned into her neck.

They shivered against each other, then lay still and silent, getting their breath back. She inhaled greedily, loving their intermingled scent.

"Natalie Lane of Heartbreak, in Sweetheart. Of Sweetheart."

She hummed and stroked his hair. They were still wet, and now sticky. She didn't give a ripe shit. "Yours, now," she replied.

He pulled back and smiled down at her. "Yes," was the simple reply, and she thought there had never been a word so wonderful.

Epilogue

"Blake? C'mon, man, stop sending me to voice mail. Listen, I need your help, no screwing around this time. I decided your insane idea was insane and called the nuclear option because I refuse to live in fear. And get this! Nonna is in on whatever this is! She knows why I'm in Venice, and Mom knows, and they're being *no* help, and if I eat any more gelato I'm gonna puke *everywhere,* so you really gotta call me back and help me figure out what to do. Blake? C'mon! Blake! Look, I know you're getting these because you texted me back that you and this Natalie Lame are getting married and I don't know why you thought that would work. Dude, if you don't want to talk to me, just say that, okay? Just be all boring and Blake-ey and be all, "You are in a mess of your own making" and something about the Duke of Lancaster and "you are terrible" and yak-yak-yak. Don't text lies, man, like you'd ever get married, and even if you *did* get married you'd never do it in a city that nearly ran me out of town with tar and feathers. Not cool. Blake? Blake? Blaaaaake!"

Romance Trope List

1. Flashbacks
2. Flashforwards
3. Hardscrabble childhood
4. Emotionally distant hero who just needs the right woman to unlock his heart (Blake)
5. The rake (Rake)
6. Tough but tender waitresses, most smarter than their customers
7. Small-town girl fleeing to Big City to make something of herself
8. Identical twins who are opposites
9. Identical twins who pretend they hate each other but love each other
10. Clueless city boy forced to work on farm
11. Farmers forced to work with clueless city boy
12. Grumpy horse who can only be tamed by (reluctant) hero

13. Hero keeping big secret
14. Heroine pretending to be someone else/keeping big secret
15. Heroine's deception makes no sense and seems silly from the beginning
16. Lust at first sight
17. Meet cute
18. Big Mis
19. Lovable farm animal brought into homes with no unpleasantness on either side of the equation
20. Kindly, paternal older man the hero takes to right away
21. Hero bonds with and loves an animal solely meant for consumption
22. Balding men are evil
23. Only after hero nearly dies does heroine realize it's love
24. Stern grandma hiding love for her family under all the stern
25. Over-the-top villain
26. Big cities are bad; small towns are wonderful
27. Hero rich but poor for convenience of plot
28. Inverted "heroine thinks hero is poor, but he's rich" trope: heroine thinks he's rich, finds out he's (kind of) poor (see #29, poor for convenience of plot)
29. Overly serious and educated older brother
30. Wisecracking "street-smart, not book-smart" younger brother
31. Heroine frequently, and inappropriately, giggles.
32. So many misunderstandings can be resolved if

characters take three minutes to just have a conversation.

33. Amnesiac sheriff
34. Hot librarians
35. Bad guys swear a lot
36. Sinister foreshadowing that turns out to not be sinister at all
37. Bodice ripping
38. Hero overestimates alcohol tolerance and has drunken rant/meltdown before horrified audience
39. The seemingly insurmountable problems of the plot are solved with relative ease at the end
40. "You just stood up to me, that was the test"
41. Big romantic epiphany
42. Geezers in love
43. No idea what they're feeling is love until it's identified at the eleventh hour
44. Family members presumed dead are alive
45. Happily ever after

Turn the page for a sneak peek
at MaryJanice Davidson's next novel

USA DEAD AHEAD

I'd never hurt her, I'd never hurt any woman, I've hurt men who have tried to hurt women and never regretted it, not once; black eyes get better and broken noses can be reset.

But this is hard. Literally, this is very very hard. Dear Abby: I'm sharing a room with my (kind of) boss who's super-cute and I haven't masturbated in ninety-six hours and she has lovely soft-strong hands and I might be getting Stockholm Syndrome because I'm looking forward to working with her tomorrow even though I'm terrified of Peeps. How skeevy is it if, while being very very quiet, I—

No point even finishing the question. He knew it was unacceptable levels of skeevy. He sighed and flopped over on his back. *Just don't think about it.* Sure. It would be just that easy, right? *Don't think about it. Don't think about Delaney just a few feet away, warm and fragrant in her bed. Don't wonder what her mouth tastes like, and the spot behind her ear, and her lovely long throat. Definitely don't wonder what it'd be like to gently rub your cheek*

316   MaryJanice Davidson

over her stiffening nipples. What she'd sound like if you slipped a hand between her legs and softly stroked her open. Nope. Don't think about any of it. Easy-peasy. And definitely don't grab yourself. A lot.

Delaney sat up, like Frankenstein in the lab after the lighting hit. Rake almost shrieked. *Oh God, she's a telepath and knows I'm a perv! My lustful thoughts were so loud they woke her up! Let death come quickly!* "What?" he shrilled from the sofa bed. "What is it? Not the face, okay?"

She didn't answer. Just abruptly swung her legs over the side of the bed, stood, and went straight to the biggest window in the room, occasionally squashing a Peep or grinding a chocolate egg into the carpet on her way but not stopping. Not even slowing. She got to the window and stood and looked and said nothing and did nothing.

He cleared his throat. "Are you okay?" *Please don't kick me out. You can't help being hot, and I can't help finding you hot, but I'd never act on it. Never unless you made it clear you wanted me in your bed. And maybe not even then because although you're hot I'm a little scared of you.*

Nothing.

She was still, so still. He'd never seen her like that, like a statue in the dark. "Delaney?"

She turned to look at him and he felt a chill; her gaze wasn't on him, not really. It was like she couldn't see him, was looking past him, or through him. "I don't . . ." she began in a low, halting voice unlike any she'd used before.

He pushed his blankets off, relieved that when she clomped toward the window like a cute Frankenstein, his penis, Mr. Roboto, turned back into *Flaccido Domingo,* and went to stand beside her. "Are you okay?"

"I don't know where I am," she whispered, sounding young and lost. And damned if she didn't *look* young in the barely lit glow by the window.

She reached out as if she was going to touch the glass, then let her hand drift back down. The woman who'd laughed when he barfed and yelled when he bitched and called him on his entitled douchebaggery was afraid to touch a window, or raise her voice, or make eye contact.

"It's always different, you know," she murmured. "I don't know where I am."

"You're in Venice," he said, and now *he* was whispering. "It's—it's okay. I mean, you're safe and everything. I'd never— no one's going to hurt you."

And God, the way her face lit up. That smile. Jesus. "Really?"

"Yeah. Really."

"No one will come in? Unless I let them?"

"No one," he promised through numb lips. *Fuck. A nightmare that she's sleepwalking in? Or sleepwalking during a nightmare? What is this?* "It's okay. You're safe. You—you can go back to bed. If you want."

"Bed?" And she flinched. Claire Fucking Delaney flinched.

"Well, you don't have to. You don't have to do anything you don't want to."

The smile again. The relief. "Really?"

"Really."

"Okay," she said, and *beamed* at him. Then she turned around and walked back to her bed and climbed under the covers and flopped over on her side and twenty seconds later she was dead asleep again. He watched her for a while to make sure she was really out; he no longer wanted to masturbate. Now he had a whole new thing to wonder about. Did that make him a good man, or just easily distracted? Both? Neither? And was he wondering about that so he wouldn't think about how scary she had been, and sad, and afraid?

What the hell was that?